I0680908

INK STAINS

A DARK FICTION LITERARY ANTHOLOGY

Volume 6

Guest Edited by
J. S. Watts

Dark Alley Press

INK STAINS ANTHOLOGY
Volume 6

ISBN 13: 978-1-946050-06-9
ISBN 10: 1-946050-06-7

© 2017 by Dark Alley Press
Individual stories copyright by authors

Dark Alley Press
http://www.darkalleypress.com

An imprint of Vagabondage Press LLC
PO Box 3563
Apollo Beach, Florida 33572
http://www.vagabondagepress.com

First edition printed in the United States of America and the United Kingdom, October 2017

10 9 8 7 6 5 4 3 2 1

Front cover art by Jetrel. Cover designed by Maggie Ward.

INK STAINS

A DARK FICTION LITERARY ANTHOLOGY

INTRODUCTION

Crossing the line.

In life, we draw many lines—lines between genders, good and evil, guilt and innocence, childhood and adulthood, real and unreal, human and non-human, life and death. It seems we like the reassuring certainty (false or otherwise) of a concept and its opposite and the clear, straight line that divides them. Sometimes, though, the dividing line is not so clear. At other times, it actually is, and yet, having drawn these lines, we cross them over and over again because humanity is curious, careless, devious, thrill-seeking and, at times, downright wicked.

So what happens if you cross the line? Does it change you and what is waiting on the other side?

In this volume of *Ink Stains,* ten contemporary authors from both sides of the Atlantic explore what it means to cross the line and the price we have to pay to do it in a collection of short stories that range from fantasy through Gothic to horror and from the fantastical to the grit of day-to-day life. Styles vary, subject matter is diverse, but at the heart of each story, there is a significant boundary, a line (or lines) that will be irrevocably crossed, for good or ill.

Sometimes crossing the line means transgression, and a number of the stories in this anthology deal with moral and/or sexual transgression. This is an adult book. It includes adult themes and descriptions. If this sort of thing offends or upsets you, you may want to walk away from these stories, or you may want to read on to find out if there was a price to pay and if it was high enough.

In the following stories, writers Monica Carter, George Kelly, Alison Garsha, Ken Goldman, Elana Gomel, Christopher Locke, Morrison, Thomas Olbert, Evan Purcell and Nicole Tanquary step over the line on your behalf to find what waits on the other side.

I should like to thank them for doing so and Dark Alley Press for allowing me to guest edit this volume of Ink Stains. I have enjoyed crossing the line from writer to editor.

J.S. Watts
Guest Editor
Ink Stains, Volume 6

TABLE OF CONTENTS

PLAYLAND

Evan Purcell

Knock.
Knock.
Knock.

I'd been waiting at the twisted metal gate for ten whole minutes before Trevor announced his appearance with his stupid three-knock code. Since we were kids, we always had that system. One knock meant our moms were coming. Two knocks meant someone needed a bathroom break. And three knocks meant that we were here and ready to start hanging out.

Trevor hid but not-hid behind a nearby tree, knocked three times, and waited for me to knock back. He looked at me, his eyes big and expectant.

I didn't knock. We weren't twelve anymore. Besides, we were standing two feet apart, with a tiny spruce between us. There was absolutely no reason for me to respond with some secret code.

"Mikey," he whispered.

The wind was cold tonight. Swirly. It didn't feel like April. It felt like the world was still trapped in the icy grip of February.

He knocked again. Three times.

I didn't respond.

"Come on," Trevor said.

"Why?"

"It's just the thing to do," he said.

The thing to do. That was like his catchphrase, but it wasn't true, and we both knew it. Everything he did—those three stupid knocks…calling me Mikey…hell, coming here in the first place—it was all a way to prolong our childhood. And it was stupid.

He looked at me, expectant.

And I gave in, like I always did. I balled up my fist and knocked three times on the metal fence.

Knock.

Knock.

Knock.

"There. Ya happy?"

He smiled. "Thanks, Mikey."

"It's Mike," I said. "And you're late."

"I know," he said. "Sorry. It took me forever to find this." He spread his arms wide.

At first, I wasn't sure what he was talking about. Then I realized… his T-shirt. He was wearing his old Playland T-shirt, the one with Laffing Sal's grinning clown face and the Big Dipper in the background.

"Nice," I muttered.

It was much too small, that T-shirt. Why did he even still have it?

Oh. That's right. He had it, because he was stuck in some sad, little time warp. We were graduating soon, and here he was acting like a fifth grader.

I didn't say that, though. I owed it to him to smile and nod and say things like "Nice."

"Shut up, Mikey," he said, half playfully and half not.

"What?"

"Sometimes when you talk to me, you sound all condescending. Like everything I do is—"

"Sorry. I didn't mean to." I paused. "That really is a cool shirt. I wish I still had mine."

He waited for a second, not quite sure how to interpret my new tone. The blank one I used whenever Mom started ragging on me for slacking in algebra or whatever.

What did it even matter anyway? I came all the way here. Because he'd asked, I drove halfway across the city and agreed to sneak into an abandoned theme park. For Trevor. Not for my own freaking health.

I gestured toward the broken neon sign hanging above us. It marked the grand entrance. As a kid, I always got so excited when I saw it. Now, it just reminded me of a pawn shop. "Ya ready?"

"Yeah."

Trevor pushed on the metal gates. They creaked painfully and swung open. Why weren't they locked? They should've been locked. That way, psychos like us wouldn't be able to sneak in and trash the place.

He ran inside without me. He laughed a little for no reason.

I paused for a second, just before my foot crossed the threshold.

What was wrong?

"You okay?" Trevor called from inside.

"Yeah, I..."

I walked in, ignoring the weird chill that hopscotched down my back.

Without the nearby street lights, all we had for illumination was a quarter moon, and all it managed to do was cast long, twisted shadows in all directions.

I looked around, checking to see if anyone was watching us. Nope. We were all alone.

"But I'm sure you remember that too," Trevor said. It was the end of one of his stories, and I hadn't even noticed that he was talking. I was sure it was some embarrassing thing from childhood, about sprained ankles or vomit or something.

"Totally," I mumbled.

It never failed. I saw Trevor for less than five minutes, and he was already talking about five years ago. No wonder it had been so long since we'd hung out.

"This way," he said. "Come on!"

I breathed deeply and trudged inside.

Let's get this over with.

"God, I almost pissed myself from laughing so hard!" Trevor said. He was running full speed down memory lane, and I was only half-paying attention.

We passed the front ticket booth, a little shack painted to look like a circus tent, and were on our way to the family fun zone.

The whole place was broken and silent, which made Trevor's voice sound even louder in comparison. "Seriously. It was crazy."

"I'm sure it was." I stepped over a fallen trash can.

"Mikey, can you please stop acting like you're at a funeral or something?"

"Fine."

He was right, of course. I was being especially gloomy. But at the same time, Trevor was acting like we just crossed over into the gates of heaven or something. He was all manic and big-eyed, like he was trying too hard. I guess I was acting glum as a counterbalance to his enthusiasm.

"Anyway," he continued, "I remember when we came here for Halloween, and everyone was dressed up…"

Thud.

Thud.

I heard footsteps from around the ticket booth, slow and trudging, and they definitely weren't mine or Trevor's.

"Shh," I said.

He stopped. Looked at me.

And I waited for more footsteps.

If it was some ancient, rotting security guard, we could get into some major trouble. Mom would take away the car, probably. I might not even get to go to the graduation parties next month. It would've been major.

But whatever. Life was too short to be afraid of shadows and things you couldn't even see. Besides, I didn't hear any more footsteps.

I shrugged.

"Anyway," Trevor continued, "you were standing right over there when all of a sudden—"

"Let's check out the old roller coaster."

I couldn't remember the name of the roller coaster—El Diablo or something—but its twisted metal loomed over us and blocked out the moon. It was creepy. It was beautiful.

I remember when they built it, too. I was so excited to ride it for the first time, but then I chickened out at the last minute, and Trevor had to ride it alone.

"You know what they say," Trevor said, "about how everything looks smaller after you grow up. Well, this thing did not shrink."

"I know, right?"

I smiled in spite of myself. Trevor noticed and took it as a sign that I was starting to enjoy our little adventure. "Hey," he said excitedly, his words spilling out of him, "remember that time you ate so much kettle corn before the spinning swings that you threw up in a perfect spiral on everybody? God, kernels everywhere."

"That's sort of an exaggeration," I said.

"Oh, and hey, remember that time we took your little cousin Taryn here, and then she got lost. And you were so freaking out. It was crazy. And then—"

"Yes," I said. "I remember that, too."

"And dude," he continued. "You were so afraid of heights. Like that one time—"

"I get it, okay?" I shouted. "We did a lot of stuff here. Now can we keep walking? I wanna get this over with."

"Oh," he muttered.

I regretted what I said almost instantly. Not just the words, though. My whole stupid tone. I was whiny. I sounded like a baby.

Trevor got quiet.

I raised my hands in apology. "Look," I said. "We're here to say goodbye to this old, crumbling place and—"

"Not goodbye," Trevor protested.

I forgot. Ever since his grandma died, Trevor had this thing about saying goodbye. He couldn't do it. He said it was bad mojo or something. He could say something else, like "See you around," or "Bon voyage," or something, but he couldn't say the G-word. I never really understood it.

"You're right," I said, humoring him. "We spent a lot of hours at this place, and we're just here to say 'See ya later. Thanks for the memories.'"

He smiled.

"And now I—" My voice cut off. I froze. Every part of me. My nerves. My heart. My...

Something was walking toward us, just behind Trevor. It was tall and white, and it had the stutter-walk of some malfunctioning piece of machinery. It had a red grin—painted on, but peeling away—and its black eyes were fixed on us.

It was Laffing Sal.

"Um, Trevor," I mumbled.

He ignored me. Probably thought I was about to complain about something else. "Look," he said. "The old log ride. It was really—"

"Trevor."

"Jeeze. Stop, okay? Stop interrupting me."

I had no other choice. I grabbed his head and turned it around for him. He saw the grinning clown approaching us. It was only a dozen feet away now, close enough for us to make out the cracks in its plaster. It stumbled, clearly rusted on its inside.

"Laffing Sal?" Trevor said.

Back when Playland was still open, Laffing Sal was its most famous figure. It was the clown woman that loomed over the spinning swings ride, rocking back and forth and laughing this horrible recorded laugh. It was just a stupid mechanical thing, though. It was never built to walk or sway its head like that or reach out toward us.

Its long fingers clawing through the air. Each fingertip was sharp. A few still had their plaster coating, but most of its fingers were just metal.

It whirred. We could hear it whirr. Like an appliance, like a sputtering, clockwork thing.

"Hello?" I called. As soon as I said it, I felt like an idiot. This thing was not going to respond to some greeting. It was...

Closer. Five feet away now. I could hear its knees clank.

"Hello?" Trevor called.

And Laffing Sal opened its mouth—still grinning, still joyful—and said, "Join me." Its voice was raggedy. Each word was a struggle.

And we didn't run. We should've run, but it was such a strange figure. It shouldn't have existed.

When it reached us, it swiped its arm through the air and clawed at Trevor's torso. There was a horrible tearing noise, and for a dark moment, I thought it was his skin. I thought that the tall mechanical thing had torn bloody gashes into Trevor's skin.

But it wasn't skin. Only cloth.

Trevor pulled away. Started running.

I ran too, of course.

And the whole way—as we ran and as Laffing Sal chased us—Trevor screamed bloody murder. But for the life of me, I could barely hear his screams over the laughter.

We reached the winding metal bars in front of the log ride. Back when this park was open, thousands of people a day would've waited between these bars, patiently standing in a zigzagging line so they could hop on the ride and get a little wet. Now, it was empty, except for Trevor and me.

It was also, thankfully, half-concealed by a fallen sign. If we stayed there and didn't move and didn't breathe, then maybe we'd be safe.

Trevor breathed, though. He was loud.

I elbowed him in the side.

"What?" he whispered.

I shook my head. Nothing.

Sal walked right in front of us. Through the space under the broken sign, I could see its clown shoes drag along the concrete.

Did it see us? No. Not likely. It didn't slow its pace.

Trevor looked at me. He opened his mouth to ask me something, but I put my index finger against my lips. He nodded silently.

Good.

Safe.

I looked back at Laffing Sal's feet. It wasn't walking anymore. its toes were pointed toward us. And its voice called out, "Join m-me."

It saw us.

With a loud, metal crunch, Laffing Sal pushed its way through the fallen sign. Neon lights fell onto the ground and shattered.

We ran. Our backs were to the log ride. There was no other exit. So the only way out was to jump onto the dry chute and slide down. "This way," I said.

Trevor looked at the sheer drop. "I don't know."

Sal snaked its way through the metal bars. It could've ducked under them, but it didn't. Taking its time, I guess.

I stepped over the railing and into the metal chute. It was basically a giant slide. What was the worst that could happen? "I'm not leaving without you," I said.

He nodded and followed behind me.

"J-join…m-m-me." Then laughter.

Because the chute was dry—had been dry for a long time—sliding down it was going to hurt. Still, it would at least be a little fun.

"Ready?"

"Uh, Mikey?"

I didn't wait. I pushed us both off. Against a rush of air, we slid toward the bottom of the ride. I smiled without realizing it.

When we got off the slide, there was no telling where that thing was. It hadn't followed us down the chute, but that didn't mean it wasn't limping toward us from the other direction. Our best choice was to find a better hiding spot.

So we did.

More specifically, I did. And Trevor followed. We crouched behind some rusted dumpsters tucked away behind the bathrooms. As far as hiding places go, it didn't have the best smell, but it was pretty hidden.

For the longest time, we waited, and the only sounds I could hear were my frantic heartbeats and Trevor's heavy breathing.

Eventually, Trevor spoke. "You sure we're safe here?"

I didn't even look at him. "Do I look like I'm sure of anything right now?"

He chewed his fingernails, like he used to as a kid. He probably didn't even know he was doing it, either. Back in Miss Phelp's third grade class, he used to do that all the time. Kids used to make fun of him, because it almost looked like he was sucking his thumb. Back then, I used to spend a lot of energy defending him from the other kids.

Back then.

I wanted to be mad at him, but I couldn't. Not now. "Don't freak out," I said. "I'll figure this out." I. Not we.

"We shouldn't have come here," he said.

"Ya think?"

"I just thought—"

"What did you think? Huh? You think we could've created some new magical memories for our scrapbooks?" I didn't know why I chose that moment to snap at him.

"No."

"Then what?" I said. "Why the hell did you want to come to a place like this? And why did you drag me here?"

He looked at me like I'd slapped him. "Because we used to have fun here, okay? Because we used to have fun."

His voice was too loud. I looked around to see if anything had heard us.

"When we were little," he continued, "we came here all the time. I used to beg Mom to take me. I loved it here. And you did, too. Don't pretend that you're above this. That you're too cool for a place like Playland. Because I remember." He tapped his temple. Three times. "I remember the look on your stupid face every time we got on the damn swings."

"That was a different time. We were kids then."

"We're still kids, Mikey. Jesus."

"Mike," I mumbled.

Slowly, he closed his eyes. His mouth got really small. It looked like he was shutting down, it really did. I thought of the time, sophomore year, when I gave him the cold shoulder in the lunchroom. At the time, I thought he was trying to look like a baby. I thought it was some act. Now I wasn't sure.

"Look. I'm sorry, okay? I haven't been the best friend. I should've..."

"Save it. We're goin' off to college soon." He inched his body away from mine.

"If we survive," I said. Probably shouldn't have said that.

"Yeah, yeah. If."

"We'll still see each other," I added.

"Maybe."

And I knew he was right. Our whole friendship had turned into a big maybe. Maybe I'll see you after school. Maybe I'll come over tonight. And more and more often, the maybes had hardened into nos.

"Mikey, what are we gonna do?"

I breathed deeply. "Okay, Trevor. Follow me. We are going to—"

BAM!

In the distance, the front gate slammed shut. Its chains tightened, and everything locked into place.

"Did the park just lock itself?" Trevor asked.

I didn't answer. I didn't need to. My head dropped between my knees. Trevor put a comforting hand on my shoulder, but I shook it off.

He looked at me, real sadness in his eyes. It looked like he'd given up, like he was about to say goodbye or something.

Goodbye. His least favorite word.

It was such a raw look on his face. Naked. Vulnerable. Christ.

"Let's think for a second," I said. "The park wants to keep us here. That...thing wants to keep us here. All we have to do is—"

BAM!

Laffing Sal's arm reached through the bars behind me. Its fingertips slashed at the back of my neck.

I screamed and pulled away. Blood trickled down my back.

"Run!"

We ran and ran, but we had no place to go. We were rats in a maze. And this maze had no exits. The park wasn't going to let us go. It wanted us dead.

We passed the zipline and the food court. The God damned spinning sombreros. We were so much faster than Laffing Sal, but it always caught up with us.

I grabbed Trevor's shoulders and stopped him. It was pointless. We were running in circles. "Trevor," I said. I could feel his irregular breathing. He was like me. He wouldn't be able to handle much more of this, either. "We can't keep running. We need to find weapons."

I looked around us. There was a lot of empty space, but not many possible weapons. Most of the small items had been picked clean long ago. There were a few trash cans, some rocks, long metal poles.

Over there! The shooting gallery. All its prizes were gone, and most of the targets had fallen off, but the guns were still there.

"The rifles!" I shouted.

"We can't shoot those," Trevor protested.

"No," I said, "but we can swing them. They're metal. Heavy." Honestly, it was our best shot.

Trevor didn't argue. We both ran to the shooting gallery. I grabbed the first rifle and pulled. With a loud click, the chain snapped apart. Bam. Instant weapon.

Trevor did the same, or at least he tried to. His chain didn't break. It wouldn't budge. "Shit," Trevor mumbled. "Shit. Shit."

Laffing Sal walked toward us. Toward him, actually. Trevor still struggled with his would-be weapon. I had to protect my friend.

"Hey! Hey you!" I shouted at Laffing Sal. "You want us to join you?"

Laffing Sal changed directions and started toward me. Its laughter turned to giggling.

"Right here," I said. Using as much strength as I could possibly gather, I spun my body in a half circle and slammed the rifle across its face.

I expected Sal to hurtle backward. It didn't. It lifted a metal finger to its face, touching the area I'd hit. It thrummed a finger against the plaster skin. And then it smiled. "P…Playtime."

I backed up two steps, but Sal was still too close. It grabbed my shirt, its fingertips slicing holes through the fabric, and it yanked me forward.

Then it let go. I lost my balance and toppled onto the ground. My rifle clattered to the side, too far away for me to reach.

In a second, Laffing Sal was on top of me. Its fingers wrapped around my throat. And it smiled. But it wasn't laughing. Not anymore.

I saw sparks, little flashbulbs of electricity on the surface of my eyeballs.

Laffing Sal's sharp fingertips clamped around my neck and squeezed. It squeezed so hard. I couldn't breathe. I couldn't swallow without those metal fingertips digging even deeper into my skin.

I was going to die. Laffing Sal had me. It was too strong. And no matter how much I thrashed around, I couldn't...

Trevor slammed his rifle against Laffing Sal's face. It didn't make noise, but I could tell he hurt the creature…hurt the creature more than I did. Chips of plaster flew in specks onto the ground.

Sal spun sideways from the impact. One of its legs twisted, and it collapsed. Crumpled.

I wanted to shout. I wanted to scream Trevor's name and do some crazy victory dance.

No time, though.

While Sal pulled itself back up, I waved for Trevor to follow me. And we ran.

"Where?" Trevor panted.

That was the million-dollar question. So far, the clown had found us wherever we'd gone.

"We're taking it back to the spinning swings," I said. "That's where it came from." I wasn't quite sure what made me think of that. It was a long shot, but at least it was a shot.

"Okay."

We changed directions. My sneakers skidded a little on the concrete. I tripped over my own stupid feet and fell onto the concrete. God, I felt like an idiot. I felt like a stupid, tripping damsel from a stupid horror movie.

Trevor reached down to help me up, but I didn't need his help. I got up on my own.

When we got to the open courtyard, Sal was already there. It was waiting for us, hands on hips, round plaster head cocked to the side. How did it get in front of us so fast? It wasn't even running. Then I realized, it was part of the park. It knew all the secret passages, all the short cuts. There wasn't any hiding place it couldn't find.

Laffing Sal didn't reach toward us this time. Instead, it waved. Casually. Simply. It wiggled its fingers in the air. "Join me," it said, and then laughed and laughed.

"No!" I shouted.

"What does that even mean?" Trevor asked. It was just like him to question the word choice of a robot killing machine.

Laffing Sal stopped. Its face twisted and it struggled to push the words through its cracked mouth. "J…Join me…in th…the p-p-park."

"Yeah," Trevor said. "I still don't know what that means."

Sal spread its arms wide, gesturing toward the empty rides and twisted shapes all around. Then, like the pulse of a living thing, each ride flashed a sign of life before shutting down.

The roller coaster first. It lit up and pushed its car around a loop.

Then the spinning swings. It flashed half its lights and spun in two circles.

Then the log ride. It pushed two of its logs down the first chute.

In a rush, each ride turned on and off. A few seconds each. Just to show they could.

Laffing Sal clapped awkwardly. "It's…f-f-fun in the s…the sun."

That was Playland's old slogan.

We backed away. I didn't know how much more of this I could handle. Christ, how could we possibly survive a fight against an entire theme park?

Laffing Sal's giant shoes thudded against the ground.

"Go back!" Trevor shouted. "Go back to your perch!" He pointed toward the top of the spinning swings. That was Laffing Sal's home, after all. Where it was supposed to stay. If we could only lure it back up there…

I looked at Trevor, Trevor looked at me, and just like that…we had a plan. Return the clown to the top of the ride, to where it was supposed to be. Trevor nodded.

Laffing Sal walked toward us. It was moving more confidently now. Its limp was less pronounced and its knees didn't clank. It slashed one hand through the air.

I headed toward the swings. My strength was sapped. I could barely move. But using what little upper body strength I had left, I climbed onto the nearest swing. It swayed under my feet.

"Come on," Trevor urged.

I started pulling myself up the chain.

Trevor was on the swing next to mine. He was a much faster climber. He was strong.

Laffing Sal was catching up, though. It looked at my swing, then Trevor's, then mine. It chose to follow me. I was the slower one. I was more vulnerable.

Hurry, Mike, I told myself.

The chain went taut under the combined weight of both me and Sal. I climbed higher and higher. My muscles burned. I wanted to stop. I needed to stop. But I couldn't.

Sal was catching up. Just below me now. So close. "Join me," it said, its voice no longer wavering like it had before. "Join me."

I reached the roof and hoisted myself up. I'd climbed enough trees as a kid to know exactly how to maneuver my body. Still, the chain shifted under me, and I almost fell.

Almost.

After one terrifying moment, I pulled myself onto the roof of the spinning swings.

I looked down, but I couldn't see Sal over the sloping edge. I could, however, see the long, deadly plummet back down to the concrete below. We were high—impossibly high—and I was starting to think that we'd made a major, major mistake.

Trevor was already there, right in the center of the roof. He wasn't even crouched down, either. He was standing tall. I wanted to yell at him. Didn't he see how high up we were? Didn't he see how easy it would be to slip…and slide…and fall onto the concrete below? Splatter into limbs and goo? Didn't he see how freaking dangerous it was up here?

I didn't yell at him. I was too busy clutching to the grooves in the roof. I was too busy keeping myself steady.

"Look," he said.

I didn't see anything. Just him, acting like a daredevil.

He tapped his foot against the circular slab at the roof's center. "This is where Laffing Sal stood before it, you know…"

Came alive.

Slowly, I inched my way toward him. He was right. The slab was about five feet in diameter, with two holes where its feet had been fastened. There was also a crack in the center, a crack that had been there a long time.

"Great," I muttered. "So what do we do?"

Trevor paused. Looked at me stupidly. We'd just finished Phase One of our plan, and I was waiting for him to lay out Phase Two. I thought he was going to say something. But he didn't. His face was frozen.

"Do we..." I started, "Do we grab it and shove it onto that slab?"

"I guess," he said. It wasn't the most confident thing to say.

"Christ, Trevor. You have no idea what we're doing, do you?"

"Well neither do you!"

"But at least I—"

Something grabbed me from behind and pulled me backward. I screamed. I twisted my body around and saw Sal's grinning face. I was close enough to see cracks. Paint chips. I was close enough to breathe in its dust. It opened its wide, gap-toothed mouth and cackled right in my face.

And pulled.

It was trying to pull me off the ride. Worse than that, it was succeeding. "Join me," Sal said. I could hear gears grinding inside. I could hear its clockwork.

God. We were so high up. If I fell, I'd die. No doubt. I wouldn't just break something. I'd break everything. I'd splatter.

I couldn't let that happen. I twisted my left arm out of its grip and grabbed its chin. I pushed against its grinning, plaster face as hard as I could. Pieces of it flaked off. Its crumbling whiteness was getting under my nails.

Sal spun its head to the side. Slammed its body against the shaky tiles underneath us.

I screamed out in pain.

Laffing Sal was strong. Ridiculously strong. It pushed me backward. My back landed on the tile—hard—and all my breath left my lungs.

I kicked wildly into the air. My feet never struck the clown, but the movement was enough to get it off-balance. It fell to the side.

I twisted out of its grasp.

"Trevor," I shouted. "Help!"

Laffing Sal grabbed my foot now. It yanked me closer.

There was no way things could get any worse.

Then I heard a click. A whirr. Flickering lights popped on from all directions. And the roof under us began to spin.

The ride had turned itself on. The whole thing spun in wild circles. Slowly at first, then faster. Its rusted innards groaned. Its lights flashed.

Faster.

God. Faster.

Laffing Sal had my foot. My ankle. It clamped down and squeezed. It would not let go. Bolts of pain shot up my leg muscles.

And in quick, jerky motions, Laffing Sal began to pull itself up my leg. "J-join me," it said.

It clung to my side now. It had me. It was going to pull me off the ride. All it would take was one, strong movement. I'd fall, and I'd die, and then it would win. The park would win.

There was nothing—nothing at all—that I could do. My hands clung to the roof tiles, but only barely. I wasn't in the right position to hold on. Even without Laffing Sal pulling me forward, it would only be a matter of time before...

I looked at Trevor, my eyes pleading for help. I needed him. For the first time in a long time, I needed him more than he needed me.

He was steadier than me. He was holding on to the slab. His hair whipped around him. His torn shirt fluttered. And he leaned toward me. "Pull Laffing Sal this way!" he screamed.

"I can't!"

"It's our only hope. Just try," he shouted.

The music got louder and louder. It sounded like a carnival. It sounded like dancing elephants.

I struggled to pull my body toward the slab. I struggled, and...

I slipped. Breath caught in my throat. "No! I can't!"

That was when Trevor looked at me. A sad realization crossed his face. His eyes darkened. And I knew—I instantly knew—what that realization was. He realized that I was lost, that he couldn't help me. If he did, then he'd die instead. The ride was spinning wildly. Full speed now. The world outside of us was a blur of lights and dancing shapes.

And Trevor was going to let me fall. Hell, it was the right thing to do. It was...If I fell, Laffing Sal would fall, too. It would shatter. Well, we'd both shatter. But Sal would shatter, surely, and then everything would stop. Trevor would be free to go home.

The right thing to do.

Trevor screamed, "Mikey. I'm sorry I brought you here."

"It's okay!" I shouted back, and it really was. I'd stop the monster, and Trevor would finally be able to move on.

"Have a good one, okay?" Trevor screamed.

"What?"

And with that, he let go of the slab and ran full-speed toward us. My eyes blurred with tears.

Trevor dove onto Laffing Sal, and I felt those cold, metal hands pull away from my skin. Then the two of them—Laffing Sal and Trevor—hurtled through the air and over the edge. I didn't see where they landed. Everything was spinning too fast.

After a few seconds, the lights dimmed. The ride stopped. Everything stopped. And there was silence.

Just as the morning sun was peeking up from the horizon, I came back to Playland. With the police, of course.

Officer Howard was the one taking all the notes. A short guy with a long face and chicken legs. Officer Geist was tall and pretty serious looking, especially with the forehead wrinkles. He seemed like a cop-type cop. Both of them had guns, thankfully. One of them had a clipboard for notes.

When we got to the twisted entrance—broken lights dangling above us—I had to stop and catch my breath.

"Kid," Officer Geist said, "you can wait outside while we check things out."

First of all, he shouldn't have called me kid. And secondly, there was no way I wasn't going to go back inside. I'd punch myself if I chickened out like that.

So we walked inside, through the gate and past the ticket booth and straight toward the swings. Geist and Howard whispered a few things to each other. I couldn't hear them. That was probably intentional.

When we got around the swings, I saw the shattered remains of Laffing Sal. It was on the ground, in pieces, just a few meters away from us. Half of its face was gone—crushed on impact—and the other half stared up at us. Blankly.

And Trevor wasn't there. No blood. No body. Nothing.

"This," I said, "was where I saw Trevor last." I didn't mention that we were standing over the mechanical clown that attacked us. I knew how cops thought, and I didn't want them to think I was some crazy person.

I wasn't crazy.

"Did you kids…vandalize anything?" Geist asked. He looked at the shattered clown.

Before I even answered, Howard had scribbled a bunch of stuff onto his notebook. Probably descriptions of my facial expressions or whatever.

"No," I said. "We're too mature for that."

They both exchanged glances.

"Okay," Geist continued. "We're going to check around. I'm sure your friend will pop up soon. Just keep tight. And if we have any other questions…" He kept talking, using that same reassuring voice that every sitcom dad uses.

I stopped paying attention about halfway through his speech. I pretended to be paying attention, but I really wasn't. You see, there was this noise behind me. Really faint, like it was coming from inside the park equipment.

Knock. Knock. Knock.

Three times. Clear as day. Slowly, I turned around and looked at the spinning swing ride behind me. No one was there. Not Trevor. No one.

"You understand?" Geist asked.

I guess I wasn't doing the best job of pretending to listen.

"Uh, sure," I said.

But I couldn't get those knocks out of my head. They sounded just like Trevor. If I hadn't seen Laffing Sal grab him and pull him through the air, I would've sworn that he was standing right behind me. Like he always did. Standing and smiling.

"Hey, kid," Officer Geist shouted to me. "You okay?"

"Yeah, yeah," I said, and used my sleeve to wipe at my stupid eyes.

"Okay," he said. "Just don't go too far, alright?" He didn't wait for my answer. Instead, he started snapping photos of some of the footprints and scratches on the ground.

Knock. Knock. Knock. Again.

It was coming from the metal base of the spinning swing ride. You know, the place with the pictures of old Victorian women swinging in front of flowers and stuff. It was coming from inside the metal.

I spun around to see if anyone else had heard that. Nope. Officer Geist was going photo-crazy with some smudges on the ground, and Officer Howard was writing God-knows-what into his notebook.

One of the swing chains started creaking from the wind.

I walked over to the swings, bunched up my fist, and knocked three times on the old, rusted metal.

Knock. Knock. Knock.

It was just the thing to do.

.

XOXOX XOXOX XOXOX X

ABOUT THE AUTHOR

Evan Purcell is a high school teacher in the beautiful Himalayan country of Bhutan, one of the happiest places in the world. Though he grew up in America, he's spent the last few years teaching in places as varied as Russia, China, and Zanzibar. He's published several romance novels, as well as over a dozen horror and sci-fi short stories. You can read more about his travels and writing at EvanPurcell.Blogspot.com

GROTESQUE

Alison Garsha

Kira stood in the corridor with her fellow course-mates, each of them waiting to receive individual feedback on the first essay of their university careers, submitted the morning before. While a couple of students made small talk about upcoming bops, she said nothing, and let her eyes drift over the grand medieval stonework of the college's interior. They settled on a portrait of a stern old man dressed in robes. His lifeless expression and the way his head seemed to slump made her wonder if the painting had been completed after his death, if she was gazing at a deceased scholar propped up in what had been his favorite chair. Suddenly, another student stepped out of the study and into the corridor, breaking her concentration. She was next.

Anxiety pricked her shoulders as she stepped into the interrogation room. The professor was still seated, studying an array of papers on her lap. She looked up. "Please, take a seat," she said, gesturing towards the sofa to her left.

She did, while her back remained rigid and upright. The professor began to shuffle through the pile of papers and retrieved a stapled bundle that appeared covered in red gashes: Kira's essay. An agonizing silence filled the room as she perused her notes through bifocal lenses. Kira could hear sporadic screeches, always in twos, through a window that looked out on the college garden. A gate in need of oiling, she thought. She wondered how long it had been crying out in distress and how a person could tolerate its incessant wailing. She tried to distract herself by studying the Oriental rug beneath her Doc Martens, until she was certain she could make out a face leering at her in the ornate pattern.

"Well," the professor began. "I can see that, for this first essay, you have immersed yourself in the required, and much of the suggested reading, with vigor and enthusiasm. Your writing is clearly expressed and shows a passion for the subject. However, I'm not sure it really works as an essay. You present points that seem to be of a related theme but without any decisive commentary on their content. Your tone is almost entirely descriptive when it ought to be analytical. You clearly have the interest, but what of your opinions?"

Kira swallowed and became aware of the dryness in her own eyes, having maintained eye contact without blinking throughout the diatribe. She closed them for slightly longer than she knew was socially acceptable, orbiting them in their sockets as she searched her thoughts.

"I'm sorry," she said, instantly regretting the apology. "I read as much as I could, but I didn't feel I had a right to an opinion on any of it."

The professor paused, appearing to choose her words carefully out of sympathy. "You must have an argument in order to make an essay your own. Use your interest and logic to guide you. That's how we do things at Oxford."

This last, emphatic line she said with finality and with little of the sympathy her previous hesitation had conveyed. Kira's eyes shot toward the rug with embarrassment, where that little face lay, mocking her.

"Thank you," she said, the moisture returning to her eyes. "I will try to write with more direction for this next essay."

The professor handed her the slashed papers as Kira stood up to leave, stepping on the rug's face as she did. She swallowed, trying to push down the tightness in her chest as she rushed off to grab lunch and review her notes before an afternoon tutorial.

"Kira, what do you make of this comparison between Wrenn and Sartre?"

She froze at the professor's question. Although she had been listening to the discussion around her, she had forgotten that she was meant to participate; this interruption had caught her absently eyeing the books that lined the shelves of the study. She rubbed the hem of her skirt between her thumb and forefinger. What did she make of it? Well, they both offered fascinating viewpoints, but she wasn't convinced that they opposed one another, not in the black-and-white fashion everyone seemed to be pretending they did. Sartre had argued more beautifully, but she suspected that this was not the correct thing to say.

She took a breath and tried to steady her voice. "Erm, I'm not sure they quite disagree. Wrenn thought that studying poetry could tell us more about early civilizations, because it was more connected to the oral tradition and the natural world. Sartre defended prose because it was more 'committed' than poetry: it could be used. He compares it to an evolved appendage...something naturally selected. But then he argues in such a poetic way, like he was trying to cause controversy."

"And why do you say that?" asked the professor, his intonation falling at the end of his question as he peered above his glasses expectantly.

"Well," she began, "he may have had communist sympathies, but he refused to pick sides. He turned down the Nobel Prize because he wouldn't brand himself as East or West. Maybe he liked ambiguity?"

"And which position is more defensible, Sartre's or Wrenn's? Which is more closely connected to early humanity: prose or poetry?" he asked with impatience, as if she should have answered this in the first place.

"I don't know. They both seem valid," she said with an air of defeat that she knew must have sounded like indifference. Her shoulders hunched in shame.

The professor clenched his jaw and inhaled sharply, as Kira tried desperately to wring the correct answer from the tattered hemline of her abused skirt. But before she could make a second attempt, he had turned to another student. This had clearly not been a satisfactory response.

The professor locked eyes with David, who had a habit of gesturing with his hands to hide their shaking. He launched into his own answer without hesitation. "If I could draw our attention to some of the inconsistencies in Sartre's argument, as pointed out by…"

And off he went. He was picking a side, something Kira had realized over the past two weeks was merely how things were done at Oxford. Firmness of opinion and eloquence of speech seemed to her the currency of academic success. She did not come from money, but she had never before felt intellectually impoverished. Then again, what David expressed was not free thinking, but the carefully selected thoughts and opinions of others. Was this not obvious to the professor and the other three students in the room? From where was she meant to draw an audacious sense of privilege over great ideas that would allow her to weigh up all the options and choose the best?

Unsure of what the right thing to say might be, she remained silent for the rest of the tutorial. She waited until she had cycled up the High Street and through a narrow alleyway, locked her bike in college, climbed the stairs to her room, and closed the door behind her before she allowed herself to cry.

She paced around the room, which felt even smaller than usual, both comforting and claustrophobic. Her feverish strides were constricted as she pinged from one wall to ricochet off the next. There was little on them to distract her: mainly posters and calendars she'd picked up during Freshers' Week. She had almost nothing of her own to personalize the drab quarters, only a postcard from her visit to Strawberry Hill House in Twickenham that summer and a few well-thumbed paperbacks.

Her pacing gradually slowed, and when she caught her breath, she settled on her tightly tucked bed, resting against the pillows that lined the wall and formed something of a sofa during the day. Her chest remained tight, and she felt choked by the enormity of her undertaking.

She had been so elated to gain a place here. Her parents had been proud, and her siblings were inspired by her success. She knew what Oxford meant to an Anglophile father and a mother who had once been a doctor. She had worked with single-minded determination to get there. She loved English and was good at it, but for the first time, she held doubt close to her chest, like a foul secret.

She resigned herself to living in the Bodleian Library for a fortnight, emerging only for lectures, sleep and sustenance. When she found herself entombed within walls of books at seven o'clock on the evening before the deadline, she had no arguments, no ideas, not a single word of text written. She had a comprehensive set of notes and a proficiency in Old English, after much gnashing of teeth. How could she possibly distil that to a mere three thousand words? Who was she even to dare try?

The lights overhead extinguished themselves one by one, as she had seen them do every evening. She emerged from her castle of books, regretting that she must leave every brick in place. Her notes would have to be enough.

She made for the exit and emerged into the library's stunning courtyard, momentarily distracted by its detailed renderings and Latin inscriptions, its Gothic splendour. Standing in the middle of it all, she felt timeless and ancient, and thought of the greater minds who had once stood in her place. *I*, she thought.

She crossed the quadrangle briskly, her thick, rubber soles making no sound on the stone floor, and saw that the south entrance toward the Radcliffe Camera had already been shut. She would have to exit through the east entrance. As she stepped outside, she became aware of the darkness of the evening. There was no moon that she could see and hardly any stars, either. Only the yellow of the street lamps in front of Hertford College provided any light. All was quiet and still. For a moment, she paused in the center of the road, sinking into the strange sensory deprivation of the night.

"Rubbish," a deep voice croaked.

She jumped and spun about, searching for the source of this interruption, but saw no one.

"When's the deadline, then?" said the voice, barely perceptible, but undoubtedly present. Each word scraped like chalk on pavement. She looked to the ground for its source, not knowing what she expected to find there.

"Up here, you silly cow," it said.

Kira looked to the skies—nothing. She glanced at the floral

embellishments over Hertford's door, then back to the Bodleian on the opposite side. And that's when she saw it.

There, nestled above the great wooden door with the coats-of-arms of various colleges, lay a row of sculpted figures. There were about a dozen of them, side by side, each an intricate, life-sized face of a particular character. Some women, some men, and others a crude hybrid of man and beast. She recognised a king, a maiden, a monk with a scandalised expression, some kind of lion with no mane and the nose of a pig…There were others she couldn't quite make out in the partial darkness. But there was one who caught her eye and refused to release it. It was a human likeness, for the most part, with black-rimmed eyes bulging from their sockets. Its eyebrows tilted, nearly converging in the center above the crimped bridge of a nose which led to flared nostrils. Its lips were twisted into a crooked smile.

It had spoken to her, although it had not moved its lips in speech. It returned her gaze, so that she felt she was the object of its mockery. She tried to tell herself it was impossible, that she had spent so much time in books that she had forgotten what it felt like to have a real conversation. And yet, its eyes stared at her with intensity and purpose.

"You spend more time here than I do! All those dusty texts, all that reading and nothing to show for it."

Kira stood in the road as if she were the one made of stone.

"I know you can hear me," the voice said. It sounded like bricks gently rubbing together and had a genderless quality. "Don't be rude, now."

Didn't they say that hearing voices in one's head was relatively harmless, as long as one didn't answer back? But what if the voice had a face?

"I…tomorrow…nine," she stammered.

"And you've written nothing? It can be done, to be sure, but why such delay? Have you no ideas of your own?"

"Not a…thesis, as such."

She heard it snicker, the sound like a boot extinguishing a cigarette on a gravel path. "How can a mind that reads be so barren?" He paused. "No, you're no imbecile; there's life in you somewhere."

"What…are you?"

"I am, in more ways than one, a part of this institution and have been for four hundred years. I am privy to the entirety of human cultural and intellectual knowledge as much as I am confined by it, to millions of tomes, which you yourself would require three thousand years to read. Maybe then you'd feel equipped to pen a simple essay."

She felt this was a bit unfair. "Mary Shelley said she was never a person of opinions—she saw the merits in both sides of an argument," she blurted, instantly fearing for her sanity at hearing herself debate with a sculpture.

"Is that who you admire, then?" She heard the voice scoff, as if coughing up sand. "Ambivalent wench. Percy, now there was a young lad with spirit and conviction, far too much for this institution back in his day. I had only to point him in the right direction."

There was a pause, during which she wondered whether it would not speak again or whether she had indeed heard anything at all. She became aware of a small group of revellers ambling along from the direction of The King's Arms. Townies, she assumed. She thought about calling out to them. But what would she say? "Help, I'm being insulted by a wall?" Instead she waited silently for them to pass, fidgeting about to create the impression that she was standing alone in the quiet street for some other, rational purpose.

"I can help you, as I've helped others before," the voice said, finally, when the pedestrians were no longer within earshot.

"Why me?"

"Indeed," it said, with a disappointed puff of sand. "Why you? You might be the dullest one yet." There was a pause. "Still, you'll have to do. I can give you what you want: the perfect essay, staunchly argued, flawlessly referenced, eloquently phrased. That *is* what you desire, is it not? To fit into this world, to flourish?"

She considered. The face was right; that was the only thing she wanted. What did her passion amount to if it did not lead to success or recognition? She could not face her professor's disappointment again. She had never cheated, never taken a shortcut before, but that was because she had never needed to. Now, feeling weakness where once there had been strength, the offer tempted her. It wasn't often that she, or anyone from her family or neighborhood, got a leg up in life. Even if this was all a dream, she wanted to see how it would play out.

"Yes," she said.

"Good," it said. "How many words?"

"Three thousand."

"Fine. Go back to college and start typing. I'll write it through you; it should only take an hour or so…Only you must do something for me in return. For now, I want you to promise me you will return tomorrow afternoon at two o'clock. I will then ask a small favour of you, which I will expect you to grant out of obligation. Are we at an understanding?"

"Yes," she said again.

"Marvellous. Go on now, run along back to your desk."

"What do you mean, you'll 'write it through me'?" she asked.

The face said nothing.

She sat bathed in the blue light of her laptop screen, staring at the blinking cursor. Her face was propped up by her left fist, and she tapped a pen against her notes with her other hand.

What she had experienced outside the Bodleian had been a simple aberration, she decided. The stress, the lack of sleep and human interaction had caused a psychotic break on the evening before a deadline. Typical! Her eyes drifted along the walls of her room and landed on a free calendar she'd received from the student union. In the bottom corner, there was a phone number and email address for a mental health crisis line. Crisis was bloody right! She would send an email rather than call, obviously.

Dear Crisis Line,

I find myself dealing with a fair amount of stress in making the transition from sixth form to university life. I believe it has begun to have a negative impact on my mental and academic wellbeing. I would appreciate information on any support services you may be able to offer, at your earliest convenience, of course.

Kind regards,

Kira

Sent. How embarrassing.

She returned her attention to the blank document that had been waiting for her. She should just start writing something, anything.

And, suddenly, she did. She knew precisely what needed to be said. As quickly as she could tap the keys, ideas synthesized and culminated into a thesis that was clear, nuanced, appropriately scaled and boldly unique. She kept going, recalling with stunning accuracy quotations and page references, flawlessly integrated within subparagraphs that upheld the main argument whilst elegantly complicating it, responding to anticipated counterargument. She stared in awe at the screen as her fingers typed, only indirectly connected to her mind, and perfectly capable of orchestrating phrasing and syntax without a single error. And so it continued, until she watched herself type a conclusion and a full page of references, adhering perfectly to MLA guidelines.

Finally, she scrolled to the top of the document and typed the title, "How Rood: Responding to Postcolonial Critiques of Animism in 'The Dream of the Rood'." She then saved the file and sent it in an email attachment to her professor. At this, she instantly felt her eyes become dry and heavy and could scarcely summon the energy to stumble over to the bed, but managed to arrive just in time to feel herself collapse on the duvet. The clock radio showed that it was only nine o'clock, and this was the last thing she saw before her heavy eyelids sank shut and her mind sank to sleep with them.

She awoke the next day at noon, feeling as she had the day she first arrived in Oxford: excited, proud, confident. It had taken a psychotic episode, but she appeared to have finally found her intellectual footing.

She opened her laptop to check for any new emails. Nothing from her professor, but this was to be expected, as she would see him in person the next day. She did see that the Crisis Line had sent her a reply.

Dear Kira,

Adjusting to university life is stressful for many students, and it is normal to feel overwhelmed. Unfortunately, the Crisis Line is intended primarily for students at serious risk of self-harm and suicide. If this is

or becomes the case for you, I would urge you to call our emergency line, which is open 24 hours a day.
Best,
Vanessa

No matter. She felt her situation had changed completely since the previous evening. Things would be better now, and with no lectures or appointments to attend that day, she could do as she pleased. She poured some cereal into a blue bowl from Poundland, where she had picked up virtually all of her living essentials on move-in day, and thought about how she would spend her free afternoon. She would read something published within the last two hundred years, and then later on, she might have dinner in hall and actually socialize with some of the people in college. That would be nice. She reached for a worn copy of *The Mysteries of Udolpho* and settled into her leisurely day.

Only once, and only for a moment, did she cast a disquieted glance at the clock as its red lights flashed 14:00.

The next day, Kira waited outside the professor's study with her course-mates, happily chatting about the year's social calendar. She was even pretending to consider attending a college ball, for which the tickets cost £150, when the professor opened the door and beckoned everyone inside. Even he seemed to be in a good mood.

"Well," he began, once everyone was seated. "We've had some very interesting essays from everyone on a wide variety of topics. David, why don't you start us off by walking us through your argument."

David did, and it was clear he had rehearsed it well. Kira listened enough to understand that it boiled down to his typical cage match of two opposing critics, with himself acting as referee. The strange part was that she was quite sure she'd never heard of either of the critics before, even as everyone else in the room appeared to nod in understanding. Had there been an additional reading list she hadn't known about? *No*, she thought, *that was impossible*.

She began to feel the familiar tightening grip take hold of her chest as she wiped her palms on her tights. There began a nervous trembling in her core and lower back. She could not recognise many of the words David was saying. Had he suddenly acquired a more advanced vocabulary? Had he started to speak in Old English?

Her hands began to shake. She had lost the train of his argument completely and could no longer recall what he was talking about. The fewer and fewer words she could comprehend provided no clues.

"Ah," she heard the professor interject. "Kira expressed quite a different opinion on historical relativism in 'Dream of the Rood'," he said, looking at her with delight and anticipation.

Historical relativism? And what the fuck was a rood? "I thought," she began, hoping the rest of the sentence would complete itself independently. It did not, and she could feel sick rising in her throat, bringing with it a tickling sensation inside her cheeks and the taste of salt. "Excuse me," she said, retching, and ran out the door, leaving a bemused and concerned group of intellectuals in her wake.

"What did you do?" she shouted to the open doorway, startling a group of Japanese tourists. She'd lost track of the horrified reactions she'd provoked in the last half hour. In her hasty cycle to the library, she had narrowly avoided a collision with a car and had nearly hit two pedestrians, besides.

The face chuckled, but no one in the crowd seemed to hear it, not even the tourists who were busy snapping photos of the library's façade. She wished someone else would acknowledge it, to give her a sense that she was not crazy. "I suppose you could say I froze you. Your intellect and vocabulary are still intact, but they will remain irretrievable. Sorry, that means you cannot reach them." It laughed again. "After you missed our appointment yesterday, I had to make sure you would come back."

"I didn't think you were real!" she exclaimed, attracting even more stares. She fished her mobile out of her pocket and held it to her ear, trying to appear casual as she spoke. "I thought it was all in my head," she said, quieter.

"You silly girl! Of course I'm in your head. And that is why I will not be ignored. You will continue to have the mind of a turnip until you do as I say. You can't get something for nothing, you know."

"What could you possibly want?"

"Oh, just a bit of fun. I want you to step in front of a bicycle."

"What?"

"A bicycle, love. You know, two wheels? Wait where you stand for someone to approach, and then jump out at the precise moment to cause a collision between yourself and the cyclist."

She winced. "But why?"

"Because I know everything there is to know about human beings, a knowledge I have acquired passively, through reading and watching. I want to act, to feel and inflict pain, to dance and fornicate and bleed. Unfortunately, it seems I can only exert my influence on precious few individuals, and it appears you are the lucky one *du jour*. I have seen many unsuspecting victims trampled on this street, but I've never caused it to happen—as much as I may have wished it!"

"You're sick!"

"You're stupid, and you will remain that way until you do as I ask. It will hurt, I expect, but I doubt you will break any bones."

Kira stood quietly, considering, but even considering was too difficult. She had to act. If she walked away in her current mental state, she might be hit, anyway. She watched as cyclists passed by, some slowing as they approached the crowd of tourists, while others prepared for a sharp right turn. She inched forward, testing her nerve with each step.

"That one," said the voice.

She looked to her right and saw a young man—fair, thin and speccy—approaching the road between her and the face. He was quick and peering in the direction he planned to turn in another ten yards. She waited until he came closer, much closer, very close, and then she sprang directly into his path.

She was knocked down instantly. Thankfully, his preparing to turn had put some spin on her helpless body upon contact, so that she landed to his left and avoided being dragged beneath the tires. She felt a horrible scraping of her limbs against the pavement and glimpsed the pulpy red mess through a rip in her thin tights. She had heard first the boy's surprised sounds, which consisted entirely of vowels, then the thump of soft humans on hard ground and the clattering of metal, followed by gasps of surprise and a noise like gravel cackling. Someone helped her up gingerly, and she saw that the boy was already standing, his jacket and trousers visibly scratched from the fall.

"Are you okay?" he said, gasping and clutching at his right side. "I'm so sorry, I didn't even see you."

"Yeah, I'm fine," she said. She was more than fine. She remembered the rood, Otranto and post-colonialism. She recalled the date of the Norman Conquest. She knew that the face that currently laughed at her pain and embarrassment was called a *grotesque* rather than a *gargoyle*, which must feature a spout for the delivery of rainwater. She recognized irony in the fact that she had endangered the boy's safety and caused him injury, and yet he was the one who apologized.

"Your leg," he said. "It's bleeding. I'll find a porter." He limped towards the entrance to Hertford.

"You're welcome," said the voice.

Once bandaged and whole, she proceeded directly to the library, having offered to pay for the boy's bicycle repair and exchanged contact information. Although her body had seen better days, her mind had returned to her, and it was ravenous. She fed it as much literature as she could cram into it, but still it craved more. It was not a search for meaning, not a philosophical quest to understand some aspect of existence, but a sheer, gluttonous growling that could never be satisfied. Not in three thousand years, apparently. And that wasn't counting the hundreds of new editions added every day, and the many rare and restricted volumes she knew the library housed, taunting her like whiffs of forbidden ambrosia. To read everything would require an eternity, and a better means of digestion than she possessed.

And so she spent five days at the same desk, poring over heavy books, savoring each word. She had stopped going to lectures out of fear of encountering those who had witnessed her nauseous exit. There hardly seemed any point to it; all anyone did was talk about what they'd read. As for tutorials: good riddance. In the silent library, there was no posturing, no pretending and no picking sides.

Her desk could not have been any less inviting to visitors. Every day she sat with her back to a shelf, entombing herself within piles of neatly stacked hardcovers on the remaining three sides. She would sit hunched over, her nose only a few inches away from the page, drinking in text like sips of fine Amontillado. She felt she belonged there, as integral a piece as the furniture, the shelves and even the books themselves. But she knew it would never be enough. She had been avoiding her stone friend for several days, but that night, after closing, she sought out the familiar face.

"My, we've been busy," the voice exclaimed. "Your cheeks have grown pale with study, and your person emaciated with confinement."

"You've memorised *Frankenstein*? I thought you preferred Percy."

"I've memorised everything, and Mary is growing on me. What have you been doing? Why aren't you off shagging that nice young lad who fixed you up after your little tumble?"

"My little tumble, that's a nice way of putting it."

"Your problem is you take everything so bloody seriously." It paused, examining her closely. "Your mind is hungry."

"Yes."

"And your body emaciated. Not quite pale, though; you have the face of the Indian subcontinent. Tell me, from which part do you hail?"

"Birmingham," she said, annoyed.

"Quite right," said the face, impressed. "But what of your belief system: Hindu, Jain, Muslim, Buddhist, Christian…?"

"None. I was never an animist, either."

"Ha! Of course not, typical human arrogance. A shame on both accounts; it might have made you interesting. Yes, I expected you to be an atheist, not of conviction, like the young Percy, but out of your own dull brand of indifference."

She was not offended by this but took a moment to consider the critique. "They're all beautiful," she said. "Why should belief matter?"

"Quite right," said the face, this time soberly. Silence. "You know I can give you what you want."

"Yes," she said, with no discernible emotion. "What do I have to do?"

"Trust me."

She spent the whole of the next day at a different desk, the one the face had told her to use, on the eastern wing of the library. She buried her face in a book and, for the first time in recent memory, found herself too excited to focus on the words in front of her. She stood up and wandered over to the stacks, weaving through them and caressing the spines as she went. Other students cast curious glances in her direction. *Let them*, she thought.

She returned to her seat and forced a few more hours of concentration until the sun no longer hung in the sky, and then a couple more until the fluorescent lights gradually flickered into darkness around her, one after another.

She packed her notebook and pen into her bag, leaving everything else undisturbed. She looked around her, and when she was sure no one was looking, ducked underneath the desk. She slid the chair inward, slowly and quietly, burrowing into a corner and concealing herself as best she could. She hugged her knees to her chest, her arms brushing the scabbed abrasions of her left leg. She waited.

She heard brisk footsteps pass, pacing along the ends of the stacks. Finally, they grew quieter and softer still, until she heard nothing at all, followed by the closing of a door and a key turning in a lock.

It was time. She reached into her bag and felt for the vial of pills and the bottle of vodka she had stashed at the bottom. She paused to savor the peaceful darkness, the musty smell of countless books, and the cold solemnity of the stone floor beneath her. She never wanted to leave. She didn't have to, the voice had told her.

She swallowed the lot and waited. It all felt remarkably literary and terribly glamorous. *Kira Bovary*, she thought, smiling to herself. It was immediately after this that she more accurately recalled the ending of Flaubert's masterpiece—the ugly, painful, ignoble death— that she first considered what she was giving up. There was nothing romantic about nausea, convulsions, or the awful, inky taste in her mouth. Her dying thoughts were an ode to her failing body, in which she would never again navigate this world.

A month later, Oxford remained much the same, but for an

earlier darkening of the skies and a wet chill in the air. Late one evening, a young woman and man walked arm in arm. Both shuffled slightly with intoxication, having just exited the passage to the Turf Tavern. The girl's black hair shone with the yellow light of street lamps and premature Christmas decorations. She wore tight jeans over plump legs, tucked into Doc Martens. She looked happy and wore a flirtatious grin, as did the boy, a slight chap with blond hair and glasses. The two walked along together, and between slurred words and laughter, it was impossible for a sober observer to discern the topic of their conversation.

They stopped short in front of the entrance to Hertford. "Remember?" the boy asked, swinging around to face the girl.

"I've still got the scar," said the girl, grinning widely. She pulled him close and went in for a snog and fumble. "Let's go back to mine," she said.

"Okay," he said.

As they turned to go, the girl looked over her shoulder at the great door of the library. She found a spot in the row of faces above it and winked.

Kira could see all of this perfectly from her new throne, but it scarcely concerned her. She had a million other things to think about and was so grotesquely happy.

✗✗✗ ✗✗✗ ✗✗✗ ✗

ABOUT THE AUTHOR

Originally from Canada, Alison Garsha moved to the U.K. in 2013 to pursue graduate studies. She has since settled into her adopted homeland, where she spends her days teaching high school and her nights writing horror, because happiness is for chumps. She is obsessed with elephants, Ira Levin, and learning languages. Grotesque was informed by her own academic experience, although it has been a long time since she has spoken to any walls: they rarely answer back.

THE YELLOW DOG

Christopher Locke

I.

I was steaming. *Steaming.* Leave it to girl-wonder to absolutely ruin my day (and it hadn't even started yet)! The point is, when I come home after nine hours of translating reams of market share analytics (don't ask; you wouldn't get it), I don't want to sit down with cute little napkins and eat a bowl of white bean soup. I don't care if the recipe is from Tuscany and was on *The Ellen Show*—*especially* if it was on *The Ellen Show*, frigging dyke. Nobody eats kale anymore. Why do I want to talk about kale and white beans at 7:30 a.m.? Besides, I want pork chops. And goddamnit, if I want to eat pork chops, I'm gonna eat pork chops! I pay for this house, don't I? Janice just lives in it.

Okay, that's not fair: it's not like she's just lying around waiting to be fucked. Though that would be kind of cool. I mean, look, she tries. Ever since that night I woke up convinced I was dying, she has really been trying to keep me healthy. Doctor said it was an anxiety attack. But I was like, seriously? Would I drag my ass out of bed at 3:30 in the morning and go to an emergency room full of crack addicts and other dumb spicks hunched over in their Fubu jackets for *anxiety*?

Anyway, as I left this morning, I could hear Janice pretending to cry near the dishwasher; you know, trying to make me feel bad about dinner, so I slammed the door to show her that that crap won't fly. I then started walking up the driveway like normal when this yellow dog came bounding out from in front of my Audi. I almost fucking shit myself. It looked young and was bouncing all around and rushed up to me. I pulled my briefcase up like a shield and told it "no," but it just kind of jumped around playfully. His tongue was like a pink party favor, and he was breathing heavy. The dog looked like a lab. It had a red collar, and I heard a couple of tags jingling around its neck, so it must have belonged to some family around here. I told it "no" again and said, "go home," but he was all smiles and playful and I felt a little more at ease. I looked over my shoulder down our driveway to see if I could spy a couple of joggers who maybe went for a run with the dog, but there was no one, so I started moving again toward my car slowly, and the dog stopped hopping and stood, looking toward the woods behind our house. He was kind of pretty, and I realized he probably just got free from his chain, and the owners were out looking for him. I called for Janice but remembered she had the TV on. When I got to the driver's door, I popped it open and slipped onto the leather seat and then slammed the door closed. I looked up into the rearview mirror, and the dog was gone. I sighed hotly out of my nose. As I started the car up and put it into reverse, I thought, *I'm not eating fucking kale.*

II.

Dinner that night was good, and, in spite of myself, I didn't think the kale was bad. Reminded me of spinach. I even had a second bowl. I grabbed the bottle of white zin off the table and poured Janice another glass, after she excused herself and went into the kitchen for more bread. *Getting laid tonight,* I thought. And if she catches a good enough buzz, we won't have to talk again about having kids. Just straight-up nasty sex, like we used to have back in college in Gettysburg. She was insatiable back then. I'm serious. Check it out. She was all pro women's rights, talked about Gloria Steinem like she invented her and even majored in Women's Studies for a while. But when we were alone…damn. That tiny dorm room of hers would be rocking all hours of the day. She usually came with her friends to the basement parties my fraternity held every Thursday. She had this unselfconscious way of moving that seemed to make everything else in the room part and give way. After spending most of the evening with my brothers on the third floor, I'd eventually come down and find her cloistered around the keg after midnight talking politics. I'd mess with her and refer to George Bush like he was a fucking hero, and she'd laugh through her auburn hair, grinning up at me. In fact, she used to always laugh at my jokes. After we started hooking up on a regular basis, I knew we'd end up married. Felt it. Marriage, back then, wasn't something that frightened me; it wasn't something that filled my dreams at night with dark shapes and indiscernible images, the dream where all I can hear is the sound of someone lightly tapping on the bedroom window asking to come inside.

III.

The yellow dog came back. Sure as shit. I was schlepping a large tin of compost out to the pile we keep turned at the edge of our property for the gardens Janice says she'll start next spring, when it damn near ran into me. It galloped out from behind a wide birch tree, and I was all like, "*Motherfucker!*" spilling the leftover veggie scraps and egg shells onto the ground. I told it sternly to "go home, get on home," and it ran around me with that dumb grin it has, oblivious. I put my head down and sighed. Then, just like that, it came over and nuzzled my hand. Its fur was soft and his breath warmed my fingertips. It felt nice. "Hey buddy," I said. He whimpered a bit, and I felt bad for him. I stroked the top of his head. "You're a good dog, aren't you," I said. Then he skittered off in the direction of the tool shed, ran a circle, and turned back toward me. He sat down on the icy grass and wagged his tail, giving me doe eyes. "Aw, buddy, I'd love to take you in, but we got cats," I said, glancing back toward the house. "They'd go apeshit. Besides, you probably belong to some kid around here, and I bet he's missing you."

The yellow dog got up and darted back into the woods, small sticks and dead leaves crackling in his wake, until he was up a small hill and behind some ancient pines, gone. I smiled. I leaned down and picked up the scraps, grimacing. I straightened up, wiped my left hand down my jeans, and walked over to the compost pile. As I dumped the heap in, wondering if I left the pitchfork in the tool shed or propped up next to a nearby tree, I gasped: behind the pile was half of a dead rabbit, its back two legs missing. Its eyes were impenetrably black. Blood dazzled its brown fur and the grass beneath it. "Oh my god," I said. "Oh my god."

IV.

When I told Janice about the rabbit she didn't believe me. So I repeated myself slowly and jabbed my thumb over my shoulder, pointing toward the body. She said okay and put her coat on and then followed me outside.

As we walked, I told her about the yellow dog I'd seen, and she became significantly more spooked, asking where it went and that we should go back inside and call the police. I told her to calm down and that the dog was really friendly to me and that it was probably just hunting. But honestly, I felt a little scared and kept looking up into the woods as we got closer to the site. I judged every sound: bird flutter, passing car, wind, for the possibility of a bark.

When we arrived at the compost, the rabbit was gone.

I looked around like a mad man, telling her that it was right there, right there. Janice asked if I was sure but then said she could see blood, which was a huge relief. I got down on one knee and inspected the ground. The cold green grass made the blood seem brighter, electric. "It was right here," I said again. Janice was breathing hard and asked which way the dog went, moving her dumb body around me, and I suddenly wanted to stand up and punch her in the face.

She stood looking deep into the woods. "Are you sure it was a rabbit," she asked.

V.

The whimpering woke me up.

I opened my eyes and lay in bed like a stone, sure of what I heard. My heart was racing. Janice was lightly snoring beside me. I then heard the whimpering again, coming from downstairs. It sounded like a dog.

"Janice," I said. Janice kept dreaming and didn't move, so I shook her hip. "Janice," I repeated.

She untrawled from sleep, inhaled deeply. "What? What's wrong," she said.

"The dog is in the house," I said.

She bolted upright. "What? Where?"

"Shh," I said. "Listen."

I continued lying prone on my back, and Janice clutched a pillow upright. Scratching sounds came from below us and then that soft whimpering again.

"Oh my god," Janice said, and she slid down closer to me.

I patted her thigh. "I'll check it out," I told her.

"What? No. Let's call the police."

"Not yet. It sounds hurt. Let me check it out."

"Don't be crazy," Janice urged and started fumbling around her bedside table for her iPhone.

"Janice," I said, "put it away."

I slowly got out of bed, trying to be as quiet as possible.

"Wait," Janice insisted.

I was looking at our bedroom door and waved back at her to be quiet. The moon lit the thin slats between the blinds and everything in the room look cut into grey strips of light. I figured it was about 3 o'clock. I slid open the closet door and grabbed the wooden shillelagh I brought home from our honeymoon to Ireland. The club's weight felt good in my hand.

As I creaked the bedroom door open, I heard the whimpering again but louder, and it sounded like it was coming from the dining room. I flicked on the hall light, flooding the stairwell, and I heard the dining room chairs jostle and then a kind of quick scuttling, like animal nails across the tiled kitchen floor. I froze. "Shit, shit, shit." I waited, my chest heaving under my T-shirt. Silence. Janice called my name and I ignored her, thinking, *Shut the fuck up.*

I walked slowly down the stairs with the shillelagh in front of me like a bat. I stepped into the living room and turned on a table lamp, and the whimpering started thrumming again, this time from the kitchen. My mouth was dry, and when I said "Hey boy," my voice cracked.

I made it to the other side of the living room and stood just outside the darkened kitchen. "Good boy," I said. "Hey, you're a good boy." I reached my arm into the kitchen and moved my left hand all around the wall frantically, trying to find the light switch before I heard the dog again. The image of it suddenly lunging from the darkness and sinking his white teeth into my throat filled my head, and I wanted to cry out. Then the kitchen exploded in light. I pulled the shillelagh back and prepared to bash the dog's head in.

Nothing.

The kitchen was quiet. Empty. I stepped onto the tiles, still holding the shillelagh like Derek Jeter. Not a single living thing stirred but me. I looked back over my shoulder, spun around, and then back toward the kitchen. I walked across the length of the room and into the mudroom. It felt cold. But the washing machine and dryer were there. Our coats were hanging on their pegs above the recycling bins. Everything looked normal. Then I looked at the front door and saw it was open about six inches. Cold air was seeping into the room. I grabbed the knob and pulled the door closed with a whump, turning the lock. *Jesus,* I thought. *how the fuck did that happen?*

I turned back toward the kitchen but stopped; both cats were now in there, huddled under the breakfast table. They looked up at me indifferently. The white one meowed silently. "Some watch cats you are," I said and went over to the sink and ran the faucet. From the strainer, I grabbed a coffee mug and got a drink. Afterward, I thought about how scared I was and smiled at my foolishness. I then retreated back the way I came, turning off each light in succession.

VI.

Janice was still freaked out after I came back to bed. I told her the dog was gone, but she said I couldn't be sure unless I checked every room and saw with my own eyes that the coast was clear. I said I was sure, and she said it was my fault the dog got in in the first place because I never lock the front door. I shot back that we live in the fucking boonies, and that no one is trying to break in and kill us. This lead to a bigger argument about who does more housework, and by the end, it was almost 4 o'clock, and I was furious. I went downstairs after grabbing my pillow and a blanket and stretched out across the couch. I started wondering if Janice was right, and the dog was still inside, so I got up and turned the lights on to double check. The house was quiet and still, and as far as I could tell, void of trespassing dog.

I managed to fall asleep at some point and had that dream again where I'm back in college at my fraternity house on the third floor. I could smell the heavy perfume of weed and the walls were covered in posters and frosted mirrors advertising beer and women in bikinis. I could feel the party thumping up from below. One of my brothers stumbled out from the main bedroom in front of me, laughing.

"We got a train going on in there, bro," he said, so I pushed the now-open door wider. I could see several members of my fraternity in varying degrees of undress half-circled around a large maple four-poster bed. Skin was slapping on skin, and I could see the naked girl unconscious face down across the mattress. Her hair was wild and splayed like the legs of a spider. Our Sergeant-of-Arms was sort of on top of her, behind her, pumping furiously.

One of my brothers—the one from a deeply religious family in Nebraska—was saying "Do it, do it, that whore loves it," his hand moving up and down on himself with greater urgency. Someone told me the girl's sister was being kept outside on the balcony, a place dubbed "The Meat Locker," and that fucking slut was next.

I started undoing my belt and the sound of the buckle clanking seemed too loud, and I woke up. My face felt hot and I was relieved I was safe on the couch. I squinted; sun was spilling into the room as Janice had already pulled the blinds up. I could hear her talking on her phone in the kitchen, but speaking like she didn't want to be heard speaking.

VII.

A town truck pulled up into our driveway after lunch. The man at my door said he was with Animal Control. He wore a denim shirt with the name Hal stitched in red above the breast pocket, and his hair was as white as his mustache. I thought it ironic that he looked like Hal Halbrook playing Mark Twain.

"Yeah, you aren't the first one to mention that," he said.

I laughed. I invited him in and we sat in the dining room. I had seen Hal around the town hall a few times, voting nights and whatnot.

When I introduced him to Janice, I made sure Janice could see the fury on my face for contacting this guy after I told her no calls. Janice went into the kitchen to make tea.

"We appreciate the call," he said. "Can you describe the dog to me?" And that's pretty much how it went for the next ten or twelve minutes: Hal asked questions about the dog; I answered.

Hal wrote in a thin spiral notebook. He finally closed the notebook and said he hadn't had any other complaints and that no dogs were reported missing in the area.

"Okay," I said. "How does that help us get this dog off our property?"

Hal paused. He said he knew this would sound funny but wanted to know if we knew the previous owners of the house, the Stewarts.

I said "no," and Janice came back into the dining room, leaned into the doorframe as she stirred her tea.

"You've been here how long, about ten years, right?"

I looked at Janice. "Yeah. I guess so," I said.

"Well, I've worked for this town for almost twenty-five, and what you're describing to me is roughly what Mister Stewart described a few years before you all moved in." Hal sipped his tea and looked me in the eyes.

"Okay," I said. "But that doesn't make any sense. This dog is like a year old or something."

"Mm-hm," Hal said in agreement. "Mister. Stewart said the same thing about the dog. Funniest thing."

Then all three of us didn't say anything for a few seconds until Janice piped up. "What happened to the Stewarts' dog?" she asked.

"Oh, it finally resolved itself," Hal said, standing up. I stood up, too.

"What do you mean it resolved itself?" I asked.

Hal sighed. He sounded like he was either really tired or thinking carefully about what to say. "Mister Stewart bought a rifle. He wasn't the hunting type. He said he would ambush the dog, said it was trying to get into the house, just like what you two described, I guess. He, uh, he tripped and fell on his rifle out there near the woods, at the boundary where your lawn meets those old pines." Hal pointed to where I discovered the dead rabbit. "The fall apparently caused the weapon to discharge. He was struck in the head. The whole thing was very sad," Hal said.

I looked at Janice. Her left hand was fluttering near her left cheek, and for the first time, I didn't know what to say.

VIII.

Hal said he'd keep his eyes peeled for the dog and would let us know immediately if he caught it. We thanked him and said goodbye. As he got into his truck and slowly backed down our drive, I knew he wouldn't come by again. Standing in the doorway with Janice, I said "So, should I buy a gun?" and laughed quickly but that only made things feel tenser.

"That's not funny," she said and moved around me and back into the kitchen.

I said I was going to take a shower.

I slid the upstairs shower door back and stepped into the tub, tufts of steam climbing up and around my body. As I lathered up, I puzzled and puzzled the whole damn thing. I was confused and alarmed but certainly not ready to chalk it all up to a phantom-dog-campfire-story. That idea was absurd. Clearly, someone living in another town lost their dog, and the thing had run away so far and wide that it became unable to find its way back. Pretty basic.

Shampoo started to sting my eyes, and as I shook my head under the warm pressure of the water, I heard Janice open the bathroom door and come inside. "Hey babe," I said. "Mind closing the door? Heat's getting out." My eyes were squeezed shut, and I could hear Janice breathing near the shower door, but her breath sounded kind of ragged. She tapped on the glass. "Babe?" I peeked my left eye open, and the first thing I thought was *why is Janice dressed like that?*

The girl from my fraternity, the one on the balcony, was standing in her sweatshirt and torn underwear. Her hair had a leaf or two muddied between the layers. She tapped on the glass again, and her shoulders were heaving up and down rhythmically, her mascara running down to her chin.

I screamed and swiped at the door, falling back against the blue-tiled wall in the process. I slipped down immediately, the built-in soap dish smashing into my back and ribs as I fell; I heard a loud snap and thought I broke the dish. My feet shot up in the air with my legs resting against the glass door with all my weight pressing on my shoulders. Water pounded my face, and I couldn't see anything.

The door slid open, and I screamed again, but my voice was strangled and high, and I felt ashamed. Hands reached in and down, and my kicking legs fell out of the tub and onto Janice.

"Oh my god, oh my god!" she screamed.

"Janice," was all I could manage to say.

She turned the knobs, and the water stopped, and I kind of slid myself up and back against the wall, causing explosive pain to shoot through my back. I was blinking wildly, and I ran my hand down my face. "Janice," I said again and heard a crack in my voice. For the first time in as long as I could remember, I thought I was going to cry and understood if I did, I wouldn't be able to stop.

IX.

After Janice assisted me in getting out of the tub, and I dried off as best I could, she helped me wince my way into bed; I had at least two broken ribs, maybe more. She kept asking what happened, and I kept saying that I didn't know. We were all out of Ibuprofen so I took a couple of Xanax that the doctor had prescribed for my anxiety and pulled the covers up to my chin. My teeth chattered, and I thought I might have a fever.

"I've never seen you look so scared," she said.

Janice wanted me to go to the ER, but I told her they couldn't do anything for broken ribs. She said she'd at least go into town and get some Advil and Gatorade, and I said fine but to please hurry back. She looked down at me with something worse than pity and sat on the edge of the bed and rubbed my hair back. I grit my teeth and swallowed.

"Janice," I said. "Remember Gettysburg?"

She cocked her head as if studying me and said, "Of course. Why?"

"Well, times there weren't always great, you know. I mean, there were things that happened that were hard…mm, bad. My fraternity wasn't full of a bunch of angels, you know?"

"What are talking about?" Janice asked. "Are those pills getting the best of you?" She smiled.

"No, no. It's just that, my fraternity was relentless. They did whatever they wanted. *I* did whatever I wanted. There's a reason I don't talk to those guys anymore," I said. I wanted Janice to tell me everything was okay and I was forgiven. I swallowed awkwardly. The room seemed compressed and tight and the fading sunlight took on a watery glow. My head felt thin and weightless as a balloon. "Janice, I did things I shouldn't have. I did so many things."

Janice looked in my eyes and in that moment, I thought she knew. She sighed and looked down. "It wasn't your fault," she said, and I felt a great release in my chest; my eyes filled with tears. "You only did what your brothers had done, and their brothers' brothers.

But things like hazing are no longer a part of the process. Things have changed, right? You told me that. You were only following tradition."

"No, no, that's not what I mean," I said, and tried to inch up but a new explosion of pain caused me to yelp and slide back down.

"Shh, try and rest," Janice said. "I'll be back in less than an hour, okay? If you need anything, call me on my cell. But really, just try and sleep." Janice's eyes were clear and bright. "I love you," she said.

X.

The front door slammed, and it startled me awake. I listened for the sound of keys and Janice's quick, nervous steps.

Nothing.

"Janice?"

I heard whimpering come from the bottom of the stairs, and I opened my mouth, too afraid to scream. "No," I whispered. "*No. Not like this.*"

I didn't have to see the yellow dog to know it was moving up the stairs, slowly, and as it lumbered up each step, its whimpering grew louder, and I could hear the light jingle of its collar. "I'm sorry," I whispered. "I'm so sorry," and I started to cry. "Please," I said, "please stay out. It wasn't my fault." I tried to sit up but slid back down. The yellow dog was outside in the hallway and it was growling. I could hear it snapping its jaws. "Get out," I shouted and lamely tossed a pillow at the door. I reached over to the bedside table and tried to grab my cell phone but only succeeded in knocking it on the floor.

The door pushed open without a sound, and the yellow dog filled the entrance. Thin streams of drool fell from its mouth.

"It wasn't my fault," I screamed. "She was just a stupid girl! She wanted it! They all wanted it!"

The yellow dog didn't wait to hear more. It moved across my floor in an instant. In spite of my terror, I was dazzled. The yellow dog's breath was hot and sour and smelled like rot. I pushed at his head, but the yellow dog calmly found my throat as if nuzzling for something good. I could hear chewing. That's when I remembered the girl's name; it was the name of a flower. Lily, I thought.

Lily.

Lily.

Lily.

)(●)(●)( )(●)(●)( )(●)(●)( )(

ABOUT THE AUTHOR

Christopher Locke is the Nonfiction Editor at *Slice Magazine* in Brooklyn. His speculative/flash fiction has appeared in *SmokeLong Quarterly, Flash Fiction Magazine, Forth, Adbusters,* and *New Flash Fiction Review.* His latest book is *Ordinary Gods* (Salmon Poetry), a collection of travel essays about Latin America. He lives in Upper Jay, N.Y.

AND HE ASKED WHY

Morrison

My name is Thomas Lyre, and I died when I was four years old.

He found it hilarious; he really did. The seamless transition into this new body, new identity, could not have been smoother. He had money, an elderly, senile mother who was delighted to see him every week, and he had made a business out of the family money so graciously given to him by his ailing mother.

There was no one who could challenge his claim.

There had been a sister, but she had disappeared years ago. Tom thought she could easily be dead, because in the four years he had been Thomas Lyre, she had never come to find him, never challenged the fact that this man was not her long-dead brother. Until such a time when she did come forward, Tom felt free to take money from his mother's hands. Free to twist this identity to his liking.

Then he had received the letter.

The first one had arrived one year ago.

The letter telling him to cease this charade before he regretted it. He was to die again, twenty years after his first death. He was to leave everything behind, or he would regret his decision to steal Thomas Lyre's identity.

It hadn't been signed. Whoever was threatening him didn't even have the gall to sign their letter.

Tom had originally scoffed at the pitiful, empty threat. But the letters had kept on coming, once a month. The same note.

It became heavily folded, crumpled, and ruined, but every time he threw it out, it would return the next month. The exact same letter he had thrown out. The second time it had appeared with his morning paper, he had burnt it. Then the next month, he received a new copy in an envelope full of the ashes and the burnt remains of the last one.

That one he had locked in his desk drawer, and the following month, he had found that very letter set on his bedside table, office drawer left open as a taunt when he went downstairs.

It unsettled Tom to know that whoever was doing this was able to access his office, his home, and he quickly began to lay off members of his household staff. Until there was no one but himself in the house.

And every month on the twenty-seventh the letter would arrive again.

Thomas Lyre died on 27th March, 1864.

He left this month's note on his desk, flattened out in front of him. Tom glared at the paper, the loopy, neat handwriting glaring back at him, and he thought of the missing sister. The whispers of her lingering in the shadows. Was it truly her? Was it the supposed darling sister? Would she have come back to remove him? He didn't know anything about her. Only that she had disappeared at the age of twenty and never returned. But he had seen her writing before. And he was looking at it now.

Leave.

He picked up the letter again. Set it down. Tried to flatten it out against the desk. Though multiple efforts had been made to smooth it out, the remnants of his temper lingered in the creases.

He would not be undone after nearly four years' success. Not by some phantom pretending to be his sister after years of being missing. He picked up the letter again, sneering at it before slamming it back down on his desk, irritated.

Tom finished his drink, ignoring the slight shaking of his hand on the glass. He set the tumbler down heavily with a lazy, dead-limbed slide of his hand before heading to bed, leaving the embers in the fire to die slowly.

Despite himself, Tom had begun to feel cautious. In all honesty, he knew that this "sister" could destroy him. She was the only one who could say for definite that this was not her brother, that her brother was dead. His darling mother was too senile, so desperate to believe that he was her child, that she had welcomed him with open arms and a hug too tight to be comfortable. However, "Thomas Lyre" was an arrogant man, sly and cunning but dulled with the copious amounts of whiskey he'd taken to drinking in the past few years. He'd become strained with nerves, worn with constant invisible eyes on his back.

Tom had long thought that if this sister was real, then she could be bought off, and even if she wasn't, then she could still be bought off. He held the belief that whoever this poison pen was would soon tire of this game.

He had enough money to have them silenced if need be, but he would wager that his original belief was correct. That the real girl was dead or married off to some family and living her own life, forgetting about the past she had had with a broken family and a dead little brother.

With those comforting platitudes to himself, what did Thomas really have to fear? Nothing. However, his confidence had faded over the continuous months of moved objects and hand-delivered letters. He drank some more whiskey in bed, attempting to keep his eyes sharp, even as he watched the wall with increasing listlessness. Despite his heavy dosing, he was taut with concern.

The house was silent as he attempted to settle into his bed, but the sounds of London drifted through his windows. The constant stream of noise was a soothing contrast to the aching silence of his home.

There was nothing to the letter, nothing at all.

A mere girl would be no threat.

No threat at all.

Tom had drifted restlessly into sleep until he suddenly startled into wakefulness in the early hours of the morning. The room was pitch black, and there was nothing out of place to have woken him, but he lay there frozen, eyes wide as though sleep had never touched him at all.

He was as awake as he had ever been, tense and ready to spring out of bed, even as he could feel the remnants of his night's heavy drinking still weighing on his limbs.

Tom shifted in his bed uncomfortably, trying to shake off the weird feeling, wincing at how loud the springs creaked in the silence. He tried to move his head onto a cooler spot on his pillow when he felt his bed shift, silently, as though someone had sat at the bottom of it. Tom looked up in alarm but could see nothing in the dark room. His breath seemed unnecessarily loud, and he tried to stifle it a little. He began to move his feet slowly, feeling around for the person at the end of the bed.

Tom felt undeniably stupid. Why on earth was he acting like a scared child? Fearing the ghost at the end of the bed? He scoffed.

Tom smiled to himself, relaxing a little at his foolishness before he heard a wet sound.

His breath caught in his throat. Though he couldn't see anyone, he could feel eyes on him, weighty as a hand on the nape of his neck.

As paranoid as he had always been, Tom was not a believer in the supernatural. He was smart, a part of the new age of enlightened thinkers.

There was someone in the room with him. A physical human being.

It couldn't be her, could it? His little lost girl...his sister.

"Lyre?" He whispered in question, no more than a shaky breath, eyes darting around in the black room.

There was no answer from the person. Tom knew it had to be Lyre, or whoever was pretending to be her, there was no way anyone else would have snuck in, and it had to be the same person who had been planting the letters. Tom's fear choked him slightly, his alcohol-weighted limbs holding him down. He let out a shaky breath.

"Lyre!" Tom said again, voice a high-pitched hiss in the blackness as he propped himself up weakly, glaring into the darkness. "You don't get to send letters and hide in the dark! Watching me sleep... Don't be such a lecherous coward! If you have a problem, at least face me."

Still there was nothing, not even a slight shift in weight, and Tom couldn't find the figure with his feet. Just as he was about to get up, a cool hand was placed on his forehead pushing him back into the pillows.

"Shh, Tom," a female voice whispered, her hand smoothing back Tom's hair and running her fingers through the tangled mess, gripping it fiercely and tugging it once before letting the strands fall from her fingers. "Is that any way to greet your sister? Not even with her first name?"

Tom tensed with fear as Lyre's short nails scraped gently at his scalp and nearly snatched her hand back when the fingers removed themselves from his hair. If she disappeared back into the shadows, he would have no idea where she was. "I don't have a sister," he rasped. "You are an intruder in my home."

There was nothing for a moment, and Tom pulled the covers up closer to him as though they might be able to protect him. He nearly screamed in terror when the weight changed, and Lyre landed right behind him on the bed like a fallen tree. The scream that Tom could feel building was swallowed into a rasping rattle in his throat as he tried to hold it in.

He felt Lyre chuckle, the hairs on the back of his neck disturbed by the warm breath of the woman behind him. The same hand that had touched his hair a moment ago sneaked around Tom and settled on his stomach.

"Oh, come now, little brother," She crooned, biting his ear, "You need to really commit to this game if you're going to play it."

"Lyre…?" Tom whispered, shaking and feeling sick to his stomach. "What are you doing?" He found his breath catching as Lyre splayed her hand, her fingers tracing his ribs as she did so.

The girl laughed again, an almost caressing sound, and Tom nearly threw up on the spot, a burning heat singing up his gullet.

"Tom, Tom, Tom," Lyre's nose brushed the base of Tom's neck, causing Tom to buck wildly in his captor's hold out of fear. Suddenly the hand that had only been resting against Tom's sunken stomach turned into an arm of steel. With a strength Tom hadn't imagined a woman could physically possess, she drew Tom toward her until his back was pressed against Lyre's torso. She felt too broad in the chest to be a woman, too strong.

"Ahh," The girl whispered, moving her head so her lips could whisper directly into Tom's upturned ear. "You're ruining the game, Tom. We could have had some *fun* before we got down to business."

Lyre's breath made Tom's skin erupt in goose-bumps, and he felt his fear increase tenfold, his heart pounding at Lyre's words. He had heard some of the things Lyre had done before she disappeared, *rumors* he'd thought, but suddenly all his doubts jumped to the forefront of his mind. Her big hands were caging him in, holding him in place with an ease she shouldn't have possessed. Tom wanted to wriggle free. He was at his best with distance, not this closeness, not with this strange woman pressed up against his back. He didn't move a single inch though, even held his breath until Lyre's next words.

"Why didn't you answer any of my letters?" She pressed her face closer, lips against the shell of his ear. "I hand-delivered them, too. Watched you open them. Watched you frown in your sleep. I know you took them seriously. They got to you." She sighed softly, mournfully disappointed. "Why didn't you leave?"

Tom then scrambled, trying to elbow Lyre and free himself, although Lyre seemed to have been expecting it. The fight for freedom was short lived. Tom yelled and bit at Lyre's restraining hands, clawing at them with his own weaker, numbed fingers. That failing, he tried to roll, using all his body weight to his advantage, but Lyre's grip was so strong that it only shuffled them along the bed.

Lyre laughed infuriatingly before securing her hold on Tom and turning her body until she was on her back with Tom pinned on top of her; Tom's back to her chest. Her arms caged him, one snug around his stomach and the other crushing around his throat.

Tom choked loudly, his hands still clawing away, but the compression to his throat was making the already black world spin and his breath rasp. He could feel his eyes rolling backwards and his body dying under Lyre's left arm, her dominant arm, and Tom finally stopped trying and went limp. Instantly, the pressure decreased, the arm loosening enough that Tom could draw breath slightly—but it was enough.

"You know, Tom, you have quite possibly ruined my *charitable* mood tonight by behaving thus?" Lyre snarled, somewhat breathless beneath him, her voice seemed to be everywhere in the dark—high pitched and serpentine in her anger. "All you had to do was play nice. And so would I. I might have even let you keep my money."

Tom made a gasping noise, throat tight under her hand, and he tried to move his legs from the tightly tangled sheets.

Lyre's temper seemed to flare with his wriggling, and she rolled him over so she was pinning him to the mattress, their legs entangling with the bed sheets, "You could have picked any other name, Tom, *any* other name in the world!" Lyre rejoined, perverse enjoyment in her voice as he wriggled in fear beneath her, "But you chose Tom. You chose my little brother's skin for your own." Tom felt Lyre lean closer. "*So, so rude.*" Her breath was hot like a furnace, scalding hot on the back of his neck. "His existence had been wiped away apart from some scratches into stone…until you." Lyre's arms tightened once again, turning into brutally constricting bars. "Until you breathed life into him again. I let you have three years. I let you have *three*. And now it's just becoming four years."

Tom swallowed, pushing back the rushing warmth of a stomach full of alcohol that had begun to slide up his gullet as he tried to reorient himself.

"And you know what happened when my little brother was four? Do you not?" She breathed. "Do you know what I am going to do to you, now that you're four?"

Tom found himself sneering, emboldened by the lie and dizzy in his stupor. There was no way that Lyre was going to kill him. She herself had only been a little girl, only about eight at the time of her brother's death. "You're not going to kill me!" He gurgled a drunken laugh. "Nasty creeping whore that you are, you haven't killed someone!"

As soon as Tom spat those words, Lyre began to increase the pressure on his face and body, pushing him further into the mattress as if to smother him and his words, "Oh but I have. Thomas Lyre died when he was four. Thomas Lyre will die at four again. You don't get to keep him. *He was mine!*" Lyre spat into Tom's hair as she pressed closer, and her anger warped her mouth into an audible sneer. "He was an irritating little boy who I had no time for! *But he was mine!*"

Tom let out a groan, the bed feeling like it was shifting under him but he managed to turn his head further to the side, dragging in gulps of air, "He wasn't yours. His name was free for the taking."

He swallowed heavily, half his face pushed into the starchy bedcovers before he added snidely in a drunken slur, "Mother was glad to see me again."

He felt Lyre shift and move off him a little, a huff of amusement coming from her before she said, "Your opinion is your own to have and mine to punish, Tom." Then the cool tip of a knife ran down Tom's neck, circling his pronounced spine. "And I am going to punish you, Tom, oh so much; I will make you regret every insult to me." The knife dug in a little, and Tom shied away from the cold burn of the blade.

Then Lyre suddenly stood, removing her knife from Tom's flesh but no doubt keeping it trained on him. "Although, I find anticipation is always worse than the actual punishment. And we have so much to discuss." The floorboards creaked as the woman walked over them, her presence in the room suddenly loud and unmissable in contrast to her undetectable, silent poison-pen of the past year.

Tom lay perfectly still for a second, silence briefly descending over the room. He could hear Lyre's lips smacking together as she tried to collect her anger, but the sound was far away, drifting, and the spinning seemed a lot worse than before. He felt a hysterical giggle squirm in his throat and wondered if she had drugged him. He briefly saw the curtain being pulled back, and Lyre's staggeringly tall figure was revealed.

"Oh dear, Tom," he heard her say. "You *have* been drinking a lot." Her figure swayed dizzyingly before he found his vision going black.

When he dazedly stirred, he was bound against a chair in his office and could see a shadowy figure sitting opposite him in his favorite armchair. Lyre had stoked the fire, if the searing brightness in his eyes was anything to go by.

Finally, he could see her properly, sitting in the bright light of the flames. She was tall, as he had previously noted from the moonlight, tall and leaner than he had previously thought. She was also wearing male clothing, inappropriately tight in his opinion. She had crossed her legs and slightly bobbed her foot as she read, looking serene and calm. She looked nothing like the strength she possessed.

He squinted at her, still unable to imagine her being able to pin him as easily as she had.

"Awake, at last." She looked up and smiled at him, her eyes glittering darkly as she looked up from a letter she was reading. In fact, he could see all his documents surrounding her feet, all his personal details and financial records spread out and examined. "I hope you don't mind." She gestured with her occupied hand to the parchment and brushed a stray curl of her dark hair back, the rest pinned up on the top of her head. "I wanted to see what a mess you were making out of my inheritance."

Tom sneered at her groggily from his seat, slumped uncomfortably against the wooden slats of one of his most uncomfortable seats for visitors.

She smiled indulgently. "I thought not." She tossed the document she was holding onto the fire before leaning forward and bracing herself against her knees. "I hope you don't mind that I used your little...*swoon* to my advantage. I thought you could do with some space. You seem to work better with distance, and me being pressed up against your back was rather too...intense for you."

Tom said nothing, attempting to wriggle to a more comfortable position, feeling more lucid. "I want you out of my house," he finally settled on saying, licking his dry lips.

Her eyebrows rose in bemusement. "Oh, of course." She smiled at him. "But it's not your house, is it? I believe it belongs to my mother, and therefore, me." Lyre stood up, walking over to his drinks cabinet and opening it. "And I have been a very obliging landlady. I have let you live here for free for the past four years." She picked up his unwashed glass from only a few hours ago, sneering at the state of it as she poured a liberal measure of his whiskey. "Your favorite, I know," she commented as she tilted it toward him in a toast. He glowered at her in response.

She strode across the room and held the glass to his lips. "You're a dead man, Tom. Drink up. There's a special place in Hell for you, and I won't send you off without a decent last drink."

He glared up at her and sneered, but she pressed the glass more firmly to his bottom lip. "That bottle hasn't been spiked like the last one. This is your last chance, Tom. I won't be playing nice for the rest of your life, so drink up."

Tom sneered over the rim of the glass, finally opening his mouth and swallowing the drink. It burned his throat with a familiar warmth, and he felt his mind sharpen somewhat. He licked his lips again, gathering himself to speak. "What do you want me to say, Lyre? Sorry?" He snorted derisively and continued with a slight slur to his words. "Do you want me to pay you money? What? What is it?" he asked, as she set the glass down on the table next to him. He strained at his bound hands, held tight enough that his arms burned at the uncomfortable position.

"Is this how you speak to everyone?" she asked, stepping backward and surveying him amusedly. "Family name, insincere apology, and the offer to pay them off?"

"It's worked before. On smarter people." He shifted his arm and pulled at his bounds again. He was sure they gave a little.

"Ah. But I'm not smart, Tom. I'm a woman. I'm hysterical. I'm silly, etcetera." She rolled her eyes and grabbed the small footstool from the armchair, then sat in front of him with a broad, toothy grin. "And in this case, you have taken something from me. You honestly believe you can pay me off with my own money?"

Tom's mouth twisted. "I'm not above begging for my life."

"Your face seems to say otherwise, but no, I don't imagine you are when it comes down to it. However, that's not what I want. I can only be paid off with what's not mine, and there is nothing that you own that doesn't already belong to me. Not even your life, dearest. You're my little brother."

"We both know I am not your brother; I owe you nothing." Tom spat, wriggling a little more. He could feel his face flushing a blotchy red.

"You've claimed to be him for this long." She pressed her hand to her heart. "I've *just* gotten used to the idea of having my brother back again." She pointed her finger at him, grinning sardonically. "Do *not* take that away from me."

Tom licked his numb lips and felt a chill run down his spine, cooling his drink-stoked bravado. She wasn't going to be bought easily. She wanted more than he would willingly give. He could feel a wave of goose-bumps running up his spine, the skin of his scalp tightening, a rush of sobriety settling like a leaden ball in his stomach. He let out a shuddering breath. "Then what can I say?"

Lyre looked at him, through him, smile fading into a distant hard-faced, stony countenance. She stood up suddenly and began to pace around him, slowly, touching a few items here and there as she did so.

"My brother's name was Tom. Thomas. Like yours." Her fingers stroked across his shoulders gently, like a spider, and he flinched at the intimacy of the act. She smiled as she continued, "*Exactly* like yours, in fact. You could have plucked it off a gravestone. As you already know. This part of the game you have already played." Her hand settled on the collar of his nightshirt. "You took my inheritance and my title from me because you are male, like he did." Her fingers dragged up the back of his neck and fisted in his short hair. "I killed my little brother for those *exact* reasons. *Do you see where I am going with this?*" she hissed, her fist tightening, twisting. "Do you see why I'm so *upset* about your little farce? Your little scam?" His nod was hesitant but sharp, a brief jerk in her brutal grip. She pulled his head back sharply once before she let go, shoving his head forwards cruelly as she did so.

Lyre hummed quietly, coming around to face him, and her blue eyes were sharp. "I *hated* him," she whispered, gently pushing under his chin with her sice-cold fingers. "He was a lowly creature who deserved nothing more than the quick end I gave him." Her brow crinkled in frustration, her eyebrows drawing in. "I spent so much time—I put so much effort into getting rid of my irritating little brother. Oh, how I *detested* him. With his *whining*, and his *crying*." Her fingers pinched his chin, and her face contorted even further, unattractively, before smoothing into a nastier looking, cruel smirk. "I strangled his pet rabbits with his shoe laces, made him cry as I replaced his little shoes. His feet were so small." She held her fingers up only a few inches apart. "Only this big," she whispered coyly. "Fit in the palm of my hand almost. So tiny."

Lyre let go of his chin, though Tom could feel the lasting impression of her pinching fingers. She stepped back and sat down on the footstool again, feet braced apart as she leaned on her knees. "How he used to sob. Sob. Sob. Sob. And he how he used to *flinch* when I came into the room." She looked briefly victorious in her viciousness. "My parents fawned over him. He was their beloved boy. The son and heir that I never was. I hated him."

"Your family is rich; they needed an heir. That is just the way it is," Tom rasped, incredulously.

"Yes." She smiled. "I was the girl. I was to sit in my dresses and be pretty. I was worthless." She responded and slouched back a little. "But I was never pretty. I didn't like dresses, and I was smarter than everyone else in the household. I was hungry for everything I couldn't have. I deserved the family name. The money. Acknowledgement."

"Which you never got, I'm guessing?" Tom sat up as best as he could from his slumped position, his fingers wriggling as the rope started to give a little.

She rasped out a chuckle lazily. "Oh, do keep on trying to pull your hands free. I can see you." She shifted her weight, smirking at him. "Don't worry, you've drunk so much of your beloved whiskey, regardless of the fact that I tampered with it, I want to see if you can actually do it." Lyre laughed, her fingers drumming an erratic pattern on her leg. "In fact, I'll help you." She stood suddenly and put her hands under his arms, pulling him up from his slump so the pressure on his muscles wasn't so demanding.

Lyre stood back and bent down to pull a small knife out from her boot. She waved the blade in front of him teasingly, before setting it down on the table beside him, behind the empty glass. "If you can get out and get this, then I might give you a painless death." She smiled at him, pushing her face close to him. "Maybe, *maybe* you will be able to kill me first." Her face creased widely with her effortless smile, amused and open. Her thumb ran under his eye. "I would love to see that. You've been such a disappointment thus far."

She went back to her footstool and kicked it out of the way. It skittered noisily across the room, scattering all the papers she had pulled out during her rummaging.

"Anyhow, you are quite correct. I never got acknowledgement. Nor all the education my brother got—and he was so young at the time. He didn't need to learn like I did, wasn't smart like I was. Like I am." She huffed and turned back to Tom, who was pulling in earnest at his bounds, eyes intent on the knife set down for him. "Thomas!" Lyre barked sharply, and his head darted up to meet hers, a fine sheen of sweat covering his face. "Pay attention to me. I do not like to repeat myself. If I have to, I'll carve what I am saying into your skin. Listen."

He bared his teeth at her and carried on, sluggishly struggling, his drugged state making his movements slow and uncoordinated. "I'm listening. Promise."

"Good." She tapped her foot. "Tom was a precocious little boy, even when he was terrified of me. He was beginning to realize that if he told someone, my behavior might stop." Lyre stepped forward, placing her hands on Tom's shoulders, and he looked up at her. "Little fool confronted me about it, when we were out near the river at the end of our property. Well, he was out. I was supposed to be reading in the house. Out of sight, out of mind." Her thumbs stroked his collarbone mindlessly. "His dopey maid wasn't paying attention to him, and I was wearing little boy's clothes…as you can see, they are my preference." Her hands clamped down a little firmer as she watched him loosen his bonds further. "He said to me in his high-pitched, whining, *little* voice that I was only a girl." Lyre bent closer. "He was the *important* one. He was going to tell about what I did to him, about the clothes I wore. And I was going to get in *trouble*."

Lyre let out a slow shaky breath. "Oh, I was so angry, so angry." She leant her forehead against his, her mad eyes instantly locking his joints, holding him still and she bit her bottom lip, pulled at it with her teeth before moving away. "Because he was right! He was completely right!" She then became quiet again, softly spoken. "And I—" She paused and an uncontrollable smile suddenly pulled at her mouth. She turned to him, giddy and hushed and began to whisper. "And I said, no one will believe you. No one will ever believe you, Tom."

Suddenly she swung her leg over his bound lap and sat heavily on him. He jerked back in surprise, the tense atmosphere breaking suddenly with her solid, warm weight physically holding him down. She perched her hands against his chest lightly as she leaned into him a little. Her breathing was shaky, her fingers trembled as they danced up his nightshirt and fisted handfuls of the white cotton, and she pulled herself up to look him directly in the eye. "And, do you know what he did?" She paused for one savory moment. "What he said?" Lyre asked, the sound was tittering, the unsteadiness of laughter dancing in her words as she leaned in toward Tom, pressing closer and breathing the next words straight into his slightly parted mouth so he couldn't miss them. So he could taste them.

"He asked why."

She laughed with a brittle edge, tried to swallow a couple of times. The motion was heavy as she seemed to pull back her mania into something tamable. Lyre then jerked backwards from him, almost as if she had been brutally yanked by her hair.

"So, I hit him over the back of the head with a rock," she rasped, licking her lips running her hands over the back of Tom's head. She ground her knuckles into his skull, "Just here." She wasn't smiling now, she was cold, blank. Tom could see the outline of her chin, the glistening of her wet lips in the darkening room. "He was my first kill. He dropped like a stone." She confessed with a quirk of her lips, continued in a reverent whisper, "And he slipped into the water so gracefully, he just—he just was…" She sighed gustily, taken with the romance of it. "*Silent* as he fell and then…then the water took his face away from me, and he was gone."

She sat silently, almost gentle in the way she relaxed. Tom tested the bounds around his wrist again and tried pulling his hands free. He felt the rope give a little.

Lyre continued to stare into the fire, not focusing on his increasing struggles.

"No one ever thought it was me. I got to live my life in a silent, quiet household. Apart from my mother's desolate wailing. My father slowly slipped away with the death of his beloved boy, left his money to mother, then to me." She turned back to Tom, smirk back in place. "And mother is almost dead now, and finally, I will be the rightful head of this household."

She got off his lap and went back to her armchair by the fire, prodding the now dying flames as she settled herself down, before folding her hands under her chin and staring at him.

"Then I heard the most amazing news, Tom. I found you. Tom. *Tom.* My little brother, alive and well and living in London." A flash of teeth in the darkening room made him flinch back. "Imagine my surprise, when I had made sure he floated down the river, broken and damaged beyond repair." She bared her teeth at him, her hands clenching around each other from under her chin. She swallowed, flinging her hands down with frustration as she stared at him.

"You see, Tom. It is not the fact you stole my baby brother's identity. Not that you gave a dead child life and yourself a way into my inheritance and my senile Mother's attentions. I can live with all that. I really can. Because I didn't love my brother. I made sure he knew it, and I made sure I got rid of him for it. What I cannot take is the insult *to me.*"

Tom stilled from where his hands were frantically pulling at the ropes, so close to wriggling one free. "Why are you taking it so personally?" he finally asked her, frowning in confusion. "Why on earth do you think it has anything to do with slighting you? I merely needed a name and an identity I could utilize."

Her scowl deepened. "Do not liken me to you, as if we are one crook to another! This is personal, because he belongs to me. He'll *always* belong to me." She jumped to her feet, eyes wild and lips pulled back in an animal like snarl. "*His bones belong to me!*" she hissed, stalking toward him. "I don't think you grasp how greatly you've insulted and undermined my efforts to remove his stain from my life, my memory."

She stopped in front of him, chest heaving before she shook herself and sat back in her chair and then sat forward, gravely as though imparting something of great memory and importance to him. He supposed that for her it was.

"And that's why I am here." She steepled her fingers, tone calm despite her wild eyes. "An insult of that measure cannot stand. It just *can't.* My precious little brother is dead." She closed her eyes slowly, tired and bone weary. "I emptied his skull of his brains and felt much better for it. Your existence is robbing me of my happiest memory."

Tom paused in his indiscreet struggles. "What is wrong with you?" He finally laughed, hysterical. He could taste the remains of whiskey around his teeth, could feel the warm heat of vomit in the back of his throat. "Dear God, you're going to kill me because of something so petty?" He laughed again, feeling demented as a cold fear sunk into him.

Her mouth soured. "It has never been petty to me. I was overlooked because I wasn't a boy and I took that back. An—and you," She barked out a coarse laugh. "And you suddenly come into my family and ruin everything! I was so upset at first! But." She took a steadying breath and tried to smile, her teeth glinting at him in brief flashes as her mouth moved. "But then I realized. I realized it is still my happiest memory, but also it is a chance for improvement. For growth and longevity. I get to relive this *glorious* moment all over again." She turned and smiled. "All thanks to you, Tom." She stood up and moved closer.

Tom's breath stilled, choked him, caught in his chest as he got his hand free. The glass was still next to him; he could see the knife glinting on the other side of it. If he got that moment to leap, he could reach it. He could escape this mad woman, kill her as an intruder, run into the street…get help.

But she smiled again in that way that made Tom pause. It was slick and wet, rabid like a dog. It made him think that he had only been able to get out of his bindings because she wanted him to.

She had never tied the rope properly.

She had been playing a game with him this whole time. He tensed, moving his drugged limbs to brace himself more solidly against the wooden chair. He could see the glitter of her dark, dark eyes follow his movements, tracing his hands as they pressed against the arms of his chair unsteadily. He readied himself to jump up, to tackle her. She licked her lips, taking a greedy taste of the air as she pulled out another knife from her pocket.

"Now, I don't have a rock this time," she laughed, pausing in front of him. "But Tom, I promise"—her knife flicked out, the small sound dazzlingly loud—"I *promise* you," she whispered, pressing the blade against his shirt. "My tastes have become much more refined since then."

He leapt.

About the Author

Morrison has just finished her master of Neuroimaging in London, U.K. In her spare time, she enjoys writing writing dark fiction about people who lack morals, are egotistical and enjoy a good rant about their own greatness. She finds her niche is in writing the drama that comes from writing mania and the lack of limits her characters impose upon their actions in the world. Her fiction has previously appeared in *Darker Times Anthology*.

DEATH IN JERUSALEM

ELANA GOMEL

Mor is suspended in heat like a fly in amber. The crowd is sprinkled with Arabs in *galabiyeh,* Orthodox Jews in dusty black coats, and young girls with navel rings. People jostle and push against each other. But Mor walks freely through the crush of bodies, buoyed by the roundness of her stomach, her gaily colored maternity dress glued to it by perspiration. People respect fertility in Jerusalem.

She is relieved when she reaches the old residential area of Rehavia, the ghostly echo of pre-war Europe lingering in the narrow alleyways lined with unkempt gardens. As she approaches her mother's house, she puts down her grocery bag to fish out the key that expertly eludes her sweaty fingers. She opens the gate into the small courtyard where a rusted bicycle rests in the meager shadow of an ancient wisteria. The heat is killing her. Leaning against the jamb to catch her breath, she closes her eyes and tries to cool off with a memory of blue steel and frozen candlelight.

The evening is almost bearable. This is the blessing of hilly Jerusalem as opposed to the swampy, humid Tel-Aviv where in summer, the heat lies on the land like a rotting corpse. As the temperature drops and the light fades to lilac, Mor takes a shower and gingerly lowers herself into the bean-bag in front of the TV. Channels flicker in a babel of voices and images as the carefully made-up anchors read out a litany of war, famine, disease, and death. Names and places change; the stories are the same.

Mor is listlessly chewing on a sandwich. She has no appetite: the heavy thing in her belly takes up too much space.

She goes to bed early. Stretching on her back, she automatically holds her breath, waiting for the baby's kick. Of course, nothing happens.

Sleepless in the dark, she touches her husband's pillow. Cold burns her fingertips.

The scrape of a chair and a man's voice saying: "May I?" She lifted her eyes and was instantly smitten.

It was summer, and the morning was hot, cloudless and blue, as all mornings would be for the next three months. But the man who sat by her in the campus cafeteria smelled of rain and fog, like the cool days Mor remembered from her two-year stay in New Jersey. He smiled: his teeth were white and impossibly even. His eyes were the color of steel.

They talked until she was close to being late for her class. The language of their conversation was English, as it immediately transpired that "May I?" was the full extent of David's knowledge of Hebrew. He was from Toledo.

"I've been to Toledo," she said. "They make wonderful swords."

"Toledo, Ohio," he corrected. "I don't like cutting weapons."

Was he some sort of pacifist? A religious fanatic? A pilgrim? Just a tourist? Mor did not care. He was the most beautiful man she had ever seen.

Just a millisecond before she absolutely had to rush, he asked her whether she was free in the evening.

She was so elated that her lecture went quite well, despite the fact that she had forgotten her notes in the cafeteria. Since her divorce, Mor's life consisted of a chain of relationships with wonderful beginnings and lousy endings. But as long as there was life, there was hope. She tried to be optimistic, just to distinguish herself from her mother. It made the guilt bearable.

They met at Dizengoff Square, which is not actually a square but the wide pedestrian overpass above a perpetual traffic jam. Its revolving fountain wobbled in the grayish twilight, occasionally coughing up a thin jet of water. There were fat pigeons waddling and cooing around. They gave David a wide berth, and Mor was struck by a longing to be with him in the magic circle of quietude that he seemed to draw around himself.

After a couple of drinks in a bar where the flashing lights and deafening noise protected her from being recognized by a nosy friend or ex-lover, they walked along the beach promenade, the black oily sea lying heavy and silent beyond the fluorescent strip of sand. Moonlight dribbled from the tarry sky.

"I like your name," he said. "Mor. Does it mean something?"

"It's a kind of spice or incense mentioned in *The Bible*," she said, searching for the English word. "Oh, yeah. Myrrh."

"Really?" he sounded interested. "I thought it had something to do with death. You know, like *mor*tality."

"Mortality, morbid, moribund." She shook her head. "You are right; it does sound like it belongs with these. Funny. I never thought about this. But it's a different root in English. *Mort*, death in French. Just a coincidence."

Her mother wanted to name her Hanna, but Daddy objected. She insisted, and so there were two names listed on Mor's birth certificate, even though she never used the other one. Another item to add to the list of grudges against her mother; another drop of sweetness to flavor her hazy recollections of the big burly man who had brought her to the kindergarten one fine morning and was dead of a heart attack in the afternoon.

The silence between Mor and David seems restful and romantic, filled with unspoken promises. Mor tries to think what to ask him next. Job, family, politics? What difference did it make? She would be happy to walk with him in this velvety dark for an eternity, just listening to the rhythmic hiss of the waves on the endless bone-white beach. But did he feel the same? He asked for her phone number, true, but made no definite promise to call. When she drove him back to his hotel (which turned out to be the Sea Crest, the most expensive one on the promenade), he politely thanked her for the perfect evening and left without as much as a peck on the cheek. She fought tears on the way back home and counted the crow's feet around her eyes as she brushed her teeth. Next day, just as she resigned herself to never seeing him again, he called.

XOXOX XOXOX XOXOX X

When the phone vibrates on the kitchen counter, Mor stares at the flashing display and tries to remember who the caller is. Her memory is holed like cheese, some memories willfully expunged, some unaccountably gone. A school friend? A former colleague? Not a relative, certainly. She has none. An only daughter of an only daughter, and her mother's entire family is buried in unmarked graves.

It does not matter. She needs nobody. She has her son.

Stroking her belly, she watches the phone quiver and jump like a living thing. When it finally calms down, she tosses it into the garbage bin.

They met every day for a week. Mor learned a little more about David: enough for her to decide he was the One. He was so reassuringly normal, so restful and commonsense, untainted by the feverish madness of the Middle East. He was an accountant, he said; and indeed, he was very good with numbers. His parents were dead, his numerous siblings scattered over an amazing geographical range, and there was no mention of an ex-wife or significant other. He read all the right books and had all the right opinions. He liked gadgets. Mor, being an adjunct professor in the department of Life Sciences, listened to his techno-babble with an indulgent smile. The only negative she could find was that he was surprisingly indifferent to good food, despite the plethora of culinary temptations on every street corner. Rice-stuffed vine leaves, couscous, creamy hummus, freshly baked pitas, honey-almond cake—he consumed them as dutifully and apathetically as if they were medicine. Mor told herself that was a necessary counterweight to her own frequent indulgences that were beginning to show in her curves. Time to cut it, and indeed, David could be a walking advertisement for the virtues of abstemiousness, so trim and fit he was.

He told her his return ticket was for tomorrow. The despair she felt was strong enough to frighten her into a recoil from her infatuation.

Did she really need him so much? She had her life, her friends, her job. She might meet somebody local, get married, have a family.

She was thirty-five. All of her school and army friends were married, most had children. The future stretched before her as blank and lifeless as the bony beach under the full moon.

For their last date, Mor put on a midnight-blue Bedouin-embroidered robe. She regretted not being the exotic, olive-skinned, Middle-Eastern type. Perhaps he would be more attracted to her, then. But the generations of her ancestors dying under the washed-out skies of Poland had left their mark in her pale skin and green eyes.

They ate at the most expensive restaurant in Tel-Aviv. David had a lot of money and spent it freely, though never recklessly. He walked her to her apartment building and pecked her on the cheek, as he did every evening. Dully, she waited for him to turn around and walk away, as he did every evening.

"Can I come up for coffee?" he asked.

Inside the apartment, he turned off all the lights, but because Tel-Aviv at night is bathed in the inflamed glow of its city lights, they were left in the orange-tinted murk seeping through the slats of the Venetian blinds. Her neighbor's cat caterwauled in the yard and fell silent. She tangled with her robe, but his undressing was quick and tidy. Running her hand over his delightfully smooth chest, she suddenly realized something she had only marginally noticed before on the rare occasions when they touched: how cool his flesh was, like a porcelain bowl with sherbet inside. Mor felt embarrassed by the drops of sweat gathering under her armpits and in the hollow of her neck. But David's body remained immaculate. His kisses were sterile; his mouth tasted of nothing.

His regular breathing did not speed up throughout their lovemaking. And then it stopped.

Mor lay in darkness, a cold, heavy body on top of her. She could hear the squeak of tires outside, the laughter and chatter of pedestrians, barking of dogs but nothing else. The innumerable small noises of the body's interior that had been the soundtrack of sex were gone. David's silken hair tickled her lips and pushed back her rising scream. And then he lifted his head and looked down at her.

"I'm sorry," he said, "but Death cannot die. Not even a little death. So that's all for me but don't worry, I'm satisfied."

She could see him clearly. His body was glowing in the dark, a bluish glow like candlelight seen through a thick slab of ice. His finely chiseled features were pierced by two black holes of eyes. The translucent flesh molded itself around the geometrical beauty of curving ribs and elegantly strung vertebrae, shining with hard steely light.

"Little death," she repeated blankly.

He sat up. Now on the left side of his chest, just above the nipple, she could see a wound-flower, a neat hole surrounded by petals of flesh that stirred restlessly, opening and closing like a sea anemone. The wound bled more metallic light.

"Orgasm," he said. "The French call it *la petite mort.*"

"And you…"

"I am Death."

In fact, he was only *a* Death, one of many. Over the next couple of days, he explained it again and again: gently, patiently, and reassuringly.

There were, he said, a number of Deaths (he talked of them in family terms, brothers, sisters, cousins). New ones appeared from time to time, and oldsters retired, though, of course, none died. Each Death was responsible for a specific mode of mortality, though in emergencies (he was vague as to what those might be), they could take over each other's domains. David's own responsibility was death by shooting.

How old was he? He did not know, could not remember. Had he ever been human? He did not know that either. Was there a God? This received a blank stare.

And, in between these conversations, they went for ice cream or swam in the sea or toured the labyrinthine alleys of Old Jaffa or made love. He brought her flowers every day. After a week, he moved in, bringing his natty suitcase from the hotel. After two weeks, he asked her to marry him.

This precipitated a crisis. She threw him out, yelling at him to go to Hell. She cried for hours afterward, only stopping when she realized, with horror, that he might have done just that. Next morning, he was at her door with a fresh bunch of flowers.

She could not say "no." She was in love. "In love with Death?" she asked herself with horrified incredulity. Of course not. In love with a nice, gentle, even-tempered, caring man, a wonderful lover, a steadfast friend, a fun companion. So what if he was the rider on the pale horse—one of the whole cavalry, actually?

And yet she could not say "yes." She procrastinated, sobbed, made resolutions never to see him again, and broke them on the spot. She pleaded with him to give her more time.

"Why can't we just live together?" she cried.

He explained that it would not be right. He wanted her to see how committed he was. And unless they were legally married, he could not give her his wedding gift. She tried to push the thought of the gift away from her deliberations—she was not to be bought, she told herself and believed it—but it sat at the back of her mind as a constant watchful presence.

One afternoon, as Mor was taking a long walk in the Yarkon Park to try to unwind after another day of painful indecision, her cell phone rang. Her mother's officious neighbor Dvora called to tell her she was worried about Mrs. Shalev's state of mind. She managed to introduce a not-too-subtle remark about Mor's dereliction of her filial duties, with the unspoken "and the only child, too!" accompanying every word.

When her mother failed to pick up the phone, Mor drove up to Jerusalem. Just as she was rounding the last bend in the highway, the setting sun shone a peculiar golden-mauve light on the smooth bare hills with their clinging clusters of whitewashed dwellings. In such moments, Jerusalem seemed not so much a city as a physical state: a lighting flicker of vertigo or a stab of pain.

Her mother was sitting in the darkened living room, softly crying. The usual half-an-hour of useless recriminations followed, with Mor getting so angry with her mother's drab misery that she felt like slapping her lined cheek. But eventually, Mrs. Shalev rallied up sufficiently to make tea. Mother and daughter sat at the spotlessly clean kitchen table with a bowl of homemade cookies pushed closer to Mor's side. This was as near to reconciliation as they ever got.

"*Ima,*" said Mor suddenly. "*Ima,* did you ever see Death?"

Mrs. Shalev, who was mechanically stirring her tea, froze. Mor felt the embarrassment of a child breaking an unspoken family taboo. But she was doubly shocked when her mother glanced back at her with a sly, almost conspiratorial, smile, as if after all that time they finally got to share a grown-up secret.

"My mother did," she said. "Your grandmother, God rest her soul! She told me about it. When they were bringing them in, in the cattle-cars, she was squeezed close to a chink in the wall so she could breathe. There was snow outside. And there was a man standing on top of a snow-drift: an ordinary man but wearing an office suit. In the depth of winter. And as the train was passing and people cried and pleaded and screamed, he was writing something in his notebook. He never raised his eyes as the train passed. That was Death, she said."

Mor felt a shiver pass down her spine.

"But she survived!" she remonstrated.

"Yes," her mother agreed. "For a while."

Two days later, Dvora called again. When Mor came, she found her mother dead in bed. The family physician called it heart failure but privately admitted that an overdose of tranquilizers might have played a part.

They went to Cyprus to get married. Israel has no provisions for a civil ceremony. In the depth of her sleepless nights, Mor sometimes imagined a council of elderly rabbis solemnly deliberating whether a Death may convert to Judaism.

After a brief honeymoon, they returned home as a married couple. Now, said David, they should have a reception for his family.

"At home?" Mor asked faintly.

"We will rent a banquet hall," David reassured her.

"A catered dinner, of course," he said casually, "say, a hundred and fifty people. No, not including your friends, we can have a separate reception for them; money's not a problem."

Of course, she thought, *who ever heard of a pauper Death?*

"No, Love, not in Jaffa, that seaside is very pretty, but it has to be in Jerusalem."

He explained that for his family a visit to the Holy City was a long-cherished dream that only the pressure of work had hitherto prevented them from realizing. Mor did not dare inquire about the means of transportation, even though David's interest in airline schedules seemed to indicate that at least some of the Deaths would be queuing for passport control at the Ben-Gurion Airport.

Standing at the entrance to the banquet hall, Mor welcomed the endless stream of visitors. The briskness of Jerusalem's mountain air was making her shiver in her turquoise dress (despite the sales assistant's pointedly raised eyebrow, she had rejected black and white outfits).

Candles burned on the tables. People with champagne flutes and plates of canapes in their hands laughed, chatted, embraced, wandered onto the jasmine-scented patio.

"Wanda, Zoe, Jerome, Ervin," David introduced them one by one even when they arrived as couples. "Mark, Yolanda, Ahmed."

Only the first names. Did it mean that they all had the same family name?

"Maggie, Ruth, Xiaowei."

How many? God, how many of them?

"Guido, Carl, Donna."

Good-looking people, all of them: youngish, healthy, smiling, well dressed.

"Liliana, Eric, George."

And properly diverse too: whites, Asians, blacks, and browns in roughly equal proportions. Mark was African-American, and elegant Miranda looked like an Ethiopian model. Ahmed would blend into any Middle-Eastern crowd. Susan, arriving on Roger's arm, belied her nondescript name by sloe eyes and *cafe-au-lait* skin.

"Kalia, Roman, Patricia."

"Nice to meet you!

"Have a drink!"

"What a lovely place!"

They all spoke English but some with exotic accents: silky French, heavy Eastern European, or guttural Middle Eastern.

"Reginald, Oscar, Victoria."

Strangely old-fashioned names but nothing old-fashioned about their bearers. Women in Fendi and Prada dresses, men in Armani suits. Glitter of jewelry and expensive dental work.

"Mikhail, Gloria, Stefan."

She had tried to guess their identities but then gave up, defeated by their impersonal gloss. But when she finally started to mingle, Mor found the answer.

At the entrance to the hall, there was an old-fashioned mirror in a Venetian frame. And in the mirror, she could see her guests as they really were.

Liliana was the Plague Queen. Seen face-to-face, she was a slightly plump woman with crinkly brown hair and laughter lines. She was reflected in the mirror wearing a blood-red cloak that dragged on the floor, leaving a dark stain behind. Her features were the same but ravaged by open sores, the lips split and oozing pus, the eyebrows missing. Holding a wineglass in a festering hand, this reflection pleasantly conversed with Mor's double.

Mor blinked and swallowed, fighting nausea.

Stefan, a balding pompous guy, was reflected with ashy, hopeless eye, his ingratiating smile—a rictus of pain, his neat tie—a twisted rope. Suicide.

Elegantly slim Ruth was transformed into a gaunt, ravenous creature. Her diaphanous dress became, in the mirror, a transparent shroud that clung to her protruding ribs and swollen stomach. Famine.

George, the only man in the room wearing a T-shirt with an Escher print instead of a formal shirt, incuriously glanced at his own image whose throat was slashed by a gaping wound. The Escher geometry was transformed into a chaos of bloody blobs. Murder.

Victoria's shiny blond hair was a couple of gray tufts on the mottled skull; her cream-and-peaches skin a wrinkled parchment; her rose dress—a shapeless stained shift. Old Age.

Mark was reflected as a walking mass of burns, bleeding tissue, and splintered bones. Accident, she thought. Zoe…the others seem to defer to her and seeing her in the mirror, with the black leather harness molding her voluptuous body, her thrusting breasts like missiles, a bracelet of rusty iron splinters around her full arm, and her face covered by a helmet-like mask, Mor understood why. War was undoubtedly high on the Deaths' social ladder.

There were, however, some visitors whose reflections left her puzzled. Maggie was one of them. When David introduced her, Mor saw a nice British woman, slightly older than the rest, looking like the aunt Mor would like to have but never did. She tried to maneuver her inside but Maggie tantalizingly loitered on the patio. When she finally walked by the mirror, Mor glimpsed a strange scarecrow figure with stick-like arms and legs, her face painted with garish whorls.

She circulated among the party, making polite remarks, feeling strangely detached (even curiosity was evaporating), when there was a commotion at the entrance. She saw David speaking to somebody whose only visible part was a pair of fluttering hands. She quickly went to David, who stepped aside and brushed past her, muttering something about "bad taste." Mor found herself facing the late guest.

He was a short man with sandy hair and blue eyes magnified by rimless glasses. He seemed pedantic and harmless.

"Your husband, I mean David…" he began, looking flustered and speaking with a harsh accent.

"All my husband's friends are welcome," she said cautiously.

"Let me introduce…Daniel," David had come back. There was a tiny pause before he said the name. "Daniel is retired. He does not socialize much."

"I thought it was my duty to come," said the short man with dignity.

Mor offered him a drink and tried to steer him toward the mirror. There was no need: he just walked there, planted his feet wide, and stared at his image.

The image was the same as the man.

And then she knew who her last visitor was.

"I'm sorry," said Daniel. "I know how you must feel. But I had to come. I'm glad David has found a Jewish wife. And I'm glad it's you."

"Do you know me?" she asked, swallowing, because her voice sounded scratchy like the squeak of a mouse.

"I know all of you," he said.

She looked around. Should she appeal to Stefan, Death-Suicide, who had helped her mother escape? Or to Plague, Famine, Accident, Cancer, even War? Any other death to keep her company but this.

"You see, I'm retired now," continued Daniel, "and looking at the whole business from an historical perspective, I can't blame myself. I only followed orders."

"Whose orders?" Mor asked sarcastically. "God's? The Fuhrer's?"

"Your orders."

"Mine?!"

"Yours, too, in a way. You're a human being, after all. You call the shots. We only do what we are told. A human hand pulls the trigger or signs an order, and we mop up the resulting mess."

"How convenient! However, I see the others shy away from you. Could it be even they don't approve of your methods?"

"Sheer prejudice," said Daniel. "Envy too. There is a great deal of jockeying for power going on among us. You'll find out. You are one of us now, after all. David's wedding gift is not to be sneered at!"

"Fuck you!" For one glorious moment, Mor was so angry that she forgot her fear. "Do you think I'm doing this to be your sister-in-law? I love David. And anyway, what are you doing here, in this city, attending a Jewish wedding?"

Daniel only smiled, unperturbed:

"I have attended a lot of Jewish weddings," he said. "And, of course, you love David. I have seen love sacrifices, stoo. Eventually they tend to benefit somebody, though not always the party intended."

They moved into a bigger apartment in Tel-Aviv, which David paid for out of pocket, despite the insane housing bubble going on in the city. Mor kept her mother's house in Jerusalem, though. He suggested she stop teaching and trying to get tenure. There was no need, he said. She refused. She needed those hours on campus when she could pretend that life went on as usual—or better than usual. She was a married woman now. She had a diamond ring, a loving husband, and money in the bank. What else could she possibly want?

She did not want to know what David was doing when she was away. Every time she came home, she was afraid he would tell her. But he never did. They watched Netflix and ate dinners that he cooked. He went through the motions of eating conscientiously, even though it was a sheer charade. Mor soon realized that not only did he not need food but that he was incapable of tasting it. Despite that, his cooking was excellent.

When they made love, David's body glowed like ice, like frozen steel, the bluish petals of the wound-flower over his heart opening wide to disclose the dark seed of the bullet inside. On the hottest nights, when Mor's side of the bed was sticky with sweat, his body was cool and sleek. He was indefatigable, he was obliging, they would have sex for hours, until Mor, wearied by the endless succession of orgasms, would doze off and wake up screaming, to find her husband alert at her side.

Once she asked him whether Deaths dreamed. He said no. Mor was sure he lied. But it was true he never slept, even though he sometimes pretended.

They were to have a party for her friends (all of whom loved David). She sent him out with a grocery list, having decided to cook herself. The idea of letting other people eat food prepared by Death made her queasy. She was chopping lettuce when the knife slipped and bit deeply into her thumb. Mor screamed and watched dark drops of blood pool in the shallow cups of lettuce leaves. And then the bleeding stopped and the cut closed reluctantly like a disappointed mouth, the skin smoothing over, the pain receding—not into well-being but into a strange sort of numbness.

They had an Indian take-away for her party.

Once a week, she goes shopping, and she always ends up with another colorful package among her drab plastic bags. She comes back home and tears the bright paper to reveal a miniature garment. The clothes are all in delicate colors: cream, lilac, forest-green. Pink and blue are vulgar. She intends to give the child a contemporary-Hebrew unisex name, like her own, fit for either gender—or none.

As she watches the TV on solitary evenings, she takes out an armful of baby clothes and keeps on folding and unfolding them, stroking them with her fingertips, checking the zippers and the buttons, her eyes on the screen. She seldom takes out the same piece on two consecutive nights. The amount of baby clothes one can accumulate in two years is considerable.

When she had a ten-day delay in her period, Mor went to a pharmacy and bought a home pregnancy test. It showed negative. She called her gynecologist. He assured her urine tests were unreliable and directed her to the lab where they drew blood from her arm. She took a long walk waiting for the results, apprehensive but not unhappy. She was thirty-three, and her friends' hints had long ago crossed the threshold of subtlety.

When she came back to the lab, they told her the test was negative. The nurse wished her better luck next time. Her gynecologist appeared puzzled and suggested another round of tests to determine the reason for amenorrhea in a woman so young. Mor thanked him but did not take the tests. When she missed her next period, she was not even surprised.

The first time she saw her husband feed was on a bright and clear winter day. She had parked her car and was walking toward a campus gate when she heard a sharp sound, which, from her military training, she recognized as a shot. Turning around, she saw people running, a small crowd milling at the sidewalk, a man down on his knees being sick, an elderly guard ineffectually pushing through the packed bodies.

A boy in a soldier's uniform lay among the parked cars, his gun beside him, splattered red and yellow. The boy had no face.

The crowd buzzed like a swarm of bees, words "suicide," "accident," "terrorist attack" mingling into senseless noise. Mor was resisting the realization that the blood and brain were not a special-effects simulation. Just as it finally sunk in, she saw her husband standing by the body.

Mor did not call out to him; she knew immediately that he was invisible to everybody else. In the crystalline sunshine, his body glistened like dirty ice. Gunmetal-colored highlights slid along his limbs. By subtle distortions, his nakedness had shed all pretense of humanity. His arms and legs looked melted-down. But the wound-flower on his left side was alive, its fleshly petals moving hungrily; and when he knelt down and dipped his fingers in the boy's blood, it flashed a deep piercing crimson. The sun washed away the flimsy disguise of his face, revealing the starkness of old bone underneath.

Sometimes they would drop in. Coming back home, Mor would find Liliana chatting with her husband in the living room or discover Mark and George sprawled in the armchairs, watching the TV or playing computer games. During the state visit by a US dignitary, Zoe showed up.

The worst of it was that she did not need mirrors anymore. She could see their real shapes flickering through the misty outlines of their fake humanity. The mist kept getting thinner. When George visited, his necktie would flop wetly, soaked with the blood seeping from the slash on his throat. When they had Ruth for dinner, the food blackened into ashes as she lifted it to her lips.

It finally occurred to Mor, eight months after the wedding, to ask David whether marriage to a mortal was an exception or a rule. She already knew that some Deaths were married to each other. Stefan, Death-Suicide, and Gloria, Death-Drowning (a bloated pallid thing under her disguise of a petite waif with huge, appealing eyes), were a devoted couple, always holding hands. But had some of them ever been mortal before joining the club?

David looked at her with expressionless eyes:

"Didn't your cousin Talma also marry a Gentile?" he asked.

She never broached the issue again.

Her cousin Talma, the one married to a nice Protestant boy from Milwaukee, came to Tel-Aviv for a visit. Such occasions are called "visiting the Motherland" in Hebrew, as if it were the land itself that was being visited, the hot dust of the country being thicker than blood, having absorbed so much of the latter in the course of the millennia. Talma and Mor sat together in Mor's kitchen, drinking "mud" coffee made by pouring boiling water over the coarsely ground Turkish blend. Ron, Talma's three-year-old, was banging on the wall with a plastic rabbit.

"So when is it your turn?" inquired Talma after the friends, family, politicos and local celebrities had been discussed, summed up and disposed of.

"What turn?"

Talma nodded at Ron, whose rabbit just disintegrated to his apparent satisfaction.

"You're not getting any younger, you know."

Mor sighed. The exile in Milwaukee had done nothing for her cousin's native bluntness.

"I have a medical problem," she admitted, only to be treated for the next hour to a long recital of Talma's friends' struggles with infertility. She was relieved when the family left, Talma's husband carrying sleepy Ron on his shoulder.

Mor was sitting in the Gilman Hall's cafeteria, poking at her lasagna and wondering whether the cardboard taste was due to the new caterers or to her changing body. She had become careless with her diet: why not, since she was neither gaining nor losing any weight, no matter what she ate? But last night while she was mechanically putting potato chips in her mouth in front of the TV, one chip stuck to her palate. Taking it out she discovered it was a piece of cellophane.

Her head remained clear even after hours of teaching. She no longer needed the coffee to which she had been addicted. This was good since it now had the same effect on her as tepid water. Sex…but she did not want to think about that.

At least she did not need to be concerned about wrinkles and sun damage. Her face creams had been tossed into the garbage bin. So had her makeup kit. She dimly remembered applying makeup for the sheer pleasure of making herself beautiful.

It was hot and muggy, the people in the courtyard were fanning themselves and wiping their foreheads. She used to wear tank tops all summer, and there would always be dark stains of sweat in her armpits. Now her beige long-sleeved dress was spotless.

Somebody plunked a tray bearing a Coke can and a pita sandwich on her table. Irritated, Mor looked up and froze. The man standing in front of her was Daniel.

"May I?" he inquired, seating himself. This was the second shock. He was speaking Hebrew with an old-fashioned accent that reminded her of her father's Yiddish-gabbling cousins.

"What are you doing here?"

"Travelling," he replied, still in fluent Hebrew. "I'm retired, you know."

"I should hope so!"

He lifted a conciliatory hand. "I'm on your side!"

"It'll be a sad day when I need you on my side!"

"You already do." He examined his sandwich and bit off a neat semi-circle of bread and hummus. His teeth, Mor noticed with a shudder of revulsion, were big, square and yellow, as if he used to be a smoker. "Look, Hanna…"

"Don't you dare call me that!"

"I gave you this name," he said.

She stared at the table, unable to meet his gaze.

"You are like a child in a new school," said Daniel. "All those secrets whispered behind your back, old alliances, old loves, old hates, and here you are, a newcomer, and nobody to explain the ground rules to you."

"And you decided to be my guide out of the goodness of your heart, I suppose."

He shrugged. "I do have a different perspective, you know. First, I'm very young. I still remember my mortal days."

"Were you human once?" she asked, horrified.

"All of us were."

Seeing her expression, he laughed.

"See? You didn't even know that. Your husband is not being very informative, is he? Well, David is singularly lacking in the two qualities indispensable to a Death: wide education and a sense of humor."

"How do you become…how do you become what you are?"

"The same way you become what you are. We are also chosen. Only we don't procreate, so the process is rather haphazard, nothing like your tidy matrilineal descent. Some of us just grow away from humankind until we discover our true vocation. It's a gradual process, you see. Kids who play with guns and explosives, this sort of things. Some hear the call but cannot make the crossover and remain stranded on your side, pathetic failures in their own eyes, never mind how many body bags they send to the morgue. Ted Bundy and such…"

"Ted Bundy," she repeated numbly.

He airily waved his hand.

"Quite a lot of those. They sense the vacancies."

"And the others?"

"Well, sometimes it is a sort of deathbed conversion, ecstatic experience, call it whatever you like. But it's going out of fashion. Most people on deathbeds nowadays are drugged out of their senses. And then, of course, there are such as you."

"Such as me?"

"Yes. Marrying into the tribe."

"Are you suggesting I will become one of you?" Mor managed to keep her voice down only because she had subliminally recognized a couple of her students at the next table.

"Absolutely. Look, you'll never be a *Hausfrau*. Not that it's fashionable in our circles. No diapers to change, and cooking gets on your nerves if you cannot taste the results. Plenty of your new relations are in-laws, so to speak. Stefan, for example, and Victoria. You should talk to her, by the way, she is a relatively new bride."

"Victoria? How can that be? Isn't she Old Age?'

Daniel nodded and finished his Coke in a single gulp.

"Then how…I mean, people have died of old age since the beginning of time."

Daniel's face grew animated as he bent toward her. "Precisely. That's the point. Deaths are not born, but they die."

"How can a death die?"

"Never heard of John Donne?" asked Daniel smugly. " '*Death, thou shalt die.*' I thought literature was your forte. Not *Christian* literature perhaps. In any case, a Death can only be killed by another Death and that under very special conditions. That's why, as you may well imagine, we have rather mixed feelings about each other. We get together out of solidarity and even affection of sorts. There is a sense of fraternity after centuries of gossiping. But we also need to keep an eye on each other. Not that it always helps. Victoria's predecessor was assassinated by Hunger and War, Ruth and Zoe, only they called themselves by different names then. We change names pretty often. I'm proud of my current choice. You're the only one to appreciate its meaning, really. *Dani-el:* God judged me."

"Oh, cut it out!" said Mor impatiently. "Cheap theology! Why would Ruth and Zoe do such a thing? What's the gain?"

Daniel beamed at her. "A very Jewish attitude, if I may say so. Practical, blunt and to the point. Well, since there are so many of us, the only way to gain influence is to enlarge the sphere of one's activity. To some extent this does not depend on us at all. You humans are our real masters, even though most of us consider you mere cattle. But that's just the deplorable lack of education, as I said. Not many of us read Hegel or understand the master-slave dialectic. Anyway, once a new modality of death is discovered, a new…executive comes into being by a process which, quite frankly, we don't quite understand ourselves. The twentieth century was a fertile one. Have you met John? In the 60s, he was about to crown himself King of Death but after the demolition of the Berlin Wall, he has been semi-retired. Tending his garden, I assume, growing mushrooms."

"Mushrooms?" repeated Mor blankly. "Oh, I see. Mushroom clouds. And you?"

"I am a different matter," said Daniel evasively. "In any case, we don't quite control the course of human history, but we can give a nudge now and then. Ruth and Zoe hoped that by eliminating Old Age, they would enlarge their own respective domains. The political situation was favorable, too. What they did not count on was that Mark's demure little bride whom everybody considered half-witted, good perhaps for crib death but nothing more ambitious, would blossom overnight into the queen of geriatric wards. And with the baby-boomers aging, she is poised on the brink of a new career leap."

"Why are you telling me this?" Mor's voice began rising again. "Are you grooming me to be your successor? If you think I'm about to take over the ovens…"

"Please!" Daniel shook his head. "A little perspective! The ovens have been inactive for seventy years! No, Mor, I'm saying just the opposite. A Death's existence is boring, devoid of pleasure, not fit for a woman like you. I don't need to tell you what our sex life is like. And no children, of course. I know what it means to your people. Your husband has trapped you on purpose, for his own amusement. He cannot love you, being what he is, but he cannot even appreciate you. You are a fighter; you are resisting being assimilated. But what if the force of your resistance is such that you'll be forever stuck in that twilight state, neither a Death nor a living woman?"

Mor squeezed her eyes shut, staring into the warm blood-red murk under her eyelids. Then she opened them and looked at the creature in front of her.

"You have a proposition," she said. "What is it?"

The red-eye flight was short: four hours. Her night was ruined, first by waiting in the lounge among anxious first-time travelers burdened by duty-free purchases and squealing babies and then by the cramped aisle seat and talkative neighbor. But she emerged into the terminal at 5 a.m., feeling no worse—and no better—than after a good night's sleep. On the Gatwick express, she watched, incuriously as the mellow foliage and the ugly rows of houses passed by.

She had expected London to be foggy and gloomy, but it was sunny and bright. Guided by her cellphone, she was in Holborn by eleven. She walked down Great Holborn Street until she came to an arched walkway leading into a cobbled courtyard. There she had to press the button several times before the grilled gate swung open.

The flat was tiny, cluttered with dusty Victorian junk. The brownish liquid in her cup was either coffee or tea: even with her taste buds intact, she may not have known which. Maggie took out the ingredients for the beverage from an open fridge that was not plugged in, its interior choked with bundles of cobwebby herbs.

"Daniel thinks the world of you," Maggie declared. The contrast between her and her place was brutal. She was carefully made up, smelled of lavender soap, and wore a neat mauve dress. As long as Mor did not look at her for longer than a few seconds, the illusion held.

"How nice," said Mor dryly. "The feeling is not mutual."

Maggie only smiled indulgently and sipped her indescribable beverage. Was she playing up her Britishness as a joke?

"Dear Daniel! He and I have a lot in common."

"How so?" Mor asked.

"We are both retired. Well, no. I'm semi-retired, I still do quite a bit of freelancing, but it's nothing compared to what it was once. I pity Daniel; so much work, and so spectacular, in such a short period, and then he is kicked out. There were certain affinities, you know, between what he did and my own skills."

Mor felt her gorge rise as the brownish liquid in her cup suddenly took on the tint of clotting blood. But the nausea passed quickly.

"It is ironic," continued Maggie affably, "I'm the oldest one and he is…no, I take it back, he is not the youngest one, even though none of them, to my mind, is as talented as he is."

"Are you really the oldest?" Mor asked.

"Yes. I was the first-born. Even before your kind was quite sure of its direction. I was there when Neanderthals scattered ochre around the skeletons of the eaten ones. I was there when shamans danced, and withered babies in their mothers' wombs, and flayed men alive without even touching them. And I still enjoy the old art. There are people, right now, dear, who are sticking needles in voodoo dolls and calling my name. Some things never change. When all the computer-guided missiles crumble to dust, I will still be there."

Maggie was smiling sweetly throughout the speech but it was not her pink-glossed mouth that spoke the words. It was the other mouth, squirming beneath her skin like a black worm: the slit in the whorl-painted visage of Death-Magic.

"But why here?" asked Mor. "Why London?"

Maggie shrugged. "The Third World is too busy aping the First World. I need believers, not superstition-mongers. This land is soaked in history that's beginning to rot like a bloated sponge. I was here before it began, and I will be here when it ends. But this is not about my plans, dear. Daniel has asked me for a favor, and I see no reason to refuse. David and I have never gotten along. His modus operandi is far too mechanical for me. No spirit. So shall we start?"

Mor nodded. Her throat went dry, and she gulped down the rest of the coffee-tea as she assumed some sort of ceremony was about to begin.

Instead, Maggie took a more comfortable position on her swaybacked couch.

"Once upon a time," said Maggie, "there was a boy who loved to play with guns. His family was dirt-poor and they could not afford buying the weapons that he wanted. His father had the only gun in the family, an old Colt Browning. One day the boy came home and saw his father sitting at the table, the top of his head blown off. He looked at his old man for a while. And then he picked up the gun lying in the pool of blood, turned around and walked away."

Maggie reached under the torn cushion and pulled out a wreck of an antique gun, rusted and bent. Mor stared at it with revulsion.

"Old tales are right," Maggie went on. "The only power stronger than death is love. When we become Deaths, old loves shrivel and fall away. But just as our bodies still bear the one mark of our lost mortality, the one spot reminding us of what we used to be, so do our souls. In a dusty corner of each Death's still heart, the one true love of his or her life lies sleeping. If it's woken, the heart will beat once and stop forever. And the Death shall die."

"David does not love anybody," said Mor.

"This gun is your husband's one true love."

Mor's fingers closed on the coarse metal. The rust stained them red.

※◯※◯※ ※◯※◯※ ※◯※◯※ ※◯※

They drove up to Jerusalem to check on her mother's house, which stood empty since the last tenant had moved out two weeks ago. The invisible Israeli fall was marked neither by the turning of the dusty leaves nor by the diminution of the oppressive heat of the day but only by the melancholy lengthening of the night. It was dark when they got to Rehavia.

She had brought a bottle of red wine and a couple of fat aromatic candles that looked almost like memorial ones, only dyed deep scarlet. David turned off the TV and stretched on the sagging couch. In the candlelight, his real face poked through his unconvincing flesh. Its sharp angles aroused her now as she had once been aroused by his bland masculinity. She brushed the bone with her lips and thrust her tongue between the lipless teeth. The metallic fingers closed around her wrists like handcuffs and with a shiver of remote pleasure she closed her eyes.

The charade was over, husband and wife were making love naked and sincere, all disguises discarded, all pretenses disavowed. The blind lead-colored balls in the sockets of his skull looked through her. And just for a moment, she was tempted by the promise of immortality: freedom from desire, escape from pleasure and pain, time itself frozen in the clarity of her indifferent vision.

Her mock lovemaking died down as it always did nowadays. She sat astride the skeletal thing.

"Don't you ever miss it?" she asked. "The little death, *la petite mort?*"

"Why should I?" he said. "I have the real thing."

"But not with me," said Mor. "And I'm your wife."

He laughed. "I did not marry you for that!"

"Of course, you did," said Mor.

Her hand snaked under the pile of her clothes and whipped out the gun. Quickly she pressed the muzzle to the wound-flower in her husband's chest and pulled the trigger.

For a second, poised over him, she thought it could not work. But then the body underneath her convulsed and dark, heavy blood erupted from the wound, warm like vomit, splattering her belly and legs. At the same time, she felt a hot explosion inside herself.

A single groan escaped her husband, the metallic bones of his face corroding and falling apart, the hard sleekness of his flesh growing soft and mushy, her fingers sinking into his arms and encountering only the pliancy of a child's bones that were snapping like twigs, while she was crying out, dying a thousand little deaths in one infinite moment of time.

When it was over, she found herself lying prone on the couch in darkness. The candles had gone out. Something scratchy was rubbing against her stomach and her thighs were glued together. She snapped on the light. The couch was littered with a pitifully small handful of bone fragments.

She took a shower and spent the rest of the night drinking tea, eating canned tuna, and watching movies in Arabic.

At dawn, she showered again and went out, into the crystal-clear light of Jerusalem. So early, the city was empty and innocent, low buildings dissolving into the pink shadows on the bare stone hills. Mor drove to the pedestrian mall in Talpiot and stood by the parapet, looking at the glorious panorama of the Mount of Olives with the dim golden dome of the great mosque and the dark lines of stunted trees winding down into the narrow valley of Gehenna.

She heard steps behind and turned. Daniel, looking fresh and dapper in a white shirt and jeans, smiled at her.

"Well done," he said.

She looked away. And then she looked back at him, incredulous.

Over the left nipple, his shirt was stained by fresh blood.

"Thank you, Hanna. You have given me a new lease."

"You?" she gasped. "Coming back?"

"No, no. My old job is done. I have simply taken your late husband's vacant place. Nature—or whoever our manager is—abhors vacuum. I am too young to retire. I knew that when there was a job opening, I would be the first on the list. I'm sure I'll significantly improve on David's performance."

"I should have known," she said dully.

"Don't blame yourself. You did not imagine this morning would see all the guns beaten into ploughshares, did you?"

The city was waking up. A car honked, a child cried, a long strident call drifted up from the mosque in the valley.

"Just tell me one thing," she said. "What was your real name?"

He shook his head.

"I don't remember. Perhaps I did until last night but now, with my new position…I remember some things. Piano playing, a woman with dark hair—my mother? Light on the linden leaves in spring. But it's fading, memory disappearing. Like that, see?"

He rolled up his shirtsleeve. On the white skin, Mor could see disjointed blue strokes—the remnants of a tattoo—that were being absorbed into the body even as she watched.

"We all have our badges," he said. "I shan't be sorry to let this one go."

Mor looked into his eyes and smiled.

"You have miscalculated, Daniel," she said. "Or whoever you are. Killing is a spur to breeding. You should have been more careful about murdering your own. And now what will you do, you and your fellow maggots, when Death becomes fruitful and multiplies? What will you feed on when life starts feeding on you?"

He stared at her uncomprehendingly.

"I am pregnant," she said.

"You can't be! You're still…"

"Death's wife. I know. But my husband died in my arms, and I am carrying his seed. I am not a pawn in your game, you smug bastard! I am the mother of the future king who will ride down this very mountain and call up the dead from their graves. He will mold ashes back into bodies and clothe burnt bones with flesh. And he will judge you as you deserve to be judged. My son is king of the living and the dead, and he will make each Death beg for oblivion before he slays you all. And you, you will remember your name when you are called to his judgment!"

Daniel's right hand crept up, the fingers melting together, acquiring a metallic sheen, fusing into a small but deadly looking gun. Mor laughed.

"I thought immunity from the family was part of the bargain! Fool that I was, to trust a Death! But I have better protection. Go ahead; shoot me! Do it! Why can't you? Could it be you are sensing your king? Could it be my baby is already stronger than you?"

Daniel dropped his hand, which slowly resumed its normal appearance. There was fear in his eyes but also something else, something that looked like relief.

"Well," he said, "this was not planned. But this was bound to happen, sooner or later. And of course, this is the most appropriate place for it. The only place. I wonder what went through David's dull brain when he decided to take his Middle-Eastern vacation. But even if he had a…guidance, this is irrelevant now. You are right, Mor. I cannot touch you. And I can feel the thing in your womb even though it is tinier than a mustard seed. But I wonder what it'll be like when it's fully grown. It's conventional to wish a prospective mother joy but frankly I wonder whether you'll have much joy in your baby. Think of your predecessors: they did not fare too well with their kingly sons who broke their hearts before future generations bestowed upon the poor women heaps of silly titles. I wonder how you'll be known: Star of the Desert, perhaps? But in any case, Your Future Majesty, though I may be bound to obey your son, I am not going to welcome him with myrrh and frankincense. And though I may be the first one to be hauled before his judgment seat, I will maintain my innocence to the end. I only followed orders."

He turned and walked away, his back ramrod-straight, as he slowly dissolved into the sunlight. Mor shrugged.

"You will show him, won't you, Love?" she said, cradling her flat stomach.

Every Friday Mor goes to the Wailing Wall, slowly wending her way through the narrow twisting lanes of the Arab Quarter's market, bright with tourist junk and fragrant with spices, coffee, and sweat. The business is not what it used to be and a couple of times she's been caught in disturbances, but she is not afraid. Nothing can happen to her.

Some of the shop owners recognize her and offer her bright blue beads against the evil eye, which she willingly buys. At the familiar corner stall, she rests her heavy belly, sitting on a scratched aluminum chair and sipping cardamom-flavored coffee from a tiny cup. She hears shots and glimpses a steely-blue apparition disappear among the fluttering rugs. She is unmoved and so is Ali who continues his rapid monologue in garbled English and waves his hands when she offers to pay for the coffee. She is encountering more and more of the same attitude – reverence mixed with fear—among Jerusalem's numerous population of holy fools, beggars, preachers, certified nuts, and would-be messiahs.

The square in front of the Wailing Wall is beaten into dusty monochrome whiteness by the pitiless glare of the noon. A couple of soldiers lazing about in their glass booth throw her an indifferent glance. The women's section of the Wall is less crowded than usual, only some Orthodox heads hidden under untidy wigs are pressed to the eroded stones like a row of bushy little animals. Their men rock on the other side of the partition, their black hats and coats greedily soaking up the heat. Mor picks up a modesty shawl from the stand to cover up her bare shoulders, walks to the wall, kisses the warm powdery rock.

"Soon," she tells the unmoving weight in her womb. "Soon, honey."

At home, she lights the Sabbath candles, fixes dinner, and sits in front of the TV, absorbing the latest litany of nuclear threats, military casualties, and political crises.

A Breaking News banner appears at the bottom of the screen when Mor feels a sickening pang in her lower abdomen. She sits up, breathless, the dinner tray pushed aside. Yes, no doubt of it, the beginning of labor, just as she had been taught in those long-ago birth-preparation classes. A wave of exultation sweeps over her, overcoming another brutal spasm that feels as if somebody has grabbed a handful of her entrails and twisted them. The hem of her dress is soaked: her water has broken.

Mor reaches for the phone to call an ambulance. A hand closes on hers.

"No need," says a familiar voice.

Deftly, Maggie rearranges the cushions on the couch to prop up her back. Dazed, Mor looks around. Familiar faces look back at her. Ruth smiles shyly at her; Victoria pulls clean sheets out of a large tote bag; Zoe plugs in the kettle in the kitchen. Liliana shoos out the men who crowd at the door. George waves at her, somebody else—Mikhail?—flashes a V-sign.

Mor pushes Maggie aside and tries to stand up. But she can't; the pain is too strong.

"Why?" she cries. "What are you doing here?"

"We want to help you," says Ruth.

"We want to be here when the king is born," says Victoria.

"We want to welcome our leader," says Zoe.

She looks at them mutely, and they look back: War, Famine, Plague. Old Age, Voodoo, all with shining hope in their eyes.

"Do you acknowledge my son, then?" asks Mor.

"He is our king," says Maggie. "We have been waiting for him since the beginning of time. And you are our queen. You will intercede for us with your son."

The labor pains are almost continuous now; she can feel the baby impatiently pushing out of her womb. There are faint screams, booms of explosions, rattle of gunfire; it takes her a moment to realize they are coming from the TV.

"But aren't you afraid of him?" she cries. "Aren't you afraid, Death that you shall die?"

She sees ambiguous smiles on their faces, but another twist of her guts makes her collapse on the couch, unable to push away Maggie's solicitous hand wiping sweat off her face. Zoe removes her helmet, and she sees the old brown bones of a skeleton rotting in some anonymous grave. The empty eyeholes are filled with light, and Mor still has the strength to wonder: is it the longing for oblivion or the certainty of triumph?

✕◊✕◊✕ ✕◊✕◊✕ ✕◊✕◊✕ ✕◊

ABOUT THE AUTHOR

Elana Gomel is the author of five non-fiction books, published by Routledge, Macmillan, and other academic presses, and of numerous articles on subjects ranging from science fiction and fantasy to posthumanism and Victorian literature. Her stories appeared in *New Horizons*, *Aoife's Kiss*, *Bewildering Stories*, *Timeless Tales*, *The Singularity*, *Dark Fire*, *Fantasist* and other magazines; and in several anthologies, including the *Apex Book of World Science Fiction*. Her fantasy novel, *A Tale of Three Cities*, was published by Dark Quest Books in 2013. She can be found on Facebook and on Twitter as @ ElanaGomel.

SOMETHING IN THE WAY SHE DIES

Ken Goldman

"Nothing can happen more beautiful than death."
— Walt Whitman, "Starting from Paumanok"

"The only way to a woman's heart is along the path of torment."
— Marquis de Sade

Fascinated, the boy watched.

On Winthrop Avenue, two speeding cars met head-on, each vehicle reduced to rubble in one horrific accident, at least horrific to those standing near the skinny kid who gawked at what followed. Many turned their heads away. Hopper Leach was not one of them.

Hopper is only seventeen on the afternoon he sees the collision. Both young male drivers must have been stinking drunk, and what were those odds during midday? The cars have nearly hit Hopper, and the boy licks his lips and breathes heavily—not with relief at his good fortune but with anticipation of what mayhem will result.

The older vehicle is a rusted clunker, its engine refurbished, judging from its unmuffled roar before it was efficiently silenced. The other car is a late-model Chevy convertible, your standard-issue cuntmobile, stocked with the requisite teenaged babes, two of them. Hopper figures the white dividing line along the center of Winthrop must've seemed only a blurry suggestion to the drivers.

The impact has sent each unbuckled boy flying to the curb, while trapping a second pair of dark-haired beauties inside the crushed rust bucket. The girls appear a bit skanky, but certainly they were doable, at least until this moment. In what had been the convertible, two wholesome cheerleader types have fared no better, their bodies crushed within the twisted lump that no longer resembles an automobile. A bloody, dark-haired girl stares at Hopper with vacant eyes. She's pretty, and she must've been something to see with her hair blowing in the wind inside the jazzy convertible. Although blood drips from her mouth in thick rivulets, Hopper cannot take his eyes off her.

Within moments, five bodies are sheet-covered and carried off by two ambulance attendants; the sixth (the dark-haired girl) remains barely alive as she's lifted into the vehicle, but Hopper sees her expire before it even moves. He knows this because the driver and the two medical attendants in the rear are shaking their heads. Death has been quick and efficient.

"That's all she wrote, eh, guys?" Hopper mutters to himself.

From the sickening crunch of metal and shattered glass, to the bloody aftermath practically at his feet, Hopper Leach witnessed the whole thing, and his reaction initially surprises him. The accident proved more entertaining than a day at the movies, and his epiphany is instantaneous. Death's beautiful hideousness intrigues him like nothing before. This is no Hollywood special effect, no crappy scene after which a director will yell "Cut!" and the young bloodied bodies will get to their feet. Nuh huh, this is more real than reality television, and the electricity Hopper feels is real, too. To anyone watching young Leach during these moments, it seems the boy's studying some captivating work of art. In that sense, to Hopper the blood-smeared asphalt could have been the canvas displaying the adolescent equivalent of a Renoir, death as envisioned through the distorted lens of heavy metal.

"Papa-oo-mao-mao," he mumbles, quoting lyrics that, given the circumstances, make sense only to himself.

Hopper stands transfixed until the ambulance pulls away, lights flashing while the unnecessary siren is silenced. He leaves the scene only because an ashen-faced officer insists that he move on, using that bullshit cop line, "There's nothing to see here." Hopper strongly disagrees with the officer's statement, but he knows visions of those ruined young bodies will repeat inside his brain in an endless high-definition replay, his mental video becoming more detailed each time it filters through the boy's imagination. Had he thought of it sooner, he would have whipped out his smart phone to record the accident so the experience would have been his to savor forever.

Plenty to see here.

Record…Remember…Savor forever…

No, can't really do that…

"Okay, kid! Times up!"

Hopper heard the Reality Actualization Navigator's voice, and he found himself back in Gruber's Arcade, Wellington Mall's latest high-tech attraction. The owner's online ads called the 40-something geek who ran the arcade a technological genius. That certainly seemed true enough, because his gallery showcased an amazing bit of impressive techno-razzle that would have given Jean Luc Picard a hard-on. Today's experience wasn't simple virtual reality, nor was it some tacky Disney World hologram. Gruber's Arcade was a whole new experience, the brave new world of Reality Actualization Infinite Hyper-Dimensional Materiality—*RA-IHDM* as local commercials christened it—and even that mellifluous mouthful didn't begin to capture the sensory adventure Hopper just had.

His parents would have grounded him for life had they known Hopper had withdrawn $50 from his college fund to spend an hour in a fantasyland of carnage, although until this moment, he hadn't realized the interest a bloodbath held for him. The elaborate fishbowl-like apparatus Gruber removed from his head seemed to know Hopper's secret thoughts. It produced the experience before him in glorious living high definition down to the last detail, recreating from some shadowy corner of Hopper's brain the smear of blood and guts and the stink of death that must have existed in the darkest nether regions of his subconscious. Subliminal maybe, but sublime definitely! Of course, Hopper knew the RA-IHDM experience existed only inside his head, but it remained difficult to wrap his brain around that thought.

"So, how was it, champ?" Navigator Gruber asked. "Did you

score the winning run of the World Series, or maybe you spent a little down time with Selena Gomez? Nothing you'd want your folks to know about, I'm thinking? 'Papa-oo-mao-mao,' as the man said." The man grinned as if he knew something of Hopper's adventure, but of course he didn't. Hopper hadn't selected a particular program, not for his first experience; these programs were more expensive, and he went into his first Hyper-Dimensional hour cold with whatever thoughts he brought with him. The apparatus did the rest. He returned the man's grin with one even wider as he constructed his lie.

"Nah. I was this astronaut heading for space." He made a whooshing gesture with his arm, Beaver Cleaver wearing The Joker's smile.

Another smile came from Gruber. "Yeah, we get that one a lot. So, Armstrong on the Moon, or maybe Han Solo piloting the Millennium Falcon? My specific programs can do it a lot better, being about as accurate as any eye-witness could describe. The older guys sometimes select Flash Gordon fighting Ming from Mars, maybe later exploring what's under Dale Arden's mini. But I guess that's a little before your time—and probably a little advanced for the uninitiated, eh?"

Hopper felt vaguely insulted. "You mean virgins?"

...and did that show?

The Navigator said nothing, but his insinuation appeared obvious. Gruber probably knew a lot about virginity. He looked the type who could wear a varsity letter "M" for his masturbatory skills.

Hopper played along and added an adult spin to his adventure. "None of that Flash Gordon crap. I was on the Challenger. You know, the space shuttle that went ka-blooey with that lady teacher onboard. Damn, was she surprised!" He had to snicker at his fabricated wise-assery.

Navigator Man looked at him hard. "Can't say I've heard anyone talk about that one, but whatever works for you is what this is about, champ. Maybe you'll want to try one of my prerecorded programs next time. They're a lot more elaborate." He leaned close as if to share a secret. "I've got assassinations and murders galore on file, if that's what you're into. Battlefields from Gettysburg to Normandy Beach, you pick the time and place. Tortures from The Inquisition, the Nazis through water boarding, for your pleasure. 'Course that stuff is usually for the adults, like spending an hour with your favorite centerfold. Some bang for your buck, if you follow my drift. Of course, I could bend the rules a little. It's just playtime, after all, a roller coaster for the mind without leaving your chair. Got your money's worth today, did you?" He patted Hopper on the back like an old pal.

Hopper's smile showed teeth. "Mister, you have no idea."

As he lay in bed, young Leach's imagination replayed the automobile accident, each time recreating a scene significantly bloodier. Of course, he could have stepped forward and been the hero during his Reality Actualization fantasy. Maybe he should have pulled one of those babes from the wreckage, performed some mouth-to-mouth resuscitation. It hadn't occurred to him at the time because he certainly would have slipped in a little tongue during his rescue, maybe even copped a feel. That dark-haired girl would have definitely been his choice, blood and all. Well, maybe next time.

Yes, there would definitely be a next time. There *had* to be.

Hopper waited until 3:00 a.m. before he rifled through his mother's pocketbook to make it happen.

"Back again so soon?" the RA-IHDM Navigator asked. "I expected you would be, but not the next day. I'm betting 'your daddy's rich, and your mama's good looking.'"

Hopper smiled, although he didn't get Gruber's reference. "Money's no problem. I've got a summer job here at the mall." It was bullshit, of course, but the geek seemed to buy it. More likely, he didn't give a rat's ass, so long as Hopper handed over the required dead presidents. He felt like a kid at the pharmacy buying condoms. "You said you have some special programs?"

The man eyed Hopper's ratty T-shirt, the one with John Lennon flashing a peace sign while standing before Lady Liberty. Unable to resist a smirk, he spoke low. "You sure you can handle the more adult stuff? It can get intense."

Hopper sneered right back. "What have you got?"

Pulling out his iPad, Gruber punched in some code. He held the screen for Hopper to examine a very long list.

"Here's a plane disaster. The program puts you onboard this jumbo while it's going down, *yee-ha!* Or, if you prefer, I can seat you on Flight 77, the first plane to hit the twin towers. The people on that flight are the real McCoy based on photos, down to the last screaming detail. You'll want to tell your friends, but I'd rather you didn't, at least not until you're eighteen. The 9/11 stuff still seems raw to folks, and I have my own PC concerns."

Hopper shook his head. The passengers' panic would have been cool to watch, but their violent deaths would have been over much too fast.

"What else you got?"

"*Plus que vous pourriez peut-être savior*, kid."

"What?"

"It's French: 'More than you could possibly know. *N'est–ce pas?* Those French have a damned bloody past. I respect that."

"Mr. Gruber, no offense, but you're fucking weird."

The geek grinned as if this were flattery. "You want an Actualization program a bit more specific, then? We've got the Kennedy assassinations, either JFK or Bobby. You're ringside in Dealey Plaza with the motorcade, or you're there in the Ambassador Hotel kitchen when Bobby gets popped. It's gripping stuff. If you're into history, I even have Lincoln's assassination here. You're close enough to the action to get spattered."

Hopper shook his head again. He didn't give a shit about politics, and American history was for his moron classmates.

The man eyed Hopper's T-shirt. "Let's try something you can identify with. You're into the Beatles, then?"

Hopper smiled. "Who isn't? You want to put me in the audience on that Sullivan show?"

"Hell, I could put you behind Ringo's drum kit! Those teenage girls moistening their panties would be screaming for *you!* A little tamer than assassinations maybe, but it's exciting to watch the young girls shriek. Love that sound!"

Hopper shook his head. "You know what I'd much rather…See, I don't mind 'extreme.' I like it."

Staring at Hopper's T-shirt, Gruber grinned. "Okay, then. How's this? You want to watch John Lennon's shooting, I'm guessing. Well, yes, I have that one too." Unlocking a huge cabinet, the man fished out a disk no larger than a silver dollar. Its label read simply 12/08/80. "This costs a bit more, but it's all here just as it happened: The Dakota Apartments, Chapman holding Lennon's album, some fans standing in the cold hoping for a glimpse. Hell, kid, when I snap this gizmo into the head set, it's December 1980, and you're an arm's length from Yoko. 'Reality leaves a lot to the imagination,' as John once said."

Ka-blam! Blood and guts. A famous man's blood and guts. The murder happened long before he was born, but Hopper licked his lips at the thought.

"Fuck yes!"

The geek held out a clipboard. "Formality. Today's adventure can be a bit riskier than yesterday's, and from what I can tell, you're into the more precarious experiences. Have to make sure I'm not navigating any poor shits with bad hearts, that kind of thing. Hell, a young and healthy heart could go pop, and even Disney requires a limited culpability agreement on their rides more daring than *It's a Small World.* Just covering my ass legally, is all, even if this shit exists only in your head."

Hopper grabbed the attached pen and signed. Wasting no time the Navigator held out his hand, and Hopper filled it with several Andrew Jacksons. The man led him to a plush armchair and slipped the headset in place.

"Okay, then, Mister Hopper. Let's keep playing those mind games together…"

It wasn't what he remembered from the old magazine photos. No smart phone videos had existed then, no instant digital snaps or selfies were around in 1980. No, this familiar yet unfamiliar scene was…***this!*** Hopper's second RA-IHDM experience was as real as real could get, and here he stood before Manhattan's Dakota Apartments waiting in the chill of a late December night for the most famous rock star on the planet.

Lennon's limo hasn't arrived yet, and Hopper has no idea of the current time, so he is as anxious, as are the few fans who stood nearby shivering in the cold. No, that is wrong. He is *more* anxious, of course. Not only does he know who was coming; he knows *what* was coming...

Girls are there, or rather young women standing in the shadows and wearing heavy overcoats because it's freezing. But Hopper sees only three of them, a small number considering they're waiting for the man who, along with his band mates, once filled Shea Stadium. That's okay with Hopper. It makes the moment more intimate, although he understands how others would misinterpret his desire to see Lennon's murder up close. Hopper doesn't care. Hell, this is make believe, his own private performance, so who's going to judge him anyway?

He looks around. Where is the night's accursed villain? Isn't that chubby assassin, Mark David Chapman, supposed to be standing near here, having waited hours to pump several hollow-point bullets into the musician's back? Bam! Bam! Bam! *Where—?*

"Hey, I've seen you before!" one of the girls says to him, but her face is hidden beneath the hood of her coat. "Yeah, now I remember! You were here a few hours ago holding John's album!"

Hopper recognizes the object he has been carrying beneath his arm. It's Double Fantasy, *Lennon and his wife's joint effort to get John back on the charts. The memory takes a moment to register. He holds up the album, realizing there's a very good reason why Chapman is nowhere to be seen. Hopper will play along, if this is the scenario that's meant to be.*

"I got John's signature on the album. It's just his scribbled name. See? He was in a hurry, but he stopped for me."

"Cool," the girl says. Hopper sees her more clearly now. It's the same dark-haired girl he noticed in yesterday's car wreck. Maybe this is some kind of technological glitch in the program—or maybe she's part of the program.

"I know you too! Jeez! You're—" But he's interrupted.

"It's John's limousine! Hey, John!" the girl yells, waving her arms at the approaching vehicle. But she doesn't run toward it, as if she knows this would be wrong. Somehow, the two other girls with her have disappeared.

The white stretch limo pulls up to the curb that moment, but it doesn't turn into the courtyard and only one figure emerges, some studio tapes tucked beneath his arm. The girl turns and watches John Lennon walk toward them, and she's still waving like a maniac. Hopper also watches as the rocker passes him, while unconsciously his hand reaches into his coat pocket. Something is there—a book! He pulls it out, studies the cover of The Catcher in the Rye.

"Yeah, that would be right," he mutters. But something else is inside that pocket, and Hopper knows what it is. Without removing the object, he understands he's carrying a Charter Arms .38-caliber pistol and that he's about to make history.

Or not. Because it's all up to him, isn't it? He gets to make the decision, doesn't he? He holds the revolver loosely. Somehow he has the assassin's memories, but that doesn't mean he has to—

The girl sees the revolver, and her eyes bulge like an insect's.

"What are you—?"

Hopper's hand acts on its own, as if it has nothing to do with him, and it's not even a part of him. The gun is in plain sight, and he's aiming it at Lennon's back as the man enters the dark alcove of the Dakota. Hopper hears his own voice call out as he steadies the .38 with both hands.

"Mr. Lennon!" echoes through the open corridor.

I'm not shouting that! It isn't me calling to him!

But it's my voice!

Hopper figures this isn't rocket science. (Well, maybe a little.) This whole scenario has been prerecorded, after all, and he's part of this program with no choice but to shoot Lennon dead where he stands. He's following a tightly written technological script like a remotely controlled puppet being made to dance. Holding the gun marine style in both hands, Hopper's hands shake badly as he crouches.

The dark-haired girl notices him, sees the weapon.

"My God! What—?"

Hopper's mouth forms words that come from some place other than his brain. They're unrehearsed, yet familiar.

"I'm going to kill John Lennon. Want to watch?" He steadies the .38 with his target's back in his site. What the hell, he tells himself, it's only pretend, no more real than some insane fever dream that he's—

BAM!

Hopper mouths the word along with the first bullet's release, and he fires four more at the shadow in rapid succession, BAM! BAM! BAM! BAM! *He wonders if that was the way Chapman did it.*

A stupid question. Of course, it is.

More real than reality...

Something's different. Lennon isn't on the ground. He isn't there at all. The limo carrying Yoko, that's gone too. But this is still the Dakota, and there's a body lying in the alcove, all right. Only he and the dark-haired girl remain, and she's there bleeding on the walkway because Hopper has pumped several bullets into her. He hurries to her, sees she's still alive.

She mutters, "I couldn't let you...You were going to kill him...I had to stop—"

Words don't come to him, not right away. He manages, "This isn't how it's supposed to...Lennon, he was supposed to...Not you!" Hopper's words drift into the night air. He can only watch the girl's life slowly drain from her.

"Couldn't...let...you..." Then: "Why...Why...?"

He can't take his eyes off her. She's watching him too.

God, she dies so beautifully.

"...and you're back!" The Actualization Navigator removed Hopper's head set, placed it on a hook, and returned the 12/8/80 disk to the cabinet. "Adventure over. So, a good time was had by all? Was it all you *imagined?*"

Hopper couldn't answer Gruber's question. The arcade's reality seemed less real than the murky Dakota alcove still inside his head. He and the geek remained the only ones inside the gallery.

"I saw a girl."

"Good for you. We have loads of pretty girls in the programs. Hell, I've had my way with a few of—" Gruber looked toward the door, but no new customers had entered the small arcade. "Anyway, I have some time. So, did Mr. Lennon ask for me?"

"You're not telling me John Lennon is still alive, are you? I mean, he died that night in 1980, right?"

The guy grinned. "Happiness is a warm gun, kid. This isn't the Twilight Zone. John's legend lives on; *he* doesn't. I know your RA-IHDM experience seemed damned real, but it wasn't. You watched Chapman do his thing, right? *Bam bam?*"

"No. I *was* Chapman! The gun, the book, but I didn't shoot him. I shot someone else—this girl..."

The man's brow knit. "You watched the murder exactly as it happened. You can't change that. You were there, but just as an observer—"

"No! *I* had the gun! *I* fired the shots! But this girl, she got in the way, the same girl I saw in the car accident yesterday. Young, dark-haired..."

Thinking that over, the geek looked troubled. "Hey, you told me you were on the Challenger. I didn't really believe that. The program wouldn't download something I have on file. You'd have to pay extra for that. I'd never make a profit if it did."

"Well, I lied. I watched this car wreck, two cars with kids my age sprawled all over the street, all bloody and dead. This one girl, I watched her die. Maybe the crash was something I created because I've never seen a bad wreck close up. I felt ashamed because...because I liked seeing it close up!" Hopper felt his face go flush. "See, this girl I saw die yesterday, she was at the Dakota, too."

Gruber walked to the door, turned the lock. Although late in the afternoon, he pulled the shutter down to close the place. His action seemed deliberate, but he appeared nervous. "You enjoyed shooting this girl, then? Like you enjoyed watching her die in that wreck you created?"

"Maybe. I don't know. Listen, I'm not some kind of sick fuck."

The guy hesitated before speaking. "The Marquis de Sade probably thought the same thing. We are what we are, kid, and what you are may exist only in your head, but it *is* what you are. I'm betting you've played your share of Tomb Raiders and Grand Theft Auto. Okay, try following this. The RA-IHDM program allows for minor alterations here and there, but it shows only what I've programed it to show. It can't be changed, no more than you could get Lara Croft to quit her swordplay to give you a blow-job. Although, maybe...Maybe the disk picked up more than your private thoughts, more than what you wanted to happen, as if you changed the channel to the director's cut."

"I'm not following you."

The man spoke low. "The program is responding to whatever urges you've got, some you can't express in any other way. Or maybe..." The geek stopped, as if some cartoon lightbulb had appeared over his head. "Maybe it's like Pepto-Bismol."

"What are you talking about?"

Gruber picked up the headset again. Almost lovingly, he studied it. "You pour Pepto-Bismol into a glass but some residue always remains, right? You wash the glass, but that pink gunk just sticks to it like fucking glue. You can't wash it off. Maybe that effect happened here. Maybe someone else left some kind of mental residue on the disk, and you picked it up and incorporated it into your own program."

"That can happen?"

"It hasn't happened before, but Alexander Graham Bell probably said that, too. I only half understand how this gear works, and I created it. There's one way to find out what happened. I've got a programmed disk I haven't used with anyone else. I'm the only one who..." He readjusted the set on Hopper's head, unlocked the cabinet to retrieve another small disk. This one was unmarked. "The only 'residue' on this program will be my own. It's a bit intense, but no charge, okay? You game?"

Hopper hesitated, then nodded.

"Fuck yes..."

"Then let's relax and float downstream, shall we?"

The red LEDs on the headset flashed on.

A dark street, cobble stoned. Old, deserted. Beneath the slight flurry of snow, Hopper lurks in some alleyway, while in the distance, he hears horse hooves, very faint. It's cold, probably early winter, and he's bundled in a heavy fur-lined coat. The street sign where he stands reads Mitre Square, Whitechapel. Alone in the shadows, he knows he's waiting. But for what?

The answer comes the next moment with the sound of clicking heels on the cobblestones. Hopper sees only a murky silhouette approaching in the darkness, but he knows it's a woman's footsteps, and he suspects who the woman is.

His ungloved hands, numb from the cold, reach into his coat pockets. He feels something sharp and metallic inside, and holding it, he realizes it couldn't be anything other than what he has expected, because now he knows also who he is...

The Ripper—Jack!

Shit. Oh shit.

Of course, he has no choice. It's in the program, and he'll do what he must do, just as he has done before. The girl will wind up dead no matter what scenario awaits. Hopper (no, Jack!) runs his thumb along the knife's blade, understanding it will be the young woman's throat he'll be cutting in one minute's time.

Will he be loving this? Should he be? Hopper/Jack no longer knows.

The woman stops before him, and he hears himself mumble, "Evenin' Miss. Cold as a bugger tonight." He has no idea where his words come from, but why should he? They're part of the program, and he's not sitting in Gruber's Arcade any more. No, he's in London, and it's probably the late 1880s, and somehow he knows this as he holds the jagged-edged blade behind his back. Surprise, surprise!

The young woman's face is partially hidden beneath an oversized bucket hat that reveals dark bangs peeking through, and she stands with the proud posture of a late 19ʰ-century prostitute, her painted smile clearly visible in the shadows.

Dark haired...Pretty...

"Cold it most certainly is. Then, will you be wanting my services to keep yourself warm, sir?"

The Cockney voice is familiar, although slurred, suggesting she's probably inebriated. But her intent is to the point, and Hopper knows her drunkenness will tragically prove her fatal mistake.

No, that makes no sense. She'll die even without so much as a drop of alcohol in her.

"Your name, Miss?" he asks, having no doubt this was the Ripper's way. Amiable, respectful, clearly cultured—all the while holding a murder weapon behind him.

"Catherine, and that is all you need to know," she answers, still smiling, although her expression now seems forced.

A good distance from the nearest lamplight, Hopper studies the empty street. "Well, Catherine, I have something for you." He feels his voice has been prerecorded, as it probably has. Reaching into his coat pocket with his spare hand, seeming to search for the currency the woman clearly expects, Hopper shows her only an empty palm.

"Sir? What…?"

"No money for you tonight. Sorry. The name is Jack, Miss. And that is all you need to know."

Her throat, so white, so delicate and perfect.

With his free hand, he grabs her, covers her face to squelch her attempt to scream, pulling her into the dark alleyway and slicing her throat with expert efficiency as she wriggles and kicks in his grasp. No longer able to scream as he releases his hand, the woman can only gurgle with blood spilling from her mouth past a tongue that dangles to her chin like a loose gobbet. But he (the Ripper!) is not finished with her. There is more to cut!

The blade slips under the woman's long skirt, and he slashes through the undergarment material to gaze upon the treasure beneath. His hands have a will of their own, while with a surgeon's precision he removes the young woman's womb, holds it high in the yellow lamplight, gagging on hot bile the entire time. His victim's meaty innards drip into the street, while what little remains of Hopper Leach's self grows nauseated at the Ripper's craftsmanship. He allows Catherine—or whatever her real name is—to slip from his grasp and tumble to the ground, her eyes opened wide and fixed on him, accusing him.

He stares right back at her, more Hopper Leach than Jack.

"Who are you really? Who the fuck are you?"

No, that's not the right question. The correct question is "Who am I?"

The answer comes with the reflection of himself Hopper catches in a nearby storefront. The dripping blade still in his grasp, he leaves the woman's crumpled corpse behind to study the window glass closely. His mouth opens in his own silent scream because…because it isn't himself he sees. It's the geek! The smirking Reality Actualization Navigator, Gruber, is grinning back at him in the window's reflection!

"What the—?"

"Pepto-Bismol! Some residue always remains!"

Like a man pulled from two different directions, Hopper seems frozen where he stands, unable to move, unable even to raise his arms. It feels his hands suddenly have been tied, and he wants this fucking RA-IHDM experience to end, he wants it to end right now, but...but God, the girl died so beautifully!

"No more...please...please..."

"And we're back! The end. *La fin.* Roll credits."

Uncertain of the authenticity of everything around him, Hopper didn't know what 'back' meant; he wasn't even sure what reality meant. Not anymore.

"I saw her again. My God, and I saw you! No, I-I *was* you! I saw my reflection—*your* reflection!" Hopper struggled in the cushioned chair. His hands were buckled.

The geek smiled, moved closer. "Did the young woman die beautifully, then? These restraints? Yes, you're probably wondering about them. See, it's for those who might squirm to the floor during the Actualization experience, another covering-my-ass formality necessary to run this place. Don't want customers demanding their money back or considering lawsuits."

"Keep the fucking money. Just unbuckle me!"

The geek's Joker smile spread. "I don't think so. You saw that pretty dark-haired girl, not once, not twice, but three times. That tells me all I need to know."

The words took a moment to sink in.

"You know her?"

Gruber's smile morphed into an outright laugh. "Oh, I know her. You do, too, if you think about it. She was all over the Internet a few weeks ago. You do watch the news, don't you?"

Hopper remembered! "Cops found some girl in the river with a rock tied to her and with her throat cut, and...and other stuff the Internet said was too awful. Cathy something..." His head clearing, Hopper muttered to himself. "The Pepto-Bismol thing...*Shit!* It wasn't only me in the program. *It was you!*"

The geek leaned close. "Right you are, Sherlock! That Catherine, one fine piece of ass ordering her Happy Meal at the mall. We share the same curiosity about pretty girls, don't we? That's why she showed up in your adventures. You think about how they might die; you get a hard-on for how it makes you feel! Death, it's fucking beautiful! You're like me, kid. More than you know."

Residue...a little bit me...a little bit you...

"You killed her?"

"Not once, not twice...Cut her throat, like our pal Jack, once for real, then over and over in my selected programs. I like watching. You want details?"

Hopper already knew the details. He'd seen the geek's work.

"No."

For some reason, the man slipped a second headset on himself. Retrieving Hopper's gear, he adjusted it on him, snapping another disk into its slot. "One last trip for you, kid. I think this next program is my best work. The body believes what the brain tells it to believe. Want to see?"

Hopper tried shaking the headset free, tried screaming his throat raw. The geek taped his mouth before he could utter another sound.

"Mmmphhh!!"

"Bienvenue à la guillotine, kid."

The man was speaking French again. Hopper had no clue what he was saying or why he had such a boner for the language, but he recognized one word.

He knew it couldn't be good.

Like some Hollywood dream sequence, reality dissolves and another scene comes into focus. Before him, a crowd shouts with a blood-thirsty fury. His hands tied behind his back, Hopper stands on a tall platform restrained by a man in black wearing a dark hood. The man whispers to him.

"Nous saluons le retour."

Hopper can't speak.

"It means 'Welcome back,' kid. So, préférez-vous un bandeau?"

Hopper recognizes the geek's voice from behind the hood. His own words are muffled and he can manage only "Mmmpphhh." The tape that had covered his mouth is gone here, but back inside the arcade, he knows the tape remains in place to mute his protests.

The hooded man whispers, "Shame you don't understand French. I asked if you would prefer a blindfold?"

"Mmmphhh!"

"No blindfold, then? You're one brave little prick. Mes compliments. Welcome to La Révolution Française and all that historical shit you probably know nothing about. Doesn't matter. These angry folks see someone they detest, and they have a lust for blood. Kind of your thing too, isn't it?" Even Gruber's nasal laugh sounds French. The man forces Hopper to his knees, constrains his neck in the small curvature while bringing down its heavy wooden companion piece that secures his head within a small hole.

Hopper sees the basket directly below, watches the enraged crowd shout. A dark-haired girl steps forward, her voice carrying above the rabble's uproar. Hopper recognizes her. Of course! Waving her fist, she screams to him.

"Sa tête, sa tête! Couper la tête!"

"W-What—?" he attempts.

The black-robed man removes his hood enough so that only Hopper sees his smile. "She's shouting for your head, Monsieur Hopper, and who can blame her? You may want to shut your eyes now. The machine is efficient, but sometimes the blade requires a second drop, and it does get messy. No need to worry. It's all make believe, all in your head." Gruber's laugh ends with a snort.

Hopper's heart beats faster than it ever has in his entire life, but in another moment, he knows it will stop completely once his head tumbles into the basket. He tells himself he isn't here, that this isn't happening, and nothing is real. But inside his brain what surrounds him seems more real than reality. Hopper remembers the geek's warning: "A young and healthy heart could go pop."

"Mmmmphhh!!!"

"Vous allez mourir si joliment!" the young woman cries out. The crowd's curses fade, and the girl's words are all Hopper hears except for what Gruber whispers to him.

"Our lovely friend is saying how you will die so beautifully."

Gruber grunts with the exertion of releasing the long handle at his side. The thick swoosh of the metal lasts only a split second as Hopper hears the blade of the guillotine fall.

It's only in my head...only in my—

✕✕✕✕✕ ✕✕✕✕✕ ✕✕✕✕✕ ✕

ABOUT THE AUTHOR

Ken Goldman, former Philadelphia teacher of English and Film Studies, is an affiliate member of the Horror Writers Association. He has homes on the Main Line in Pennsylvania and at the Jersey shore. His stories have appeared in more than 870 independent press publications in the U.S., Canada, the U.K., and Australia with more than thirty due for publication in 2017-18. Ken's tales have received seven honorable mentions in The Year's Best Fantasy & Horror. He has written six books: three anthologies of short stories, *You Had Me at Arrgh!!* (Sam's Dot Publishers), *Donny Doesn't Live Here Anymore* (A/A Productions), and *Star-Crossed (Vampires 2);* and a novella, *Desiree,* (released by Damnation Books, and by eXcessica Publishing for Kindle). His first novel *Of a Feather* (Horrific Tales Publishing) was released in January 2014. *Sinkhole,* his second novel, was published August 2017 by Bloodshot Books. Many of Ken's stories can be found on Amazon.com at https://www.amazon.com/Kenneth-C.-Goldman/e/B004QVWTTE. Stop by and scream hello

Sylvester

Nicole Tanquary

Bill couldn't afford to stay in Boulder Heights much longer. There'd been all kinds of media attention about the little girl he'd taken in July; the disappearances of blonde, blue-eyed cuties like her always got media attention. The black little girls and daughters of Latino migrant farmers, not so much. That was his usual game, and they could be good, very good. But there was something about the girls hidden in the bland McMansions, the mass-produced gardens, and rolling lawns of Boulder Heights that attracted his attention. Excited it. Here could be a challenge.

He walked around the neighborhood at an easy pace, getting a feel for the place. It had rained earlier in the morning. Shiny puddles were collected on the sidewalks, soaking through the bottoms of his sneakers. According to the street sign, this place was called Hook Circle; most of the houses were only half-built, set in scrubby fields that opened to picturesque forest views. Bill had lived near a forest once, a real forest, so the scrap-trees trees of Hook Circle had a whittled and thinned-out look to him.

Still, it was a nice set up. Maybe the parents would assume their girl had gone off for an adventure in the woods and gotten lost in there somehow. That's what they'd tell themselves, at least. They didn't like to think that people like Bill existed. Or, if they did think of him, it was only in vague and uneasy thoughts. When all was said and done, he was more shadow than man. Shine a bright light at him, and he would practically disappear.

Disappear, but remain very much alive. He had to be that way in this day and age, when parents were paranoid and mostly kept their children indoors, as if monsters were lurking behind every bush outside their windows.

Yes, it was a dangerous game. But when planned correctly, the payoff was oh so *sweet*. Sweet eyes and soft skin…

Bill started to jog, his steps brisk and his bald spot gleaming. Soon there were twin stains of sweat beneath his armpits. Summer days like these brought out the adventurous middle-aged homeowners of Boulder Heights, trying to work off their dinners and food-splurges, though their bulges never seemed to get any smaller. Dressed like this, in baggy pants and a sweatshirt, he fit in here like a hand in a glove. That was just how he liked it.

As he was turning onto Hook, he spotted something that made his mouth twitch into a smile. There was a girl, dressed in capris and a soccer jersey several sizes too big. She was pacing the sidewalk, not in a straight line but a restless zigzag, peering into the shadowy hedges and corners in her neighbors' front lawns. Whenever her head turned, her ponytail swung against her neck, smooth and slick with sweat. *Ah,* thought Bill, his lower abdomen lighting up in a warm glow. She would do just fine.

As he watched, she paused, cupping her hands around her mouth. "Sylvester! Sylvester, where are you?"

Bill continued his jog, slowing just a hair as he passed her. At the sound of his footsteps, she turned and started toward him, saying, "Excuse me, sir?" He paused mid-step, panting lightly, hands on his hips. "Have you seen a cat around? A biggish cat, black with white on his belly…" She trailed off and lowered her head, already knowing his answer from the look on his face.

"Sorry, I don't think so. When did you see him last?"

"Yesterday morning. He went out on patrol, and he hasn't been back since. I'm worried one of the monsters got him."

Bill raised his eyebrows. "Monsters?"

The girl had already lost interest in him. Her gaze moved over his shoulder, tracing the side of a house where wall met flower bed. "Yeah, he's always fighting with monsters. I'm gonna keep looking now," and she was turning away from him, half-heartedly. "Thanks anyways."

Bill rubbed a hand across his forehead in mock-thought. He was glowing from his own sweat now…the anticipation. Summer days and summer girls always filled him with this kind of feeling, this glow. "You're probably not going to find him just walking around. Cats can cover a lot of ground. Have you asked your mom or dad to drive you around the neighborhood?"

The girl bit her lip, something like anger passing through her face. Maybe it was resignation.

"Mom works all day. She'd only get home after dark." Bill nodded in sympathy.

"That's a shame...you know, my car is parked just around the block, on Hedgewood. We could go looking together."

She gave him a look. "But aren't you jogging?"

Bill shrugged.

"It's okay. I'd rather help you than jog. I mean, I know what it's like to lose a pet. My dog got run over by a car when I was your age..." He paused, pursing his lips in sadness. "He was my best friend, the best dog ever. If I can help you find your cat, it'd be like...getting a chance to save him, you know? It would make both of our days a lot better." He rubbed a hand along his forearm, the skin blushing red. Getting a kid to come with him always made his skin itch; he didn't know why.

She wasn't completely sold on the story. He could see it in her large brown eyes, the way they flickered to the left, to what he assumed was her house, in the very back of the cul-de-sac.

Fortunately, he knew a line that would bring her around: "I just don't want your cat to get run over, like my dog. Being on the streets can be dangerous for something so small. And we adults aren't always careful when we drive."

That did the trick. The idea of Sylvester the cat broken and smeared across the pavement by a car's tires was too much to bear, so they started toward Hedgewood together, Bill moving briskly, the girl trotting at his heels to keep up. He had a good reason to move quickly. The less time she had to think over her decision, the better.

"So, how'd you get Sylvester? What kind of cat is he?" Keeping the girl's mind on the cat was going to be his best bet for getting her into the car, he knew that from both experience and intuition.

She shrugged to herself, her ponytail bouncing as she walked. "I found him in the woods last summer. He was fighting with one of the monsters I told you about. He was bleeding all over the place; one of his teeth had been torn out. The monster was gonna kill him. So I threw a rock," she stopped long enough to mime the throw with her arm, "and it hit the monster right in the eye. Burst it open, and yellow gooky stuff went all down his face. So the monster turned and started coming after me, and that was when Sylvester used his knife to stab him in the back and kill him."

Bill smiled. The things kids thought of these days. "I didn't know cats could hold knives."

"Sylvester's only a cat some of the time. He can be anything he wants. He just stays a cat whenever Mom comes home." Maybe what they were searching for wasn't a cat after all, but an imaginary friend, Bill thought. Not that it mattered; it was all the same to him.

They turned a corner onto Hedgewood, a winding, impractical suburban road that snaked through all of Boulder Heights. Despite the earlier rain, a couple of sprinklers were going on the spots of lawn, water draining out of the drowned grass and moving along the gutters in sluggish trickles. That, and the noise of distant traffic, were the only sounds on the whole street. People just didn't come outside like they used to on these gorgeous summer days. Too busy with Facebook and Netflix and whatever else Boulder Heights people did.

He felt in his pocket for his keys. "Well, this Sylvester sounds like he can take care of himself. Did he say why he was hanging around in Boulder Heights, of all places?"

The girl smiled down at her feet. "He was just here to kill the monster, at first. But I saved his life. As a thank you, he said he'll stay in this dimension and keep me safe, for as long as I live."

Dimensions, where did she get that from, the Syfy channel? "Well, that'll be a long time, won't it?"

The girl gave him the look children occasionally give adults, a look that said, "That's not the point, dumbo."

"Sylvester's lived a long time. Thousands and thousands of years. So he doesn't mind waiting until I die. Time feels short to him."

Bill could see his car now, a red minivan whose back spaces he had converted to suit his needs. He pointed it out to the girl, who spotted it and started grinning. Kids were never sure if an adult was lying to them or not, so they were always happy to have proof that Bill wasn't leading them on. Plus, the car wasn't one of those shady white vans their parents always warned them about as part of their stranger-danger training. No, minivans were standard fare for suburbs like these, and the familiarity of their shape always had a bit of a lulling effect.

Her trot speeded into a sprint, as she ran to the door and then hopped from foot to foot, waiting for Bill to catch up and let her in. "Come on. We have to find Sylvester!" she called. "He could be in danger! The monsters might've hurt him!"

Bill winced, wondering if any housewives had heard the girl's raised voice.

"Hold on. I'm coming." Finally, he got to the car and popped open the side door. She clambered in and pulled the seatbelt over her chest, clicking it in place. He got into the driver's seat and closed the door behind him.

There. No more pretenses necessary. Child locks were all in, and she was small enough that when he drove to someplace quiet, he could climb back there and drag her into the space where he had taken out the back-back row, the space she hadn't noticed yet. He flexed his fingers on the wheel, grinning despite himself. There was a state forest on the other side of town, one he'd spotted on a map. It'd been full of thin dirt roads, leading to deep, wooded areas, places with no people. Places, in fact, where it would take a very long time to find a body.

Turning the car onto a road heading out of Boulder Heights, he couldn't help one last question. "His name. Sylvester. Is it after the Loony-Toon cat?" He could see the girl make a face at him in the rearview mirror.

"No, it's after Sylvester Stallone. He likes watching Stallone movies."

Bill blinked, wondering if he could chuckle. Stallone, huh? The kid was well-versed in the movies, apparently. He hadn't taken her mother to be the type to let her watch a Stallone flick, but hey, surprises happened every day.

The girl fell quiet after that, her eyes glued to the window, roving back and forth as they drove in search of the cat. A tenseness had come into her shoulders, and Bill thought he caught her looking at him out of the corner of her eyes. She was beginning to wonder if she'd made a mistake. *Too late, sweetie,* he thought. *They all think that, always too late.* By now, his skin had heated from a warm itch to a burn, a delicious burn that lit up everything in his body.

After another minute, she spoke up. "I don't think Sylvester would go this far."

"Oh?" Bill said nothing else, and the girl shrank into the back seat.

Another minute passed. "Can you take me home?"

Again, Bill said nothing. There was no need to.

He could see the girl working out the situation in her head: young kid's faces were always easy to read, all the emotions right at the surface, not buried under years of mistrust and bad experiences. After a moment, she tried the window. To his surprise, it rolled down just a crack, and she had time to call out "SYLVESTER!" before Bill rolled it back up and locked it shut. He swore aloud, his grin pinching down into a frown. That had been clumsy. He *thought* he had locked all the windows. Maybe he was slipping a little in his older age.

"No more of that," he said. "We've almost gotten to where we need to be. Just keep quiet, and everything will be—"

There was a shadow standing in the middle of the road. The silhouette of a man with his head down and his shoulders hunched forward, and two orange eyes that *burned.*

Bill turned the wheel in his hands to swerve and avoid hitting the thing. Except, the shadow leaned *toward* him in the swerve and outstretched his arms, graceful as a praying mantis. Bill thought he could even see the glint of claws.

The thing's hands ripped into the side of the minivan and clung on, the momentum swinging the van around to the side until, at last, it was dragged to a standstill. Then the shadow pulled off the door with a crunch that set Bill's teeth on edge in a fierce clench.

There was a swirl of motion, of black limbs flowing against leather seat cushions. A moment later, and the silhouette was standing outside again, holding the girl close to him. Except, it wasn't a silhouette anymore. It was beginning to take on details.

Bill screamed and floored the gas pedal, but Sylvester had set down the girl and slashed his claws back into the minivan's metal hide. The wheels spun and burned themselves on the road, but the thing's grip held firm.

Finally, Sylvester let go and, in the space of a second, circled around to the driver's side, wrenching open the door and wrapping a hand around the front of Bill's jogging sweatshirt. Bill didn't realize he was still screaming, his eyes bulging and his pupils fully dilated, taking everything in with the intricate level of detail you can only see right before your death. The hand that held him was *huge,* like a catcher's mitt, except that the nails were hooked and silvery...

A moment later, and Bill felt pavement beneath his shoes, as Sylvester lifted him bodily from the car and set him on the ground. Sylvester's upper lip curled back, and all the teeth were not only visible but *gleaming,* they were so white. Bill had thought that only happened in books. Or maybe in Stallone movies.

"You like taking little girls from their homes? You like playing around with them, huh, you sick fuck?" Bill's hands went up to Sylvester's wrist, desperately trying to pry off the grip and get back in his car and *drive away,* away from the imaginary friend that wasn't imaginary after all, that could shape-shift and was from a different dimension and hunted monsters and was real, real as the edge of a knife on a throat...

"Look away, Sarah," Sylvester called, his eyes flicking to the girl for a moment before traveling back to Bill's face. He released his grip just long enough to move his hands to Bill's neck. Then he clenched down.

The body that a moment ago had been warm and sweaty was now carved of solid, hardened, crystal-bright pain.

And then it was simply nothing. Like everything below his neck had been chopped clean off.

Sylvester lay him down the street, then stood, his head tilted to one side. For a moment, he watched Bill gasp quietly to himself. Finally, he moved to stand behind Bill's head and crouched, their eyes locking together. Bill would've tried screaming again, if he thought it was going to be of any use, but it wasn't; he could see the end clearly in Sylvester's eyes, bright with rage.

Sylvester was swallowing it back, though, and when he reached down, he only grazed his claws against Bill's chest instead of digging them in and tearing his heart out through his ribs. "If you had so much as *touched* her, you'd be dead right now, you motherfucker," he whispered. "As it is, with a broken spine, you won't be moving around on your own anymore. Have fun with that."

Then he turned and walked back to Sarah. With each step Sylvester took, he shrank, his ears growing to points and fur spreading up and down the length of his body. Bill's eyes rolled in his head, fixed to the cat's back legs.

Sarah didn't start following after Sylvester right away. She was standing still, looking down at Bill, still splayed out on the road. "You didn't kill him, did you?" she asked, finally.

"No. He's just paralyzed. Forget about it, hun. He's not important."

After another pause, she began to follow Sylvester back down the road, the summer sun burning their shadows into the ground. Bill's eyes were swimming in gray fuzz, so he closed them and rested the back of his head against the pavement. The solidness of it steadied him, if only a little.

He thought he heard the girl ask what motherfucker meant, and Sylvester answer that it was nothing she needed to know. It was one of those words you had to use with people like *him*. And sorry that he was gone for so long; he'd been hunting.

I've been hunted, thought Bill. It was this thought that broke through the gray and, at last, brought out his own rage, shrieking through his bloodstream with adrenaline he could no longer spend, not even in the smallest leg twitch. DAMN IT! *THIS WAS NOT HOW IT WAS SUPPOSED TO END!* He was supposed to *get* the girl, that's always how it worked out before! What the fuck even WAS this?

You'll have enough time to answer that question on your own, buddy, he thought he heard someone say, before the fuzz filled his eyes, and the world faded away beneath it. Hopefully someone would find him.

Unless maybe a monster got to him first.

)(O)(O)( )(O)(O)( )(O)(O)( )(

About the Author

Nicole Tanquary lives in upstate New York State, where she has worked variously as a geochemistry lab assistant, a teaching assistant, and a non-fiction editor and writer, and is currently employed as a writing tutor for Syracuse University. Writing speculative fiction in her spare time, she has sold and published short stories to a menagerie of venues, the most recent of these including work with *Fantasia Divinity Magazine, Deadman's Tome,* and *Not One of Us Magazine.* A more complete list of projects she has been involved in can be found by searching her name on Amazon.com. Other things she likes to do include long hikes, playing with her pet cats and rats, and eating ice cream.

Blood Rush High

Tom Olbert

Blood dripped from the fangs of shadowy demons, their eyes dancing red flames. They crawled from stygian pits, from seething black viscous pools, reaching up into silver moonlight, the sweet blood of hapless human prey dribbling from their curving claws...

Caitlin moaned as she woke, dark dreams dissipating like black smoke in the grey-filtered evening light. Gavin laughed softly as his muscular body slid across the stale-scented sheets, his strong arms embracing her. "Stop," she muttered through her laughter as he bit into her neck, his strong hand kneading her breast, his calloused fingers playfully squeezing her nipple. "Will you stop," she protested, half in jest, pushing him off. "Will you look at the time? If we're late again, Greeley'll have our heads!" He groaned and swung his legs over the edge of the bed, leaning forward and rubbing his head.

As she gathered scraps of hastily discarded clothes and dressed from what she could put together from the disarray, shadows of sensuous nightmare began to mingle with slowly coalescing shapes of solid memory. The blood of dream demons and drug rush merging with the screams of the dealers she and Gavin had killed the night before. Sweet screams and geysers of blood. She smiled. *Blood looks so black in moonlight,* she realized, slipping on her trousers, blood still splattered on the cuffs. Against dark blue, it looked so damned red. The ebbing sun's golden rays seared her eyes as they washed dark, intoxicating shadows across Gavin's rippling muscles. His tattoos. His scars. Scars from the Gulf. From the streets. She wanted him. He pulled her to him, his tongue down her throat as he ran his fingers through her hair. *No. Not now.* "Not now," she insisted, pushing him away. He sighed. The two laced joints still smoldered in the ashtray, which she picked up on her way to the john.

"What's your rush?" he asked playfully, as he followed her to the bathroom. "No, strike that. I know what your rush is." He chuckled. "It's mine, too." He slipped his arms around her from behind, nuzzling her neck.

"Will you stop?" she protested, pulling away and dumping the ashtray into the toilet. "We have to look presentable," she said, flushing the two joints. "Those bodies are going to be found soon, you know."

"What's left of them," he said, choking down a laugh and belching, as though with indigestion.

A half-formed memory slipped through her mind, like a dark shadow in fleeting light. The sweet coppery taste of dripping raw meat, the taste lingering in the back of her mouth, even now as she smacked her lips. She trembled lightly as she shook it off. *Just blood rush dreams,* she thought, tying back her hair. She looked in the mirror, switching on the dim, flickering light bulb. She winced. Her eyes were bloodshot and dark-rimmed. Her cheeks sunken. God. How long had she been working the night shift? Seemed like forever. It also seemed like she wanted it never to end. The night's wild light, silver and blue and red and…the sweet, black, black blood…

"That's my girl." He whispered, kissing her on the neck and nibbling her ear lobe, as if he could read her thoughts.

She smiled, running her hand along his coarse beard stubble. *He's ruined me for other men,* she thought with resignation. Even the memory of her ex-husband now sickened her. So soft. So damned clueless.

"Get dressed," she ordered, pulling on her shirt. As she straightened her badge, she noticed a spec of gore over the number and wiped it off with a tissue. She sniffed and cleared her throat. The memories of the night before came through louder and clearer, like blaring sirens in her head as she pulled on her gun belt. The terrified eyes of the men she'd killed flashed through her mind, like a snatch of shining silver racing through her like a rush of electricity. It got her blood flowing again. She drew her gun and loaded a fresh clip. As she holstered the gun and slid the baton into its ring, she glanced over at Gavin's belt. "There's blood," she said, pointing at the handcuffs he'd used to smash-in that guy's face the night before. "Clean it."

He smiled at her, rubbing the bloodied cuffs together and chuckling, a twinkle in his eye.

They gathered at Andy's Café as they always did when their shift ended. The screams of the protesters had faded to a dull thrumming a few blocks away. A meagre rustling, like wheat in the wind. Wheat, ripe for hewing. She felt a smile coming on as memories flashed through her mind. Repeating muzzle flashes from rooftops in the dark night. Molotov cocktails exploding in the dark streets like Fourth of July fireworks. Some punk's head exploding like a bloody piñata as she squared him in the infra-red scope between the cross-hairs and pulled the trigger. Her heart raced even as Andy brought another round.

"Drink up, boys and girls," Andy said with a broad grin crossing his wide, rubbery face. "My best," he said, handing out the beer bottles. "On the house."

"To Andy," Gavin said with a smile, raising his bottle in toast. "Best friend a cop could have!"

Caitlin and the others raised their bottles in toast, shouting Andy's name. "Nonsense," Andy said with a smile. "Nothing's too good for our brave fighters in blue, protecting our businesses from those scum out there. Now, don't go away. I've got something very special for you, seeing you've been out there working up a hearty appetite half the night."

"Oh…some of those fire-grilled bits, Andrew?" Donovan said, salivating as he rubbed his meaty palms together.

"That's why you keep comin' back, am I right?" Andy said with a laugh, heading into the kitchen. They all started pounding their bottles on the table, clamoring for a taste of Andy's fine grub. Nothing else like it, anywhere, that was the God's honest truth. Caitlin's mouth was watering at the thought of it. Delicious, those juicy bits of meat, fresh off Andy's flaming grill. She could never get enough. Though somehow, it never filled her. It just left her wanting more. Like fuel for hunger's fire, she just had to keep feeding it. So, out into the wild, rushing, screaming night with Gavin and the boys. The rush filled her. Memories were vague and smoky, like ashes the morning after. But, the rush sated her hunger somehow.

Andy came back a few minutes later carrying a tray of steaming meats, his apron splattered with dark red juices. "Eat up, kids!" he said, laying the tray down in the middle of the table and handing out the forks. "Fuel up for another night's hunting! And, keep shooting straight!" His trademark phrase.

"God bless Andy!" Monahan shouted as he speared a steaming hunk of meat and crammed it into his mouth.

They all dove in. Caitlin picked at hers. She could never figure out what the hell kind of meat it was. Kind of like chicken, kind of like pork. But, different. The shapes were weird. Little tubular cuts, that reminded her of calamari. But, the tasty, succulent moistness that melted in her mouth was nothing like that. And, the char-blackened crisp skin crunching between her teeth. Thick, meaty chunks that had been shaved off bones she had a hard time picturing. The ribs were the best. Becker was gnawing on one now, the reddish grease adhering to his meaty chops, his reddened drool dribbling onto the table. *The rib of what animal,* she wondered as she stripped one with her teeth, licking the sweet juices from her lips and savoring the taste as it slid down her gullet. Yes, it ignited the blood, and made her stomach growl even as the tray was emptied. She had to have more.

She finished her beer in one belt. They all did. The air shimmered with a deep, dark buzz, like a steamy wash of shadow. Street lights shone dully through the windows, as through smoke and moist summer heat. A deep breathing and the pounding of blood raced through her head and ears. The shadows around the other tables, long since emptied, seemed to grow darker as they bled across the floor, drawing closer. Hungrier, it seemed.

"Ready to roll?" Gavin asked with a low whisper and a wolfish grin, laying his hand on hers.

She smiled back, the hunger rising in her mingling with the stirring memories of the last few hours. "You know it."

XXXXX XXXXX XXXXX XX

The blood rush was at its peak as they strung up the prey. In the deep shadows in the rubbish-strewn dark corner under the bridge, live men hung by their wrists, strung up like sides of beef.

They all moaned and begged, blood streaming down their naked bodies, pretty black rivulets, sweet as trickling molasses. Caitlin drooled and trembled with hunger as Gavin and the others howled with laughter. The steak knives Andy had provided glistened like silver in the moonlight. Caitlin's hand trembled with ecstasy as she took hers. It had been a rite of passage, she thought as she licked her lips, looking at the stupid, mewling, terrified faces of the scum strung up for the kill. Now, it was an addiction. It was what she lived for. She didn't even remember who they were or where or why they'd pulled them over. Protesters, agitators, dealers, pimps, johns....Who could remember? Who cared? They were all the same. Meat. Was it even real, she wondered, or a dream? Who cared about that? It was the rush. The rush was all that mattered, the only thing that was real.

It all blurred into a wild dance of sound and harsh light and racing shadow and surging pleasure. A madly rushing pitch-black wave of darkness and sweet, splashing blood. The cutting, the screaming. Gavin, and the others...Monahan, Donovan, Becker... their eyes were red flame in the darkness, their bodies morphing into black shadow. Their teeth flashed white, becoming long, silver fangs. Their fingers lengthened into curving, tapering black claws, dripping with blood. They were like wraiths of boiling pitch jacketed with shimmering waves of silver. And, she was one of them.

Eyes stared in terror out of a bloodied human face as she hurtled closer...

She awoke to the annoying beep of a cell phone. She was in her bed, Gavin grumbling in his sleep beside her. Morning sunshine stabbed her eyes and made her head throb as she threw off the clinging tangle of sheets and staggered about, looking for the phone. "Yeah..." she groaned, her voice like gravel, her head pounding as she winced in the light. "Who the hell is this?"

"Caitlin? It's Robert." She smacked her lips in disgust at the sound of that mewling cock she was ashamed to admit she'd been married to.

"What the fuck do you mean, calling me at his hour," she demanded, trying desperately to discern the clock as her eyes adjusted. "Haven't I made it clear I'm still on night-shift? And why the hell isn't your sheister attorney making this call?"

"It's Brigitte." She froze at the sound of her daughter's name, the phone nearly slipping from her numbed fingers.

"God…wh-what's wrong?" Her heart was slamming her chest as she imagined the worst. If that whining little pantywaist or his new little office slut of a girlfriend had let anything happen to Brigitte, she'd…"Is she all right?"

"She had a terrible nightmare, woke up screaming. We couldn't calm her down. I've never seen her so scared. She insisted on talking to you."

She could hear the worry in his voice, and it scared her. She knew Robert would never allow her one second more than her court-appointed time with Bridge, unless this was a real emergency. "Put her on!"

Her pulse raced as the seconds ticked by. "Mommy?" The frail little voice on the other end of the line set her heart quavering in a way it hadn't for so long. The rush of the night before retreated as Caitlin thought only of her little girl.

"Mommy's here, baby. What's wrong?"

"The monsters. They tried to get me. They're going to get me!"

"Honey, there are no real monsters, remember? They're all in your head. It was just a bad dream."

"No, they're real! They are! Please come. Please, Mommy…I'm scared."

Ice ran through Caitlin's gut, which never happened. Brigitte's trembling, anguished voice cut through her like knives. She'd never heard such terror in her little girl's voice before. Her sweet angel…so pure…the one thing the evil in the night couldn't touch…that one thing that was forever, that was good and incorruptible. She could barely fill her lungs enough to speak.

"Mommy?"

"Mommy's coming, angel," she finally forced out. "Be good. Be brave. Mommy's coming."

She ran to the bathroom, horrible visions racing through her head. If that bastard had done something to Bridge. If he'd let that slut of his do anything, she would kill. She would...

The sight in the mirror that met her eyes as she turned on the bathroom light made her freeze. She was drenched in blood. It covered her face and hands. *God, is it real? Oh, God, Oh God, Oh God, Oh God...*

She threw herself in the shower, trying to scrub the memories away...The lingering nightmare shadows that bled away like the cloudy crimson water circling down the drain. *Not real,* she kept thinking as the water pounded on her face, and she tried desperately to wash the dried blood from her hair. *Not real. Not real. God, don't let it be real. Mommy's coming, baby. Mommy's coming.*

Robert ran out to meet her as her car pulled into his driveway. She'd barely avoided several collisions as she'd barreled to his house, the siren wailing all the way. "Where is she?" she demanded, getting out of the car.

"In her room," he said, sweat standing out on his forehead. "Jan's with her. She just keeps calling for you."

"Get out of my way!" She pushed past him as she ran up the stairs into their old place, in his nice, safe neighborhood. How trapped she'd once felt here. How desperately she wanted to get back in now.

"Caitlin, for God's sake, leave your gun in the car! I don't want Brigitte exposed to..."

"Shut up!" she screamed, unable to bear his mewling voice anymore. What had she ever seen in him? Oh, he was all kind and gentle, and good looking enough, but his weak, bleeding heart ideas turned her stomach. He knew nothing. He lived in a dream world. Whatever evil had touched Brigitte, it would have slipped past his nose, and he wouldn't have questioned it. His kind never did.

"Caitlin, please calm down!" he called after her as she bounded up the stairs to Brigitte's room. "I don't want her scared."

She could hear Brigitte sobbing as she approached. "I want my mommy…"

"It's okay, sweetie," she heard that little slut Janice answer. "Mommy Jan's here. It's okay."

Caitlin pushed the door open and saw that red-haired slut holding her baby on her lap. That lap, where that bastard Robert had…Her blood boiled. "Get away from my daughter!" she shouted, pulling Brigitte from Janice's arms. She desperately wanted to bludgeon the little whore, to see her bleed. But, all she could feel a moment later was Brigitte's warm little body against her, Brigitte's tears on her cheek. It had been so long. "Mommy's here, baby," she whispered, holding Bridge close and stroking her hair. "Shhh…It's okay now. You're safe. Don't cry."

Brigitte's little hand touched Caitlin's face as she pulled back to look at her. Her warm little smile was golden sunshine…something Caitlin had done without and hadn't missed in what now seemed like forever. As she wiped the tears from Brigitte's face, Brigitte's big, pretty eyes widened, her face twisting into a mask of horror. The child screamed, as though the devil had appeared before her. "You!" she screamed. "You're not my mommy! You're not my mommy!"

Caitlin's blood ran cold through her hands. "Sweetheart…I'm your mommy. I'm right here. It's okay."

"You're not her! You're not!" She cringed in Caitlin's arms, pulling away. "It's the monster! Get it away! Get it away!"

Robert pulled Brigitte from Caitlin's arms and turned his back, shielding their little girl in his arms. Janice had pulled back behind Robert, clinging to him, as though for her own protection. The look on her face was almost as terrified as the one on Brigitte's. "Caitlin, for God's sake," Robert said, turning to her as he held Brigitte's head to his shoulder. "Get out. For God's sake, get out."

Caitlin staggered out of the room, numb as she nearly fell down the stairs, clutching the bannister. She tried to drown out the sound of Brigitte's crying but could not. Dear God, what was happening? *Brigitte…My sweet little angel…*

She cried as she staggered towards the door. She froze, her eye fixing on the mirror in the front hall. That fancy, ornate mirror she'd always hated. What was that abomination she saw staring back at her from the glass? A face not of flesh and blood, but of boiling pitch, flaming red eyes and white fangs stained with blood. *No!* She clawed at her eyes and shook her head. When she looked again, she saw her own face looking back from the mirror. She ran from the house, back to the squad car. She was panting, her face broken out in a cold sweat as she pulled out of the drive, crashing through a fence post on her way out, the tires screeching out onto the street.

Dear God, was she losing her mind?

"Bless me, Father, for I have sinned," she muttered, crossing herself in the confessional. "It's been…It's been…I don't know how long it's been. I…please…"

"You are deeply troubled, child," Father MacKinnon said softly, his face silhouetted through the screen. "What was your sin?"

"I…I'm not sure. It's getting hard to tell where nightmare ends and reality begins, Father. But, I…I think I killed someone."

"Under authority?" he asked, tight-lipped. "Or, was this an act of murder?"

"I'm a police officer, Father."

"Is that you, Caitlin? You haven't been here in quite a long time."

"I know, Father." She looked down, cradling the small crucifix her mother had given her. She'd hung it from the rear-view mirror in the squad car, like a good luck charm, never carrying it for so long. "I couldn't find any answers here, Father. I stopped looking here a long time ago."

"And, now?"

"Now…" The tears came. She used to scoff at tears. They were for children and cowards. Now…it seemed they were a treasured bit of a fast-waning humanity she'd taken far too much for granted. "Father…my daughter screamed and told me she was afraid of me. She called me a monster. Am I a monster, Father?" She looked up at him, trying to discern his expression through the gray shadow obscuring his face.

"Do you believe in monsters, Caitlin?"

"I know they exist, Father. I tell my sweet little girl they don't, but I know better. I see them every time I go out on patrol. Filth. Scum. They wear human bodies, but they're evil. The smell of evil comes off them like rot from a dead body." Her hatred flowed, coursing through her blood, and again her blood raced as it had night after night… The nightmare rush memories resurfaced and her teeth clenched in a cruel smile. She found herself chuckling. She glanced up at Father MacKinnon and saw him pull back, crossing himself. *Oh, God, not again,* she thought, cold horror racing through her blood, drowning the fever of the rush.

Her breathing was labored as she left the confessional booth and staggered, light-headed toward the baptismal font. Crossing herself, she reached out a hand, hesitantly toward the water. Something pure. Some touch of grace. Her eyes widened as the water seemed to ripple, then boil at the proximity of her fingers. *No. No, no, no, no….*

She ran from the church, the sun as burning acid to her eyes.

The demonstrations had flared up again, feeding off the anger at the latest police shooting, like a raging fever that fed on itself.

The fires and the screaming raged long into the night. Caitlin, Gavin and the others were in the thick of it, smashing heads. It came alive inside her, the fire and the hate. To hell with the shields and the safety of numbers. Fly free. Swing. Swing. Swing. The lights flashed across her eyes as she swung her club. Warm blood splattered her face. She licked it off. Warm and sweet. She laughed wildly, the old familiar madness flowing over and through her, washing away the fear and weakness that had afflicted her before.

She froze at the sight of a teenaged girl strewn on the pavement, blood streaming from a gash on her head. Anger and fear intermingled on the girl's face, her blood splattered across the bright yellow cardboard placard lying on the pavement beside her. "Stop Killing Us," it read. A woman reporter ran through the mad rush of the crowd, her microphone now more a bludgeon than a recording instrument as hands tore at her fine, cream colored blouse and scarf, and her long, flowing black hair. The woman tried to shield the girl with her own body, apparently hoping her presence would stay the

clubs of the police. Their eyes met. Caitlin and the reporter woman…
her eyes were dark and angry, sparkling like black stars. There was a
power in those eyes Caitlin had never seen before.

A police staff swung down at the woman's head. She crouched
low, shielding the girl. Caitlin moved on reflex, blocking the blow
with her own staff. She recognized the face behind that blood-
splattered glass visor. Donovan. He snarled at Caitlin with a bestial
hatred. *How dare you deny me prey,* his wild eyes seemed to scream
into Caitlin's mind.

The staff fell from Caitlin's numbed fingers as she saw Donovan's
face consumed in pitch black shadow, his eyes exploding with red
fire, his canines gleaming white sabers. She reacted, a power flowing
through her, lashing out like a bolt of lightning. A surge of darkness
and silver that boiled through the night air like a living wave.
Donovan was sent flying backward, his 230-lb frame lifted like a
leaf in the wind, bodies crashing against each other. Caitlin gaped,
disbelieving. Donovan struggled to his feet a few yards from her,
fallen cops and protesters strewn across the pavement around him.
The hulking cop glared down at her, throwing aside his helmet and
striding toward her, his teeth bared, his eyes flaring with hate. Caitlin
trembled, feeling…something. Like a wave of power and darkness
flowing from him. She steeled herself, feeling the same darkness
rising within her as she prepared to meet him.

"No!" Gavin shouted, stepping between them with arms
outstretched, his face strained, his eyes wild. *What in hell are you
doing,* he seemed to scream in her mind, his eyes stabbing into hers.
Was she actually hearing his thoughts? She lifted the injured girl from
the pavement and with the reporter's help, tried to get her to safety. A
few of the cops converged, but stopped when cameramen moved in.

"Get those damn cameras outta here!" one of the officers shouted.
The girl limped, her face twisted in pain as Caitlin and the reporter
moved her toward one of the many ambulances that had moved in.

Caitlin! An angry voice stabbed into her mind, painful as an
electric shock passing through her head. She shook the voice off and
pressed on. Somehow, she knew the voice was Gavin's.

ЖФЖ ЖФЖ ЖФЖ Ж

"Miss, would you like to give a statement?" the reporter asked as the girl's leg was set and bandaged.

"Could this wait, please?" the paramedic said, waving her off. She sighed and tapped her microphone, apparently realizing it was broken. She handed it off to a cameraman, throwing up her hands, rolling her pretty eyes. Caitlin couldn't help but smile. She hadn't smiled since that living nightmare with Brigitte. And, then the church... All she'd wanted to do after that was lose herself in the chaos and the wild rush of the night. Now...now, dammit, the pain came rushing back. She'd let herself get soft, damn it to hell. She'd lowered her defenses, and all she could see was Brigitte's fear, all she could hear was her scream.

"Are you okay?" an unfamiliar voice asked, a soft hand on her shoulder. She started.

It was the reporter. Her expression seemed genuinely concerned. Those eyes. Those, dark, lovely eyes in her triangular face with its high, artful cheek bones. Those soft lips. The way the flashing blue lights played over her soft brown skin, sparkling in those eyes... Caitlin tore her eyes away. God, what was wrong with her? "I'm fine." Caitlin muttered, turning away.

"Officer," a tall man in a state trooper's uniform said as he walked up. Caitlin looked up at him. He looked strong; a capable, confident-looking cop. Handsome, for an older guy; a darkly complectioned black. She'd heard about him. Williamson. The new commander assigned by the governor. He didn't look like a guy who frightened easily. But, those eyes of his at the moment carried a strained expression of fear. The fear she'd sensed in Father MacKinnon in the confessional. "Your name, officer?"

Her mouth went dry as she removed her helmet and tucked it under her arm. She cleared her throat. "Kelleher, sir. Caitlin. Tactical."

"You want to tell me what the hell happened back there, Officer Kelleher?" Her mind raced. She didn't know what to tell him, or even what she should. Her eyes reflexively darted around, looking for Gavin. He was nowhere to be seen. She couldn't see Donovan, either. Yet, somehow, she could sense Donovan's presence...his hatred... circling her like a wolf waiting to pounce. "I'm waiting, Officer

Kelleher." Williamson barked. She met his eyes and started to open her mouth, not having the vaguest idea what to say.

"Excuse me, Captain…" the reporter cut in. "I'm Jacqueline Esperanza of KTTL…"

"I know full well who you are, Ms. Esperanza," Williamson said, sighing in weariness. "And, you're not supposed to be here."

"It's all right, Captain. As you can see, I'm without a microphone. I'm here strictly as a witness. One of your riot officers very nearly killed this young woman here. When I tried to come to her aid, he tried to kill me, too. Officer Kelleher saved both our lives."

"Is this true, Officer Kelleher?"

"I…" she hesitated, looking at Esperanza.

"It's true," the girl being patched up by the paramedics said as they tried to load her into the ambulance. "That crazy white motherfucker cop tried to smash my head in. I'd be dead now if it wasn't for her." She pointed at Caitlin. Caitlin's face flushed hot.

Esperanza took out her notepad. "May I quote you on that, Miss…?"

"That's it, Ms. Esperanza," Williamson cut in. "You just went from witness back to reporter. I will have to ask you to leave. You… get that woman to the hospital," he said, addressing one of the paramedics. "We'll get her statement later. Officer Tate, ride with her," he said to a police woman standing beside him. Tate climbed in as they closed the doors. Williamson glanced behind him as the riot cops moved in behind a wall of plastic shields. He pulled out a handkerchief as teargas canisters sailed overhead and the protesters pulled back. "Officer Kelleher, you are on restricted duty pending further investigation."

Caitlin's heart sank. "Sir, I…"

"No argument. Ms. Esperanza, please instruct your cameramen to surrender their film. We will be needing it."

Esperanza's eyes flared, her mouth dropping. "Captain, I strongly protest this flagrant violation of my First Amendment rights!"

He sighed and rolled his eyes. "You can file for the return of the film, ma'am. But, for security reasons, we will need to inspect it first."

"And, edit it?" she asked, a sneer on her lovely face.

Williamson stared coldly at her. "You need to leave, Ms. Esperanza. Right now." He walked off. Caitlin glanced around and saw Williamson's men collecting the confiscated film.

"Shit," she overheard Esperanza muttering as she pulled out a phone and texted something. "I assume they won't confiscate this, too?" she asked, holding up the phone in front of Caitlin.

"I wouldn't." Caitlin cleared her throat and shrugged. "Thanks for that," she said, having a hard time getting it out.

"It doesn't begin to cover my debt to you," Jacqueline said, stepping closer.

Caitlin suddenly felt a slight and unfamiliar uneasiness, like a cold tingling passing through her as she pulled back a bit. "Uh...that was pretty gutsy, what you did back there, trying to protect that kid. Dumb, but gutsy."

"Not bad for a civilian?" she asked with a slight smirk.

"I thought you reporters were only supposed to observe and record."

"We have our limits. I do, anyway." Jacqueline covered her face with her scarf, the stench of teargas getting worse.

"Back here," Caitlin said, taking her by the arm and urging her further away.

Jacqueline sniffed and tossed her hair, wiping aside a tear. "That guy you saved me from is quite a piece of work, trying to butcher a young girl."

Caitlin stared at her, suddenly eyeing her with suspicion. "Looking for a quote?" She asked.

Jacqueline stared at her and sighed, slinging her expensive-looking suede handbag over her shoulder. "Look...I'm not the enemy."

Caitlin took a deep breath, trying to let the heat and the blood rush pass through her. At the moment, and for the first time, she wasn't quite sure who the enemy was. "I'm sorry," she muttered, the words catching in her throat. Apologies were for the weak, and the soft. Yet, this woman was neither. Caitlin was having a hard time meeting the other woman's eyes, yet somehow very much wanting to. "It's been a damn hard time out here. Once the blood catches fire and flows...once you and your buddies are in danger, it's damned hard to just turn off the juice, you know? No offense, but you wouldn't understand."

"Maybe I'd understand more than you think," she said, running a long-fingered, graceful hand through her hair. "I've been embedded with troops in the Gulf. I've seen the killing up close and personal. Believe me, I know what death looks like, and I definitely know how it feels to fear for your life." Caitlin saw the truth of that statement in Jacqueline's eyes. She'd never met anyone quite like her before. Jacqueline lit two cigarettes and offered Caitlin one. Caitlin reflexively hesitated but accepted. She needed a good drag right then, if only to kill the smell of the damn teargas. "So…" Jacqueline said, letting out a long blow. "Looks like we're both benched for the rest of the night. May I buy you a drink?"

Caitlin narrowed her eyes. "Seriously?"

"Why not? I owe you a debt, and besides…" She slipped in a bit closer, gently brushing aside a strand of Caitlin's hair and leaned toward her ear. Caitlin felt the warmth coming off her. "You're damn pretty for a cop."

Caitlin stepped back, blushing hot. "Uh…I don't think so. You need to back off."

"Do I? What's the matter?" She smirked. "Scared?"

"Hell, no. I just…"

"You just what? We both know something's there. I saw it in your eyes." Her's softened a little. "So, why not? God won't like it? Your comrades in arms won't approve? What?"

Caitlin sighed and bowed her head, wiping sweat from her upper lip. "Look…this is not happening, all right? I mean…" Her head was spinning. "You're hot and all, but…" She couldn't believe what she was saying. "I'm a cop, for God's sake, and you're a reporter covering my department. We can both get fired here. This cannot happen."

Jacqueline took off her press badge and took Caitlin's helmet from her. "We're both off the clock," she said, pitching the badge into the helmet and tossing both aside. Caitlin couldn't help smiling. "Look…Either you're my story or you're my date. You can't be both. I'm not trying to pump you for information." Caitlin believed that. She looked into those deep, dark eyes again. She'd known this woman a few minutes, and already she trusted her more than she could remember trusting anyone. Except, on the force. "So?" she asked, drawing close.

Caitlin shuddered a bit as Jacqueline's hand stroked hers. She felt as foolish as a schoolgirl. She started as she sensed the cold caress of shadows off in the darkness and thought she could feel hot breath down the back of her neck. Her eyes darted across the dark street, beyond the ebbing flames of the waning riot. They were out there. Circling, circling. She looked at Jacqueline and saw the concern in her eyes. And, the desire. Caitlin wanted to be with her. Mainly, she wanted to be away from here. "Okay."

Jacqueline took her to a bar on the other side of town, clear of familiar faces and haunts.

It felt strange, at first. Alien. But, it was somehow a refreshing change from Andy's. Caitlin looked around, sipping her bourbon. The casual banter of civilians. It was more…more human, somehow. The television carried the newscast of the riots. Caitlin looked away, taking a swallow, the liquor rush sloshing through her brain. She sighed. It was like trying to quash one addiction with a far weaker one. She swished the bourbon in the glass. She couldn't even get drunk. It might as well be tap water, beside the fire in her blood, that even now seemed to be lapping at her heart…calling to her to run to Andy's and join up with Gavin and Donovan and the others.

"You look a million miles away," Jacqueline said, sipping her brandy and laying a hand gently on Caitlin's arm. Her touch was fire. Caitlin's heart raced. That was stronger than the blood rush. That was stronger than anything she'd felt before, even from Gavin. And, it was growing steadily stronger, every time she looked at Jacqueline. Every time she studied the dancing flames in her eyes or let her gaze travel along the artful curve of her neck, the gentle slope leading down into the creamy recesses of her delicate blouse. She wanted her.

She finished the bourbon in one gulp. "Can we get out of here?" Caitlin asked. Jacqueline smiled, and their fingers interlocked.

In Jacqueline's apartment, they lay in fire. Fire that consumed and grew like an inferno.

Caitlin moaned in pleasure. Pleasure born of pain and ecstasy that came from inside her, not from the dark storm she'd channeled before, with Gavin, the blood rush in her veins. This was the humanity she'd felt when she'd had Brigitte. The life inside her.

Jacqueline taught her, entering her in ways she'd never thought possible. Strength and tenderness and kindness and wildness all meeting as one, a passion terrifying in its truth. She'd never felt so much at one with a lover. Never with Robert. Not even with Gavin. Gavin had been the cup bearer that had brought her the flaming elixir of the rush. The rush used and discarded her, like a spent vessel. But, never had she felt so alive. Through the sweat and the pain and heat…the softness…she wanted it never to end. Jacqueline's lips against hers. Jacqueline's breasts against hers. Jacqueline inside her. She inside Jacqueline. She tasted Jacqueline, and she was sweet as honey and intoxicating as strong, sweet wine rushing to her brain.

She screamed in joy, remembering the day Brigitte was born, and feeling she was born now.

They lay together in the morning light. Soft, golden light. Light that no longer stung her eyes or made her long for darkness. Jacqueline gently stroked Caitlin's hair. Caitlin softly laughed and playfully nursed Jacqueline's nipple.

"Behave," Jacqueline playfully scolded.

Caitlin turned and slid her arms around Jacqueline's narrow waist as they lay face-to-face. "Thank you," she whispered with a smile.

"I feel I should be thanking you," Jacqueline said softly, stroking her finger around the line of Caitlin's jaw.

"I feel…alive," Caitlin said, barely able to contain the tide of joy rising in her heart. "I feel free." She kissed Jacqueline. She didn't need the blood rush anymore. Ever.

"Brigitte," Caitlin whispered as the little girl knelt at the foot of her bed, saying her prayers. Caitlin clung to the trellis outside her daughter's window, precariously balanced. Robert had been refusing her phone calls and had gotten his damnable lawyer to slap a restraining order on her. Her visitation rights were suspended, and she damn well couldn't afford a lawyer capable of getting that overturned. "Brigitte," she called out again, terrified Robert or his precious Jan might hear.

"Mommy?" Brigitte called out with cautious hope in her little voice as she looked around and saw Caitlin at the window. She ran over eagerly and pressed her little hand against the screen. "I prayed you'd come."

"Shhh...Keep your voice down, Sweetie," Caitlin said, gently pressing her hand against Brigitte's through the screen. "Mustn't let Daddy or Jan know I'm here."

"Why?"

"It's a secret, baby, okay? I'm sorry I couldn't come sooner. I tried, but...something got in the way. Something bad."

"Something bad was here," Brigitte said, her voice low and trembling. "Something that said it was you. But, I knew it wasn't. It was something so, so bad." Brigitte's lip trembled, her face wrinkling as though she were about to cry.

"I know, but it's okay now, baby. The monster's gone, and it won't be back. It's just me now, okay? Just us. Here...I brought you something. Raise the screen just a little. That's it." Caitlin reached carefully inside her jacket pocket and handed Brigitte the little doll she'd bought for her. A cheap little thing, but Brigitte's face lit up when she held it.

"Thank you, mommy!"

"Shhh...quiet, Sweetie, remember?" She glanced at the bedroom doorway behind Brigitte. "And, don't let Daddy or Jan see it, okay? But, you're welcome, baby. Keep it close, to remind you of me and how much I love you, okay?"

"Aren't you coming back?" Brigitte asked, sounding very sad.

"I'll work on it, baby. I will."

"Promise?"

"Cross my heart." Caitlin smiled and blinked back tears, Brigitte's face blurring. "Mommy has to go now, but I'll be back as soon as I can. I wish I could kiss you, but...just know I love you always. Sleep tight, baby. No more bad dreams, okay?"

"Cross my heart. Bye, Mommy."

"Bye, Sweetie." Her heart felt lighter than air as she climbed down the trellis to the dark driveway. Nothing else mattered anymore. No more running into the darkness. She was home. Whatever it took, she was home. She started, her blood running cold as Robert faced her in the driveway.

"What the hell do you think you're doing here?" he urgently whispered, looking up at Brigitte's window. "Are you trying to scare her to death?"

"Robert…you don't understand."

"You're damn right I don't!"

"Please…Bridge wasn't scared this time. She saw me…She saw *me*." She started crying and brushed the tears away. "She called me 'Mommy.'" She started laughing and crying at the same time, the tears flowing.

Robert's eyes softened. "Caitlin, I think you need help."

"Yeah, well…" She brushed away the last of the tears and cleared her throat. "I'm getting some. But, for Brigitte's sake, I–I want to find a way back to her, Robert. I want you to help me find it."

"You've got a strange way of asking for help," he said, looking back up at the window.

"I just couldn't wait. Look, I–I lost my way, all right? Things got dark and crazy for a while, but I'm back now. Can you see that I'm back?"

He sighed, looking into her eyes. "Yeah," he whispered. "I'm seeing the old you peeking out a little, at long last. But, I'm not sure…"

"Please…" She clenched. It was damned hard for her to beg, especially to Robert. But, where Brigitte was concerned, her pride was nothing. "Supervised visits, anything. I just need to be back in Bridge's life again. She called for me, Robert. Even though I wasn't there when she needed me, I'm here now. I want to be with my baby."

"Robert?" Jan's voice called down from another upstairs window. "Who are you talking to?"

"No one," he called back as he stepped in front of Caitlin to hide her from view as she slipped into the shadow of the house. "Just a neighborhood watch guy. I'll be in in a minute."

"Okay," she said in a cautious tone as she turned from the window.

"Caitlin," he whispered, turning back to her. "We will talk about this later. We…we'll try to work something out, I promise, but you cannot pull stunts like this ever again, you understand?"

"Yes." She nodded, resisting the urge to hug him in gratitude. "I promise. Thank you." She slipped quietly back into the night as Robert went back into the house.

Caitlin's stomach felt cramped and queasy as she walked into Andy's with Jacqueline. They'd taken her off restricted duty, and the night shift had gone more or less quietly. No violence with Williamson in charge. The demonstrations had continued without much trouble, Jacqueline covering the marches, she and Caitlin sharing the odd stolen glance across the barricades.

Gavin sat at their usual table with Monahan, Becker and Donovan. Donovan cast her a hateful sneer as she walked in, just as Andy brought the boys another round of beers. The shadows gathered around their table and around the bar, the corners dark and cold, the air growing colder. "Well, look who decided to join us," Donovan said with a wry smirk, taking a swallow of beer. Caitlin felt cold and numb as she and Jacqueline sat down at another table. She glanced around and saw the few other patrons leaving. Why had she come? It had been Jacqueline's suggestion. Curiosity, maybe. For Caitlin, it was perhaps a way of testing herself. Of finding out once and for all if the old addiction had indeed lost its power over her. Her skin crawled as Gavin walked over.

"Caitlin, long time no see, stranger." His voice was low and steady. Caitlin almost couldn't work up the nerve to look him in the eye. But she forced herself to, for Jacqueline's sake. "And, keeping interesting company, I see. Jacqueline Esperanza." As he looked Jacqueline over, Caitlin felt her reach for her hand, and Caitlin clasped hers. The other guys were chuckling over their beers. "Been a while since the Gulf."

"Not long enough," Jacqueline retorted quietly, her dark eyes glaring coldly up at him. Caitlin tightened her grip on her hand.

"Still smearing America's warriors, I see."

"Still slaughtering women and children, I see." The other three cops started to get up, but Gavin held up a hand to restrain them.

"That's it," Andy said, walking over and jerking his thumb at the door. "You two…out. You're not welcome here."

"Just as well," Jacqueline said as she stood. "The food's probably swill anyway."

They all stood. Caitlin pulled Jacqueline aside and stepped protectively between her and Gavin. Her hand had gone reflexively to her gun. "My door's still open, babe," Gavin said, his face a cold mask. "You'd be wise to walk through it." He held out a hand.

Caitlin looked deeply into his eyes. Cold, hungry eyes. "Go to hell." Gavin's eyes flared with hatred.

"Out," Andy repeated, more urgently. "Now."

Jacqueline looked like she wanted to get up in Gavin's face some more, but Caitlin pushed her toward the door. "We're going," she said. She took Jacqueline by the arm and walked her quickly across the dark street. "We shouldn't have come here," she said quietly, her blood chilling. The looks in the eyes of Gavin and the others still burned in her memory. "Jacqueline…" Caitlin took her by the shoulders and faced her. "You need to get out of town. Right now. Ask for a transfer, an out-of-state assignment, anything. Right now, Syria is safer for you than here."

"Honey." Jacqueline took Caitlin's hand in hers and stroked her face. Her expression was tense and concerned. "You're terrified."

"I am. Please, you have to go."

"I am not going anywhere." Her eyes were focused and determined. "Nobody runs me off. And, I am not leaving you. Especially now."

"It's my fight, and I don't want you in the middle."

"Hey, I thought we were past that." Her eyes softened. "Your fight is my fight." She brought her lips close by Caitlin's, her finger stroking her chin.

Caitlin desperately wanted to give in to her, but she knew she had to get her to safety. "Jackie, please…you don't know…" Jacqueline kissed her, long and hard, their hearts beating against each other. Caitlin held her, close. She knew she couldn't let her go. Damn.

꙰꙰꙰ ꙰꙰꙰ ꙰꙰꙰ ꙰

Lights flashing, spinning. Blue. Red. All washing into shades of gray. Nightmare rush. Waves of fear washing like caressing fingers over Caitlin's heart as she walked, numb through cops and photographers, flashbulbs popping. Yellow tape. Guys laughing and telling jokes. Nightmare. Not real. Not real.

But, it was real. Real as the blood splashed across the walls of Jacqueline's apartment. As real as Jacqueline's dead eyes staring at the ceiling as they zipped her eviscerated corpse into a body bag. Talk and flashing. Talk like droning insects and background noise. Dust swept away in the tide of life. On and on. Caitlin felt nothing as she walked out into the night. All she could feel was lying dead behind her. The night embraced her like an old friend, the cold wind caressing her. Lights and cars and buildings and people were nothing. Space itself was nothing. She moved as through a dream, as though the physical world was nothing. She sought who she sought, even as she felt their voices calling to her in her mind, mocking her. Taunting her.

There they stood, in the street, the shadows bowing before them like supplicating worshipers. Gavin. Monahan. Becker. And, Donovan. Donovan's smile was broad and red. Jacqueline's blood still trickled from the corner of his mouth. He laughed, his eye twinkling in merriment. Gavin stared at Caitlin. *You had your chance,* his eyes seemed to say.

Her eyes locked with Donovan's. They both knew. At that moment, they both knew what was to come.

The basement of Donovan's apartment building was a maze of shadows. The bulbs cast only a dull, sickly yellow pall. She hunted with her gun drawn, her back pressed to the wall. The water rushing through the pipes, the scuttling of rats in the shadows. Through it all, Donovan's mocking laughter wafted through the darkness like a skulking whisper. *Come,* his thoughts echoed in her mind, mocking her. *Come and get me.*

A wave of darkness seemed to sweep through the corridor. One by one, the lights went out, until only one sputtering bulb remained. That one went, and she was in pitch blackness. Her breath trembled, cold sweat covering her. *Still,* she thought, trying to still her rapid breathing. His approach was like a slithering shadow, less than a breath of air. She spun, flaming red eyes baring down on her in the darkness. She screamed and fired, the muzzle flashes illuminating something horrible coming at her: fangs framing a drooling maw. The darkness was alive, and it was hungry. Her bullets were as useless as flecks of shadow. She screamed in pain as razor-sharp talons cut deeply into her chest and throat. The pain was fire and hot steel cutting through her. The hatred that welled up in her at Donovan's slavering laughter raged into a far stronger inferno bursting outward from her.

How can I still be alive? she found herself wondering. She'd felt his damnable claws shredding her heart. She should have died, as Jacqueline had died. But Jacqueline hadn't been like her or Donovan. Jacqueline was human. Caitlin and others like her were a breed apart. Her body was what her mind wanted it to be. All she touched was what she wanted it to be. She understood now. She struck back. Not with her weak human flesh and brittle bone, or her frail toy of a gun, but with something far greater that flowed through her as it had before. The darkness and fire raged through her and became her. She tore into him like a ravenous cougar into a lion, two beasts of fire cloaked in shadow, tearing into each other, talons like sabers. Tear. Tear. Tear. *Die, you bastard!*

The lights came back on as the darkness retreated. She was drenched in blood, hers and his. Her head throbbed, hot blood pounding trough her temples. Her lungs labored furiously as she sank slowly to her knees. Her uniform was in shreds, but she felt her wounds…which should have been mortal…healing. Severed tendons fusing, severed veins becoming whole instantaneously. Her heart throbbed as she looked down on what was left of Donovan's body. The dark power that had lived in him had departed his shell and now lived in her, her dead enemy's strength adding to her own. His vacant eyes stared up as Jacqueline's had done, and again Caitlin was reborn. She threw her head back and screamed in joy, like a wolf howling at the moon. Her stomach growled, gnawing hunger. She pounced on his torn body and feasted.

)O(O( )O(O( )O(O( )(

"Father MacKinnon?" her voice trembled breathlessly, the phone shaking in her hand.

"Caitlin?" the priest asked. "I've been so worried. Where are you?"

"Uh…" She looked around, leaning in exhaustion against a building side. Somewhere. Some dark, moonlit neighborhood. The world was hard and closed again. Some part of her that was still human was desperate to emerge. And to hide from Gavin and the others. Away from the blood rush and the shadow, she was apart from them. Off their radar. "I'm not sure. I need your help, Father." She sobbed, tears streaming down her face as she looked up into the clouded moonlight. "I really need your help."

The afternoon sun was slipping toward the horizon, its red-golden light glittering in sparkles on the lake. Her hand trembled on the tea cup. Father MacKinnon gently laid his own hand there to steady it. She looked, hesitantly into his gentle gray eyes. He wasn't afraid of her anymore. Yet, she sensed a hint of caution there as well. She looked out the café window overlooking the lake. Birds flew overhead. Life went on. A part of her resented that. "So," she said with a deep sigh. "Am I crazy?"

Father MacKinnon leaned back in the booth with a gentle smile. "My business is the soul, Caitlin. My atheist friend here looks to matters of the mind," he said, casting a glance at Professor Curtis Havers, the distinguished, middle-aged black man seated beside him.

"When I pick up the tab, I'm his 'atheist friend,'" the university professor said, blowing gently on his coffee.

MacKinnon laughed gently, obviously trying to lighten the mood. As if that were possible. He sighed, looking down. "Who's to say whether you're crazy, or whether I am, Caitlin? Since we seem to have reached an impasse between the possible and the impossible, I felt Curtis and I perhaps both were needed."

"Father…" Caitlin began. "On the phone, you never really answered my question. I figured it was a question that only you could answer."

"Is there really such a thing as a demonic acolyte?" he asked quietly, adjusting his glasses. "Are there really people who channel the power of Hell itself? Well…" A pensive sadness came over his face. "We're not living in the middle ages, Caitlin. The days are long gone when the church espouses such beliefs. But…" He looked out over the lake, sipping his iced tea. "'There are more things in heaven and earth, Horatio…' As a physicist, Curtis, what's your take on what Caitlin has described?"

Professor Havers took a deep breath and leaned back, the tips of his long, slender fingers drumming together over his dingy shirt and ragged cardigan. "Well, we know there are many dimensions folded up inside the visible universe. Levels of reality that we can't really comprehend, let alone enter. If you want to call those other dimensions Heaven or Hell, that's really up to you. I suppose it's as close to a definition as science can provide."

Caitlin looked at him. "But could people tap into those other realities somehow? Draw power from them?"

"No, I don't see how. Although…" The physicist leaned his whiskered chin over his fingertips, staring at the tabletop. "The human brain does function at quantum levels that we don't fully understand. There are all kinds of theories, though I strongly doubt any normal human brain could actually—"

"But what about an abnormal brain?" Caitlin cut in. "Could there be people—a small number of people—who are…different?"

He leaned back and sipped his coffee. "Interesting question. I'm a physicist, not an anthropologist. But, a few of my colleagues in the biological fields might suggest that human evolution might be splitting off in branches we don't suspect. Could there be a breed apart among Homo sapiens, maybe even a whole new species of human that's capable of, as you put it, tapping into other dimensions of reality? Well, extremely doubtful, of course, but I can't absolutely rule it out. And…" He leaned forward, scratching one greying temple. "Might there be some form of inhuman intelligence in those other dimensions for such people to channel? Well…" He stared off into space, dreamily. "That's really impossible to say."

She leaned her chin in her cupped hand and looked at Father MacKinnon. "Father, you said you couldn't tell me if I'm insane. Am I evil?"

"Caitlin…" he shook his head. "We're all sinners. Which among us is purely good or evil?"

"I've known a few that were pure evil," she said, remembering a father who'd horribly abused her mom, and all the two-legged beasts she'd seen on the streets since. "There seem to be more and more of them every day." Her heart began to race again, the old familiar fire of the blood rush beginning to surface again. MacKinnon and Havers pulled back from her a bit, as the old familiar expression of fear returned to their eyes. "Is it wrong to want to kill evil?"

"It's not wrong, Caitlin," Father MacKinnon answered. "But it is impossible. Evil can't be killed with hatred, because it feeds on it. You can strike out in anger and hatred and kill a man who has committed evil acts, but the evil in him just comes back stronger in another form. Sometimes, inside you."

The words sank into her like bullets. She was still trying to extract them when someone turned up the sound on a streaming news broadcast. "Riots exploded again as the police opened fire on demonstrators." Caitlin's blood raced as she looked at the screen over the bar, the familiar scenes of blood-letting raging like a fire. The announcer's voice droned on: "This follows the gruesome discovery of Captain Marcus Williamson's eviscerated body hung from this bridge." Caitlin's blood froze solid as she recognized the bridge, and the exact spot where she and Gavin and Donovan and the others had hung their victims on those wild nightly hunts.

"Caitlin…?" She almost didn't hear Father MacKinnon.

The announcer droned on: "We can't show you the details, but, written in the Captain's own blood, on the wall beside where his body was found, were the words: 'One is down. Three await you here.' Experts have theorized a ritual significance…"

Caitlin shook off her numbness and bound out the door, almost knocking over a waiter on her way out.

It was as before. She moved as through a dream, time and space parting for her like water before the prow of a boat. She alighted like a ghost borne on night winds on the summit of the suspension bridge on a dark, moonlit night. The city lights were distant glimmers across the silver sparkling of the river.

And, there they stood, waiting for her. Gavin, Becker, and Monahan. "I see you got our invitation," Gavin said mockingly.

"Why?" she demanded, the sight of their hateful, leering faces, Williamson's blood still lingering on their hands and lips, making her boil with rage. "He was one of us."

They all scoffed and spat. "He wasn't one of us, and you know it," Gavin said. "The uniform doesn't make you one of us. Cops are a breed above the scum who crawl the streets, of course," Gavin said, passing his hand across the line of cars passing like tiny rows of ants so far below. "But our kind—you, us, Donovan—we're a breed apart from a breed apart. That's evolution, babe. The stronger predators devouring the weaker ones, until a stronger species emerges. But, you?" They all three glared at her. "You betrayed your own. It's time to pay."

She took off her gun belt and tossed it over the edge. Becker sneered. "This is an execution, not a challenge, bitch. You really think you can survive three against one?"

"Three against two, asshole," she retorted, letting her anger flow hot and swift, but channeled. "Don't forget: All that bastard Donovan had, I now have." She raised her hand, and the dark shadows crept up the bridge at her command.

"Including his memories?" Gavin cut in. "Do you remember the delight and pleasure he felt when he butchered your pretty little Jacqueline?" Becker and Monahan drooled and grinned like animals. Her blood burned. She wanted desperately to tear Gavin's guts out but fought to channel her hatred. "By right, the kill should have been mine, but he begged me for it. I was in a giving mood." He smiled. The others chuckled.

She lunged at Gavin's throat, as he had obviously expected. At the last second, she turned, a living wave of shadow, and slashed Becker's throat with her talons. *Die!* A quick flash of black claws and blood splashing black in moonlight, and what was left of Becker plummeted from the bridge toward the river, a now empty shell, opened and spilling its contents like loose garbage dumped from a scow.

"Bitch!" Monahan roared in rage, leaping toward her, the darkness flowing through him taking the form of a gargantuan beast, like a gigantic hell-hound, eyes and fanged maw roaring with blood-red flame, claws extended.

She moved like a wave of darkness, the dark energy fleeing Becker's emptied corpse still flowing into her. *Come*, she silently commanded, drawing on the power that filled the air around her like a viscous black cloud, silvery bolts of energy shooting through it, into her. *Come!* She tore wildly into Monahan as she had into Donovan, siphoning Becker's dark power and turning it upon Monahan. Monahan was like some monstrous, brutish thing, half-way between a gargoyle and a giant wild boar, snarling, clawing, acid spit sliding down bloodied fangs. In mid-air, they fought in fury, like two dragons locked in combat, two combatting waves of darkness opening around them like monstrous wings. She screamed as she tore and tore and tore, opening him up like a ravenous wolf devouring the flesh of its enemy.

As his dissected body resumed its now barely recognizable human form, the darkness leaving it as he, too, fell toward the distant river, she drank and drank and drank the dark wave of power until she was full and glutted, her mind a swirling wave of silver and lightning. Lightning bolts streaked the sky, as though at her command. She screamed in ecstasy and reached her blood-drenched arms toward the lightning-wracked black sky.

A wave of raw, dark power slammed into her like an explosion as Gavin attacked. He was like a black, winged demon, claws slashing deep, with keen skill and precision. She screamed in pain as she spun from the air like a wounded hawk, clutching the suspension cables and trying to pull herself up to the bridge summit. She felt her blood draining away, her wounds bursting wide. Gavin's damnable darkness filled the wounds, prying them wider. The bastard wasn't allowing her to heal herself. He laughed as he alighted on the bridge above her, withdrawing his dark power like a receding mantle of shadow, resuming human form. "Thank you," he taunted. "I knew you'd kill those two clumsy fools, as I knew you'd kill Donovan. Now, the power of all three is in you. And, when I kill you, I'll have it all."

She gritted her teeth and writhed in pain as he crushed her fingers under his foot. She felt the bones cracking. He eased up the pressure, and she let her injured hand pull back, dangling high over the river with her remaining hand. She looked down, at the black, silvery water so far below. Did she have power enough to survive the fall, despite her injuries, she wondered. *No matter,* she thought, looking up at his cold, hateful face. *Better to die than let him win.* She let go.

His fingers were like steel claws as they clamped like a vice around her wrist. "You don't cheat me by the simple trick of dying, girl," he taunted, pulling her up by the arm and heaving her onto the bridge summit. She moaned in pain, her broken ribs cutting into her chest wounds. She vomited blood as she looked up at him, his cruel expression blurring through the pain. "You could have had it all," he said, his anger sputtering out in spit as he bore his teeth. "I would have shared power with you. We'd have spawned the new breed, you and I. But, you chose that little slut over me? Over *me?!*" he roared, his eyes brimming with fire and darkness. She roared in pain as he kicked her in the side, again and again.

She looked down and pulled her mother's crucifix from her pocket, cradling it in the palm of her hand, the moonlight glinting off its gold surface. *What I believe is,* she told herself. *All that I touch is what I believe.* She concentrated. She forced herself to focus, even as his attack became more viscous. *Believe.* The cross glowed like molten gold in her palm, the glow exploding into brilliant golden fire as the cross grew and mutated in her hand into a long, slender golden dagger. She channeled her rage into a single roar as she rolled and plunged the dagger upward into Gavin's heart.

His face blanched white in shock, his eyes turning inward as he toppled backward off the bridge, falling dead as a stone into the river. She exhaled and fell exhausted onto the summit platform, the knife slipping from her grasp and turning back into the tiny cross it had originally been. Her wounds healed, her broken bones knitting inside her as Gavin's released darkness flowed into her. So much. So much.

"No, let me alone," she moaned, trying to ward the darkness off, even as it permeated her. "No more!" But, the darkness would not be denied.

She staggered into Andy's Café in the dead of night. Her head reeled. She didn't know why she'd come here, yet she did know.

There were answers here. The center of everything she needed to know, somehow resided here. She sensed that clearly now.

She staggered past the bar into the darkened kitchen and made her way to the walk-in freezer. She pulled the door open, the cold white light stinging her eyes as the refrigerant mist chilled her flesh. She looked away in revulsion at the half-stripped human corpses hanging like gutted cows from meat hooks. She vomited as she slammed the door behind her. She fell to her knees in the darkness and prayed, clutching the crucifix to her heart.

"We're closed, Officer Kelleher."

She gasped and looked up, recognizing Andy's voice. He turned on a light, and there he stood in his bloodied apron, staring coldly at her.

"You," she whispered, getting slowly to her feet.

"Now, you shouldn't have opened that," he said with a slight smirk. "A good chef never gives away the secret of his signature dish." He smiled, broadly and coldly.

"Andrew…" She paused, suddenly realizing she had no idea what his last name was. "You are under arrest for murder."

He laughed merrily, taking off his apron and tossing it aside. "I think you might have a hard time staying on the force, considering you've helped digest the evidence." He chuckled and clapped his hands. Her stomach heaved again. "Especially considering you're covered in the blood of three of your fellow officers. I'm really going to miss their business." Her blood chilled. The coldness coming off him was a thousand times colder than the freezer. The shadows gathered black and deep as ink around the little man.

"What in hell are you?" she asked, barely able to raise her voice above a whisper.

He laughed and spread his arms wide, as the room—all of space, it seemed—collapsed into a raging maelstrom of darkness. Pitch blackness and swirls of sickly blood-red flame circled Andy like a whirlpool of cosmic fire, like a sun collapsing into a black hole. Like the pit of Hell swallowing the world. She screamed as Andy morphed into something completely inhuman. Eyes of pure blood-red fire, bursting out of an immense, ebony-black skeletal face, all bone and fangs. A thing of shadow and fire, like she'd seen flowing through Gavin and the others. And, through herself, she realized with horror. But gigantic, and pure. The source of the dark power, she realized. The power itself, now in its true form.

"You see only a reflection of what your puny mind conceives me to be," the monstrous apparition said, rising up out of the fires, a towering black shadow, now taking solid form and looming menacingly over her with its long, curving black talons like a cat crouching over a mouse. Her knees turned to putty. It laughed, and the cold laughter cut through to her spine, as she sank to her knees, unable to look away from those blazing red eyes. "This is the gateway into my realm. You opened it for me. For a hundred million years, I've waited for you little bugs to pull yourselves far enough out of the slime to hear me, see me, feel me..." The thing roared in fiery laughter and the cosmic pit grew wider and deeper, trying to pull her in. She held on, a prayer lodged in her throat. She thought only of Brigitte.

"Your new breed channels my essence," the monster said. "Your kind will devour this miserable dust speck of a planet." It opened its clawed hands, the churning fiery darkness around it turning into visions of cities dissolving into mushroom clouds. "And, carry my essence to the stars, spreading through your continuum like a plague." Its red eyes flared as the vision turned to ghosts of spaceships rising on columns of fire towards the stars twinkling in the inky blackness. "You are the one I've awaited," it said. She trembled as it pointed a long, clawed finger at her. "You are the strongest of the strong; the first of my carriers."

"No!" she screamed, holding the crucifix high against those damnable eyes of flame.

The monster laughed. "You think you can hold me at bay with that? I've had two thousand years of practice twisting that into any form that suited me." The fiery vision turned to ghostly trains of medieval crusaders, knights in armor with bloodied swords setting cities ablaze, fire roaring through the night. The flames morphed into pyres of living death surrounded by men in Puritan garb. The fires round their screaming victims morphed again into burning crosses surrounded by men in white sheets and pointed hoods. "You are mine," the monster taunted. "Your race is mine, no matter what you want."

"I'll die first!" she screamed, clutching the crucifix to her heart.

"What a waste that would be, when I can offer you what you want most. Your precious Brigitte."

Caitlin paused, her eyes wide, her heart throbbing with hope. "What?"

"Let me inside you. I'll fill you with more power than you could imagine. You'll butcher Robert and Janice and have little Brigitte all to yourself. Half of her is like you, remember. She'll grow up just like Mommy." It chuckled, drooling flaming black blood, and her heart turned to ice. "You'll raise her, and when she grows up, the two of you combined will channel me and dominate this world."

She turned away, cold iron claws gripping her heart. She clenched her eyes, tears streaming down her cheeks as she realized she would never see Brigitte again. She opened her eyes and looked down at the crucifix in the open palm of her hand, the crucified image of Christ looking up at her. "Never," she said, the crucifix turning back into the golden dagger in her hand. "Never!" she roared, turning and lifting the dagger aloft.

"NOOOOOOOO!" the monster roared as she plunged the dagger into her own heart.

The monster screamed as the dark whirlpool contracted around it and collapsed in on itself. There was a thundering explosion, like a white-hot nova.

The gaping, smoldering pit that had opened like a giant sinkhole in the heart of the city, swallowing Andy's Café would remain a mystery.

Brigitte cried as she set the doll her mother had given her in front of the gravestone. "To remember me, Mommy," she said, wiping away the tears. "I'll love you always. Cross my heart."

"It's time to go now, Sweetie," Janice said, holding out her hand. "Come now."

"One more minute," Brigitte said, looking up at her daddy. "Alone. Please?"

"All right," he said, putting his arm around Janice's shoulders and turning her away. "We'll be right over there."

As Brigitte reached out to touch the gravestone, her fingers passing over the lettering of her mother's name, the doll bled. Brigitte's gaze wandered over to the cemetery path, zooming in like a camera and fixing on the soft, pulsing warmth of Janice's throat. Brigitte's stomach churned with a deep and sudden hunger. She licked her lips, and her blood burned.

XOXOX XOXOX XOXOX X

About the Author

Tom Olbert lives in Cambridge, MA, home of Harvard, MIT, kooky liberals and wacky street performers. When not working or writing science fiction and horror, Tom might be found volunteering or marching in demonstrations for progressive causes, like environmental protection and human rights.

Tom's fiction can be found in Mocha Memoirs Press, Lillicat Publishing and Phase5 Publishing.

The King's Viceroy

Monica Carter

Marcello slouched over the long, oak library table and searched through his novel for the son he had lost. The pages turned on their own, barely touching his fingertips, as if the lips of a mistral wind perched on the windowsill and blew through them. He scanned each sentence looking for the little boy. Not a sign of him, his precocious little Giovanni, lingered within the words he'd created. No scuffed-up knees from playing by the riverbanks, no pomaded stubborn cowlick ready for Sunday service, no toads or frogs captured in a jar and shown with pride to his squeamish yet dignified mother. This boy, a secondary yet vital character he had carefully woven into the fabric of his venturesome tale, had disappeared. He loved Giovanni as much as he loved his flawed protagonist. Had Giovanni exited his story without a word of thanks and left behind a feeble and tatty tale? How could his protagonist be anxious about his son Giovanni's journey into the Black Forest if Giovanni is gone?

Then, Marcello lurched up and surveyed the space around him. Perhaps Giovanni wanted to play a game like little boys often do. Yes, he wanted to play hide and seek with Marcello. A smile spread across his thin, many-angled face at the boy's cleverness. And his own. Indeed, he was a fine writer for creating such a boy.

The library, busy with the muted bustling of intellectual calisthenics, suddenly appeared as a giant labyrinth of hiding spots for the boy. Marcello knew every detail of Giovanni he had thoughtfully given him, along with reddish-auburn hair, spindly energetic legs, large dark-lashed eyes and skin the color of goat's milk. This was a stunning, impressive young lad; an eleven-year old interested in the constellations, dragons, and men with the beastlike strength of his father. And now, this tiny pebble's absence threatened to destroy the stone house of fiction he had created. Giovanni could be anywhere in the city's library. Down a dusty aisle and ensconced in the fables of Aesop, or scrunched in the bowels of a ship as a stowaway listening to the rants of Ahab, or detaining a prisoner, his sister, in the verdant environs of his home listening to his mother, George Sand, call for him from a distance.

After a fruitless search down the identical book-crammed rows, resentment twisted around Marcello's heart and squeezed. None of his characters would ever dare to leave him. This was the fault of another. Evil lurks within the annals of knowledge, and some possessed academic has absconded with poor Giovanni. Another less-talented author, starving for a nod from the literary gods and whose marrow of creativity had been sucked dry by the greedy mouth of survival, could have sensed the power in Marcello's young Giovanni, a complex and clear voice filled with richness. Of course, he had gone. Marcello sunk back into his chair and realized, after perusing the library's inhabitants, there simply wasn't anyone to accuse. Would he not do the same thing if, suffering at the altar of imagination, desperate enough? The faint grip of sympathy tugged at his conscience, and he decided that Giovanni was a contribution to the less artistically fortunate.

But the dilemma remained that his publisher expected this book by tomorrow morning, and he had no time to recreate Giovanni, and any attempt would finish with an anemic version of the original. Anxiety overtook him as possibilities whirled in his mind. Just at the moment when he thought he must call his publisher and tell him it would not be ready, which would surely mean no money for this month's or last month's rent, a fragment of a conversation echoed in his head. At a party given by a society patron some months previously, a young writer, successful and prolific, approached Marcello to compliment him. But he also had said that the time in between Marcello's published works was too long, and that people's memories were short. Intrigued by this, Marcello asked how he could produce works so quickly. And he replied with this: "The King's

Viceroy, two streets up from the main boulevard. In the alley behind the used bookstore."

Marcello shoved his papers in his worn satchel, which had ceased being a satchel since the clasp and strap broke off last summer, and hurried to the main boulevard that coiled through the town. He tipped his hat to most of the ladies he passed because, even in haste, he was still a gentleman. The hands of the clock on the tower were close to striking six, and he knew that if it were any type of business at all, it would close at six. It was Friday night, and nobody wanted to work while the whole town gorged on sausage and ale, as was their ritual since a distant relative of King Lupercalia built the town's first sausage factory after he settled here in the 1500s.

But dear God, Marcello was hungry. He needed to finish this story by tomorrow or...

No hot juice exploding in his mouth upon the first bite of a sausage, no bitter, cold ale flowing down his throat, and no small attic room with a small window to look out of, late at night, while he dreamed of his next book. If he didn't finish the novel, Soldini wouldn't ever receive him in his office again, which meant he would never pay him again. Marcello missed deadlines often. If his story was not ready, he must submit to its gestation regardless of Soldini's threats or promises of money. Marcello prided himself on this artistic tenet that made him unpopular and poor.

These thoughts occupied him until he reached the middle of the alley where he came upon a dark green door that resembled a giant replica of a fine leather book cover. A cold gust whisked scraps of newspapers and granules of dirt past Marcello as he held his hat on his head and squinted at the faded gold script on the door, "The King's Viceroy." Below that, in smaller letters, he read "Home of Gently Used or Forgotten Characters."

Not finding a knocker or doorknob, his fingers grabbed onto the door and pulled it open.

Marcello made out shapes of furniture in the dark room, which had one small lamp hanging from the ceiling.

"Hello, Marcello. A bit of writer's block, I presume?" A soft yet deep voice annunciated these words as if he had created each one, and then a man stepped into the yellow cone of light and stood behind a small counter.

"Not writer's block, no. How did you know—It doesn't matter. A young man," Marcello saw the hair that matched the yellow of the light was combed back and the speaker's eyes were a cloudy gray-blue, so faint in color Marcello felt his head grow hot under his hat, "recommended me. I, well, this might seem a…a bit…strange, but I have lost a character. And I am on a deadline, a very important deadline—"

"I understand. Here is a permit. Go through the curtain and peruse at your leisure. I am here to aid writers in their quest for the perfect story. If you see something that interests you, we will discuss the purchase."

Marcello nodded, unsure as to what he meant or even where the curtain was. Just as the thought traveled though his mind, above a red damask curtain was a sign lit up in red letters, "Browsing Room." Marcello looked at the permit: *Good for One Entry to the Browsing Room. No refunds. Exchanges only. Characters sold as is. Not responsible for characters' behaviors in fiction or otherwise. Please, no touching. Take the card only. Thank you. The Management.*

Pulling back the curtain, he thought he heard someone whisper in his ear, "Don't do it!" He turned around, and no one was there. Upon entering the room, which was also dark, like the city streets just before the forehead of the sun disappears into the horizon, he was struck by all the lamps hanging down from the ceiling. Each one spotlighting a mannequin and a small card hung around each neck. He didn't know where to begin. People of all types stood before him—a dowdy grandmother holding a frying pan, a Cossack with a walking cane and a pipe in his mouth, a butcher with a bloody splattered apron and a smile, a prisoner in shackles holding a tin cup, a tiny baby sleeping in a crib. With each mannequin he passed, he heard a cacophony of voices and sounds while he felt a cold wind blow through his body. He heard the town clock strike seven and knew there was no time to question or worry, he must find another Giovanni.

He spotted a shorter mannequin, hiding behind what looked like a medieval beggar. What luck! It was a young blond boy. The card read: *Young male, eleven years old, needs supervision.* Supervision? That must mean he needs a writer to watch over him, to make him useful. Marcello smiled because the harmony of the universe was finally working in his favor.

He ran through the curtain and demanded, "I'd like the rest of the information on this one, please."

"Of course. Take a seat." The man motioned with his eyes, which had a faint glow about them, to a chair next to a small table. Marcello took a few steps to the other side of the room and sat down. The man came out from behind the counter and pulled over the other chair at the table, setting it directly in front of Marcello. A look of confusion must have crossed his face because he said, "Don't worry. It's not a painful procedure. I simply need you to relax and take a short nap. I will clap my hands, and you will have all the information about the boy right there in your mind."

"You mean to say that it is some sort of hypnosis? Say, where exactly do you get these characters anyway? That is, do you invent them yourself? Is there a place you order them from? I am a bit taken aback by this whole experience—"

He was fiddling with some sort of object on chain that Marcello couldn't see clearly. The man looked up casually. "Sometimes they wander in from the used bookstore. Sometimes writers who decide not to use them drop them off. Just depends." He glanced at Marcello, laughed and then said, "Don't worry. I have checked each one out personally, and they are all fine. Very serviceable."

The bell in the clock tower struck half past the hour of seven, and Marcello would have to work all night to fix the story. He had no choice.

"You've done this before?"

He looked Marcello in the eyes, the blue of his eye becoming milkier and brighter. "Many, many times." He shut his eyes for a moment, and the room dimmed. As his eyes opened, he held up a tiny glass ball on a chain. It slowly began to swing from right to left. Marcello followed it, as he knew he should. The man's soothing voice wooed him through an idyllic version of Corvetto, his favorite fairy tale from childhood. Just as the end was near and Corvetto was to give the palace to the king, he awoke suddenly.

The chair was gone and the man stood behind the counter, polishing his little glass ball. Marcello, strangely invigorated, asked the man how much he owed.

"Don't worry about that, I've already taken what I needed." His eyes pointed directly at Marcello. "Anything else?"

"No, no. That's it?"

"That's it. Return to your story, and you will find everything you need. Now please, I must close for the evening."

The bells rang eight times, and Marcello exited out into the dark alley. There was a chill in the air as he walked back to his room. He had no time to waste. Soldini expected the book in the morning. Marcello worked through the night. Wherever there was a scene where Giovanni had been, this new character of the same name, fit in perfectly. This boy was so alive, so original, so vivid, that Marcello doubted his own worth as a writer. Who would have thrown this wonderful character away?

The next morning, while the sun warmed up the town, Marcello packed up his finished manuscript. He bounded down the streets until he reached Soldini's office. Up the two flights of stairs and through the busy front office he went, ignoring anyone asking if he had an appointment. Soldini, always dressed as if he were attending the best dinner in his life, greeted him with a nod. "Marcello. Have we a book to give me?"

Marcello's entire face crinkled and creased with an enormous smile. He set the manuscript gently down on his desk. Soldini glanced through the pages. "We have been busy, haven't we?

"I believe, good sir, you owe me my advance for finishing on time."

Soldini stared at him for a moment too long and Marcello worried that he had made some other mistake. His smile weakened.

Soldini reached for the gold key in his vest pocket and opened the top drawer. He took out two stacks of crisp bills and handed them to Marcello.

"You realize, Marcello, if I don't like it, there will be no more money for you."

Marcello's smile broadened again so confident he was of the novel. "I hope it is to your liking."

He walked back to his building, knocked on Signora Gratti's door. He handed her the rent for this month, last month, and even next month.

Her eyes widened and her jowls jiggled as she shook her head. "I cannot believe it! Have you struck it rich? It doesn't matter. I knew my Marcello would pay."

Later that day, a messenger knocked on Marcello's door. Marcello read the message once and then a second time to make sure he read it correctly. Soldini had loved it. The best novel he'd read this year. He put a rush on the printing, and it should be out in two months. So awestruck was Marcello that he grabbed his hat, leaving the messenger standing in his doorway, and ran to the King's Viceroy.

The man greeted him again as if he expected him. Marcello kissed him on both cheeks. When he touched the man, a menacing darkness loomed like a shadow in his mind, and his heart turned to ice. Marcello ignored his body's reaction, thinking it was the potent combination of anxiety and excitement at the thrill of artistic triumph and not the result of his contact with the wicked soul of fate. The man smiled and the viscous whiteness of his eyes shimmered like the sun reflecting off the frozen tundra. Marcello was too filled with joy to be frightened. He thanked the man again and started for the main boulevard.

Marcello bought himself a hand-sewn satchel made from the finest Italian leather. He bought two suits of silk, a cashmere coat, and a pair of leather shoes. With his shiny new black hat and shiny black shoes and shiny black suit, he treated himself to the best sausage in town and two glasses of the King's ale.

Tonight, I celebrate. Tomorrow I begin a new novel.

And he did just that. He woke in the morning refreshed and full of enthusiasm to write. At his desk, staring out over the rooftops of the town, he wondered what to write about. Marcello was never one to have a lack of ideas. He knew that with this novel, he yearned to create an unforgettable character, one that would burn so brightly that Sir Lancelot and Hamlet would become mere flickers behind his archetypal hero.

He decided to put pen to paper and fill the pages until he wrote himself into a good story. Once he began writing, his hands scribbled nonstop as some creative muse possessed him. He fell into a trance until the sun began to set, and its light slowly retreated from his room. Once he read what he wrote, a whimper escaped his mouth like the sound of a wounded coyote. It was the boy, his ersatz Giovanni! It was the same character he had put in his new book. How could he be so careless?

He cursed himself for wasting a whole day on a character he'd already used, especially one that wasn't meant to carry the hefty weight of a protagonist. There was nothing to be done now, he conceded. Tomorrow he would start anew.

The next morning when the sun rose, Marcello sat at his desk. Again, he struggled for ideas and again, he decided to allow the words to guide him into a story. The words tumbled out as if the pen was filled with them instead of ink. His hand cramped, but he didn't want to stop. The muse was a noble yet infrequent visitor. As the sun waned toward evening, Marcello finally put his pen down, weary with exhaustion, and read what he had written.

There he was.

The words were different, but it was the same story as yesterday. A young scamp of a lad returns from school one day only to find his parents gone. He waited days and days. He implored neighbors and friends to say if they had seen them. They never returned and were never sighted in town again. The boy couldn't believe this was true, because every day, they told them how much they loved him. The rest of the pages were filled with all the places he searches for them.

It was too much for Marcello. He slipped his feet into his new shoes, doffed his hat, and ran to the King's Viceroy. Surely the man would know how to cure him of this wretched affliction.

Marcello rushed in and took his hat off so that the man could get the total effect of the pained look on his face.

Stepping out of the darkness, he appeared. Dressed neatly in black, hair slicked back, and those terrifyingly luminous eyes.

"Marcello, may I help you?"

"Yes! I cannot write any story without the boy. You must take him out of my head! If you don't exorcise him from my mind, my life as a writer is over."

"I cannot do that. No refunds or exchanges."

"But I don't want a refund! I didn't even pay for him. I don't want another character. I simply want to rid my mind of his presence. You must help me." Marcello straightened up as he noticed that he had crumpled with desperation.

"I cannot do that. I am not responsible once they leave the store. That was explicit on your browsing permit." He fixed his eyes on Marcello, and Marcello, dejected, put his hat on his head.

"Please, you couldn't hypnotize me again? Just as you put him in my mind, you can take him out. Please!" Marcello was relieved that there were no mirrors because the sight of him begging would plague him for eternity.

"Dear sir, I am not here to solve any writerly problem that arises. You needed help, and I helped you." The light above him turned off, and a green light turned on above the door. He had was no longer visible and even the quiet inhalations and exhalations of his breath could not be heard.

Suddenly, a voice filled the room. "The door will lock in one minute. Thank you for shopping and please exit. Have a nice evening."

Marcello pushed the door open, and it slammed shut; behind, the sound of a large lock slid into place. Hopelessness weighed too heavily on his heart and lungs, making it difficult for him to breathe. The rest of his writing life lay at the moody hands of a young boy who'd lost his parents. Then, he wondered if he might take a break from writing. Yes, a brief respite. Let his mind and body recover from this anguish. If he stayed away from writing long enough, maybe the boy would leave his mind out of boredom.

Marcello lazed in cafes, watching the people of the town walking to and fro to places where they lived their lives. He walked along the river for hours and took train rides to nearby towns for adventure. Even with all of this, he could not stop thinking about his writing. He mourned the loss of the one thing he loved. Perhaps if he read something written by someone else, it would distract him from his melancholy.

His own book sold well, and this gave him momentary pleasure. Yet his success made him want to produce another novel, just as good or better. Back to melancholy he went.

In the bookstore, he browsed the aisles. In the front of the store, he came upon a stack of green leather books. He picked one up and the clerk reassured him that he would not be disappointed with that one. It was brilliant. When Marcello read the first pages, a sense of recognition crept into his consciousness. Had he read this before? Had a writer told him about this? It was strange how familiar it felt.

He looked to see who the author was. S. Fox. He knew so many writers, but had never heard one utterance of an S. Fox.

"Say, have you met this Mr. Fox?" Marcello inquired of the clerk.

"No one has. A true mystery."

Marcello reread the first few pages and knew he had heard or read this story before. But his mind was empty as a dry well, so empty he couldn't lift one bucket of memories up out of it to help him recognize where the story originated. Convinced that he knew of it, he headed to La Scrivania where most of his writing acquaintances sat outside, debated and sipped espresso.

They nodded and groused their greetings when Marcello sat down. He ordered an espresso as well and asked if any of them had heard of S. Fox.

"You mean the guy who is selling more books than you?" One writer responded.

Marcello then asked if anyone of them had read this book by S. Fox. A rumbling grumble of nays rose and then diminished. What about the writer himself? Had they ever met or heard of him? Another swell of nays. Marcello went on to explain the plot of the story and then inquired of the sundry group if it sounded familiar. With this last question, a silence ensued while suspicion entered into their minds as they stared at Marcello. They shook their heads and returned to their conversations. Marcello, embarrassed by his own anxiety, left the café and walked home.

He lay down on his small bed and wept because he wanted to write, but the boy wouldn't leave him alone.

When he awoke the next morning, the sun had already pushed its way through his window. He put his feet on the floor. His furry scrap of a cat, Pinocchio, yawned and sauntered over to lick his ankles. He bent down and petted Pinocchio, saying "Without you, I would be totally alone." Pinocchio figure-eighted in and around his legs, purring at Marcello's praise.

Only too soon did the novel by S. Fox control his thoughts again. Marcello decided to look through his old notebooks. Maybe an idea would inspire him to write a new novel, bring back his imagination since the boy had captured it.

He scanned the pages, his eyebrows expressing either approval or scorn—arched for approval and slanting down to his nose for scorn. Then, there was an idea he began to read that was too familiar. Suddenly he realized it was the plot of S. Fox's very novel. An expression of incredulity broke out over his whole face, and he called Pinocchio over to look. Pinocchio trotted over and rubbed his leg in comfort.

He wanted to go directly to the bookstore and then to La Scrivania to prove that wrong had been done to him. This charlatan S. Fox had pillaged him! When he put on his custom-made shoes, he realized that people would mock him. A writer whose book is selling well cannot accuse another best-selling author of stealing his idea. It was ludicrous. He would have to find another way to trump this S. Fox.

Determined to overcome this assault on his pride, Marcello sat down to write immediately. He was quickly pulled into his trance where he let the boy lead him as if it were his story, but this time Marcello did not object. Months passed by, notebooks were filled, pens went dry with use and Marcello appeared gaunt and sallow. The boy led him through churches and markets in villages as he asked about his parents. He dragged him through fields in the coldest of winters and on the darkest of nights, he made him ride for hours in the hot sun on the back of a lettuce truck heading to the city, he pulled him through the rocky terrain of treacherous mountains where the boy's question echoed in the valleys when he cried it out. At the finish of each day, Marcello was exhausted.

In need of encouragement that he could still write, he walked to the bookstore to see how his novel was doing. Upon entrance, he ran into a pile of green covered books stacked up to his waist sitting right there on the floor. The moment he saw S. Fox, he flipped open the book. Another book, another plot and as Marcello read, he couldn't help but know everything that was going to happen next. All the while he had let a second-rate character traipse him all over the world, this scoundrel had penned another opus.

In utter panic, he dashed home and pulled out his notebooks full of ideas, and there it was, in black and white, the very same story. He flung himself on the bed, and Pinocchio jumped up and sniffed his face, wondering what was wrong. Marcello was so dispirited he could not even run his hand down Pinocchio's back. His life might as well come to an end because his imagination had been stolen.

Even though he was a man not much for the drink, he needed one. He was nearing hysteria. He listlessly headed to a place where people would not know him, a place where the vagabonds gathered and drank.

Once he arrived at Il Fondo, he sensed the coarseness of poverty all around him. The stale smells of men who slept outdoors, their loud, damp laughter and the sticky feel of the tables and chairs. Even the darkness was coarse. No sign of imagination anywhere. Marcello sat alone and drank ale till they closed.

He shouted in the streets while he ambled home, accusing the fox of stealing his imagination. He fell asleep without taking off his hat.

He arose the next morning, his head filled with pain. He loathed the sunlight and the noise outside from the village. He must go to the King's Viceroy to demand the boy be removed from his consciousness once and for all so he could return to his normal life.

When he got there, a sign hung on the door that stated:
CLOSED INDEFINITELY

Marcello never wrote again. He lost his room and wandered the streets with Pinocchio following behind him. He slept outside, and when he was thrown a few coins, he went to spend it all at Il Fondo.

During his wandering one day, he spotted the man from the King's Viceroy at the bookstore amid a boisterous crowd. In the window, a large sign advertised the chance to meet the famous author, S. Fox. The man was dressed impeccably, and his face looked as if he had just returned from the spa. He smiled and used his quill to scribble his name in hundreds of books. Marcello's fingers curled into his palms as he pulsed with anger. Marcello waited for him.

Once Fox left, Marcello followed him until Fox reached an alley where no people were around. Marcello grabbed his shoulder and spun Fox around.

"You! You took the most important thing I had. I demand it back," Marcello spat out.

Fox, after recovering from the shock of Marcello's appearance, smoothed out his clothes and said, "I did not take anything. Did you honestly think that I would give you a character for free? That these fictional people can be bought and sold? It was a fair exchange. You were desperate, and I exchanged your imagination for the character you begged for."

Marcello wept. Not a soul would believe a vagabond over a famous writer. He picked up Pinocchio and walked away. When he went to sleep that night, he dreamed he was looking for his imagination but couldn't find it. During his quest, he met the little boy. The boy took his hand and said, "We can look for what we have lost together." They walked on, and Marcello admitted that he was looking for his imagination because he wanted to create characters again so he wouldn't be lonely. The little boy said that he knew just the place where he won't be lonely and where he would fit in with all the others. Suddenly, they were in the King's Viceroy's browsing room. All the characters he never had a chance to create were crowded around him. Pinocchio sniffed around a mannequin and rubbed its legs. Marcello took a closer look and saw that it was his own auburn haired Giovanni.

The King's Viceroy, now owned by Soldini, had reopened with a plethora of gently used characters. One day, S. Fox came in, looking for a character. He spotted Marcello, and said, "I'll take the hobo in the corner."

Marcello never woke up but wandered through his own stories searching for an ending.

XOXOX XOXOX XOXOX X

About the Author

Monica Carter is a writer, poet, and reviewer. She was a PEN Center USA Emerging Voices Fellow, a Lambda Literary Foundation LGBT Emerging Voices Fellow, and a fiction graduate of the prestigious PEN Center's MARK program. Her fiction has appeared in literary journals including *The Rattling Wall, Black Clock, Cactus Heart, Bloom,* and the anthology *Strange Cargo.* Her nonfiction has appeared in publications including *Black Clock, World Literature Today,* and *Foreword Reviews.* She presently serves as a judge for the Best Translated Book Award in fiction, curates Salonica World Lit, and is the program coordinator for Lambda Literary's LGBTQ Writers in Schools program. She is also finishing her first novel. Visit her at www.monicacarterthewriter.com

A Sign of Death

George Kelly

"Every time I get an autograph, I feel like I'm taking home a little piece of that star."

— Joshua Morrow

Arthur only entered the shop to avoid Billy Dockland. School didn't start for another twenty minutes. He had plenty of time. He pretended to look around at all the secondhand items—racks of clothes, shelves of books, a corner of miscellany—but he kept glancing outside. Billy was hunched over at the empty bus stop, marking the red bench with his tag: *Billz*. Then he capped his black felt-tip pen, pocketed it, and admired his work. Moments later, two other boys joined him.

Arthur picked up a T-shirt and held it up to the light, as if wondering whether it would suit him or not. He looked past it and saw Billy shadowboxing one of the boys.

Yesterday, on his way to school, Billy had seen Arthur's new football sticker album, something his stepdad bought him on the weekend along with packs of stickers.

Arthur had it clamped under his arm, excited about showing his friends at school and maybe swapping some of his duplicates with them, but when Billy saw it, he slapped it out of his grasp and laughed like a maniac. It splatted into the mud, and Arthur had to wipe it up with a handkerchief his mother had given him. He said, "Why'd you do that?"

"It was just a joke," Billy said. "Don't take it so serious."

"You've ruined it!"

"It's a little stain. You're such a girl."

Arthur said nothing, just pushed past him and went to school. He wasn't scared of Billy, but he didn't want to fight him either. He had an idea Billy could hit hard. Most probably his dad or older brothers beat him every evening, and he was used to punches.

Billy wasn't even that bad at school, especially in science class where he usually applied himself and had what their teacher called "an innate aptitude for chemistry," but out in the streets, before and after school, Billy always showed off to his dumb friends.

And now, Arthur wanted to avoid another confrontation with him.

Inside the shop still, he started to pay attention to the items on the shelves, thinking he might as well look around now that he was in here. He came across a cool Polaroid camera. Nobody used them anymore; this was old-time stuff, the kind of thing his stepdad would be interested in maybe. Everyone had a camera on their phone these days, even on their iPods and computers and tablets. Arthur had three of them altogether.

But this was vintage. He held it up, feigned taking a photo and imagined the image being spat out like a tongue, Arthur needing to wave it around for a few minutes.

It was a novelty thing, but seemed cool. Too much money, though. Ten pounds. He barely had two pounds. And that was a week's pocket money.

Looking further along the shelf, he picked up another curious piece: a small black notebook of some kind. On the front, the word *Autographs*, which made it another ancient item straight from history. Nowadays everyone took pictures with celebrities—usually on their phones or tablets, never with Polaroid cameras—and that was it. Nobody bothered to collect autographs anymore. That was from before his time, in the old days.

He flipped it over—only £1.75. Maybe he could start up a new trend.

His mother said fashion was cyclical; it faded from popularity and then returned years later even stronger. What if he managed to make autograph-hunting cool again? Then he could be like, fuck Billy. Everyone would think *he* was the interesting one.

Tomorrow the Arsenal team was attending an evening event in his local town hall. He could sneak out after dinner and start filling the book with famous signatures.

He took the book up to the front counter, which was manned (or WOmanned, to be more accurate) by a friendly-looking dark-skinned lady with a short, natural afro, dark eyes, who was wearing a blue and red cardigan over a white T-shirt. He liked her casual style.

She smiled, and it was bright; he warmed to her instantly. "Hey," she said.

"Hi," Arthur said, handing over the notebook. "Just this please."

She held it up and chuckled. "I was wondering when this would go." She leaned forward and lowered her voice to a whisper. "It was left here by a crazy witch…"

"What, a *real* witch?" He'd never met one before.

"Well, I doubt it," the woman said, punching the price into the till. "She came in here with a bunch of items in a bag. She was a little—" The lady spun her index finger by her temple. "She said the autograph book was cursed. That's £1.75 please."

Arthur dug into his pocket for the money. "Cursed? How is it cursed?"

"She said it collects lives. Whoever signs it, dies apparently."

Arthur passed over the money and took the notebook. He stared at it, wondering how many souls it had collected so far. He opened it up and realized at least five pages had been ripped out at the front by the previous owner. "Do you think it's really cursed?"

The lady laughed again; a gentle sound. "I'm fairly certain it isn't."

"I hope not," he said. "I don't want to kill anyone."

"Here." The lady picked up a pen and signed the book on the first page. "I'm the first person to sign it. And look, I'm still alive, right? Don't worry about it, it's fine."

"Okay." He wondered if he could ask for some money back now that she'd tainted his book with her signature. He wanted celebrities in here, not shop workers.

"Is that all?"

"Yeah," he said. "Thanks."

She smiled, and he instantly forgave her for writing her signature in his book. He wished he were twenty so he could kiss her on the lips. She said, "Let me know if I die."

"I will," he said. "Bye," and he slipped the notebook in his bag, and thought nothing more of the curse. Like the lady said, the witch was probably just a nutcase.

Tomorrow night he'd sneak out to the town hall and begin his collection.

Rain lashed against him like hundreds of tiny water bullets.

Arthur huddled under a bus stop, just across from the Transcontinental, the hotel the Arsenal team was reported to be staying at. On another night, the streets would probably be lined with autograph hunters such as himself. Or, at the very least, picture hunters, the paparazzi, groupies, and fans. But the weather tonight was too shitty for most people to leave their house. He'd considered staying home himself—especially when he heard the first crackle of thunder—and then he caught a glance at the autograph book on the side of his bedside cabinet and snatched it up. He couldn't let the thing go to waste.

After telling his mother he was off to bed, he slipped out the back door with the stealth of a ninja assassin. His mother wouldn't notice his absence, as she rarely checked on him in the night. She usually watched her soaps on TV with his stepdad, Darren, and then retired to bed for a loud session of *bang-bang-bang,* goodnight, turn off the lights.

On his way to the Transcontinental he passed the charity shop he'd bought the notebook in. Earlier, on his way to and from school, he'd peered inside to make sure he hadn't accidentally killed the lady who worked there—or she hadn't killed herself, seeing as she wrote in his notebook without his permission or even a request from him to do so.

But she was very much alive, standing behind the counter reading a book.

He decided the story from the crazy witch lady was just some kind of folklore thing or just a prank. Or maybe she was off her medication like the lady suggested.

Now, clutching the black notebook to his chest, he saw a couple of the Arsenal players exiting tinted SUVs and entering the Transcontinental through the back entrance.

He whipped up his hood and sprinted across the road, the wind cutting at his face, the rain like sleet, a slap to the jaw. He caught a group of three footballers by their cars.

"Hey," he said, panting. "Could you please sign my autograph book?"

The three players glanced at each other, smirking, probably wondering what kind of lunatic bothered with signatures these days when he could simply take a picture.

Still, each of the players signed their name, with no message, in the book.

"Here you go, kid," the last one, a striker, said, handing it back.

"Thanks." He beamed, looking at the signatures and then slipping the book into his pocket. The Arsenal players smiled, and one of them ruffled his shaggy brown hair.

"Get home safely," the striker said, and they ambled off into the hotel.

Grinning, barely caring about the rain anymore, Arthur jogged across the road to the bus stop. In the light, and under the roof of the stop, he twisted from the rain and looked at the book again, admiring the intricate scrawls of the three famous footballers.

He was so enthralled with the signatures he only gave a fleeting glance to the shadow cutting across him. Then he felt a nudge in his side and turned to see Billy.

"Yo, what you got there, fucky-roo?" he said. Billy liked to join swear words in odd combinations, as if it made him cool or something. Arthur thought it probably did.

"It's just a notebook. It's nothing."

"Let me see it."

"You'll think it's boring," he said, trying to shove it in his pocket.

Billy grabbed it, pulled it away. He flipped it open, perused the first few pages, then barked a laugh. "What in the holy shit-stain is *this?* You collect autographs?"

"I'm starting." He held out his hand. "Give it back now, Bill."

"Don't you want mine?"

"It's only for famous people."

"I'm gonna be famous one day."

"But you're not now. Give it back please."

"Hold up." He turned away from Arthur—letting rain get on the book in the process—and produced a biro from his pocket. He scrawled his signature graffiti mark over two pages: *Billz.* Then, on the third page, he signed his real name *Billy Dockland.*

Then he handed it back, grinning. Arthur stared at it. "You ruined it!"

"Don't be a prick-rot," he said. "I just made your thing priceless."

"Whatever! I'll see you at school." Arthur stuffed the book in his pocket and walked off, heading home through the rain, hoping Billy wouldn't decide to follow him.

When he arrived at his house, he snuck through the kitchen again, and silently padded across the carpeted hall to his bedroom. Inside, he checked the book once more.

And as he saw Billy's signatures, he thought: *I wish it were cursed. That would teach the little prick-rot to ruin my fucky-roo book.*

The next morning before school, he admired the autographs at his desk.

Then he flipped open his sticker album, the one his stepdad had bought him. He already had four Arsenal players, including a duplicate of the striker he'd met outside the hotel the night before: Ranell Johnson. He peeled the back off and stuck it next to the signature, making it seem official. He wished he had the other two to fill in, but maybe he'd get lucky with the next pack of stickers. Or maybe someone at school had them. He'd try and swap some of his other duplicates for the two remaining Arsenal players.

For now, he had to be content with Ranell Johnson being his only one.

He stuffed the autograph book in his backpack—down low, way out of reach from Billy and his sticky, wandering hands—and then left for school, skipping his breakfast.

As before, he checked on the dark-skinned lady in the charity shop. The one with the short Afro and warm smile, just like how he expected a friendly aunty to look like.

His own aunties were mostly miserable and chunky and alone, whereas this lady, in contrast, was alive and healthy. Which meant she hadn't been struck dead by the book.

Billy was also alive. It didn't take long for Arthur to find this out, the legend himself marking up a bin near the school with his black felt tip, bent over in a crude manner, his crack showing at the top of his tattered tracksuit bottoms, like a child plumber. When Billy spotted Arthur coming, he straightened, capping the lid on his pen.

"Hey, fuck-lips," he said. "Get any more autographs yesterday?"

"Nah."

"Where you going?"

"School," he said, not stopping to talk.

"I'll see you in English," Billy said and returned to his graffiti work. It might not have been so bad if he'd drawn a picture or done something arty. But instead, he just wrote *Billz* in a terrible attempt at calligraphy. He might as well have just drawn a cock.

Then again, Billy had never been the kind of guy to do a self-portrait.

In school, Arthur found himself checking his notebook hourly, as if he expected it to be missing. Or maybe something kept pulling him in—the so-called killer curse, perhaps. But when he looked at it, nothing happened. He just saw swirly handwritten signatures.

Lunchtime flashed by in a blur.

Near the end of break, he spoke to a nervous kid in 7c and asked if he wanted to trade football stickers. The boy—short, stumpy, with glasses—said yes, then kept twisting away to look through his pile of duplicate stickers, not letting Arthur see them. He had the attitude of someone who wanted to keep all his secrets to himself, even though nobody cared or wanted to know. Finally, after a drawn-out negotiation process, Arthur bartered a fair exchange for the two Arsenal players who'd signed his notebook.

Later, in the comfort of his room, he'd stick them next to their autographs.

After school, Billy approached him. "Did you hear?"

"Hear what?"

"You got shit-bricks in your ears?"

"Hear *what*?" Arthur asked.

"Ranell Johnson. He died in a car crash."

"You're lying," he said, an automatic response.

"Real fuckin' squares, I'm not playing. He's dead, bruv."

Arthur saw the truth in Billy's dark pigeon eyes. He opened his mouth to talk, but nothing came out. His chest felt heavy all of a sudden. He brushed past him, got on the first bus, and went home. In his bedroom, he sprawled out on his bed and closed his eyes.

Tears sprung at the corners and ran slowly down his cheeks to his neck.

I killed him, he thought. *I killed Ranell Johnson with my book.*

But how?

And why only him?

He figured it out a few hours later.

It was the sticker. Something about the combination of both the autograph and the football sticker to showcase Ranell's face was enough to trigger the curse and kill him.

Or was it simply a coincidence? That would be preferable. He didn't like the feeling that he'd killed, accidentally or otherwise, one of his favorite footballers. And coincidences happened all the time, didn't they? He remembered hearing stuff about nine-eleven, how there were people who had never once missed work, but they called in sick to the towers on the morning of the attacks. That was coincidental *and* good fortune.

But luck could be bad, too. Maybe this was just a messed up one-off.

His stomach churned. He couldn't eat, couldn't think straight. His mother raised him to be a good boy, one who followed all the rules and always tried to please people.

Now he might be an inadvertent killer, a kind of accidental murderer.

He had to know one way or the other.

After dragging his notebook from his backpack, he fished in his pocket for the football stickers. He had two Arsenal players, and what he did next would potentially kill one of them. More than likely it wouldn't; probably it was all a coincidence. But just in case—if, in fact, he did have some kind of murdering machine—he needed to choose.

Between the two, Paul Splint and Jan Lagos, he preferred the latter. Jan Lagos was a six-foot-six Norwegian left-winger with a wicked cross and a cool tattoo that covered his whole left arm. He was worth £35m. But could he pick in such a biased way?

This was a man's life after all. He needed a fairer system than his preference.

So Arthur assigned the players with either heads or tails, then flipped a coin. It seemed to spin in the air for an eternity, mocking him. Finally, it landed on heads. Shit. That meant he'd be consigning Jan Lagos, his favorite of the two, to the hands of fate.

With an impending sense of dread, he peeled the sticker and stuck it down.

Then he went to bed, wondering if Jan Lagos would haunt his dreams.

First thing the next morning, he checked the news.

Filled with anxiety, a cloud of nausea bubbled up from his stomach to his throat. He held a hand over his mouth, keeping down the vomit. The news trickled through item after item, bouncing from war to economic instability to celebrity mishaps. Frustrated, he urged the news lady to get to the point and let him know whether Jan Lagos was dead or not. She seemed to be talking about everything but the most pertinent thing of all.

By the end of the segment, the newscaster hadn't once mentioned it.

That meant he was okay. Arthur jumped up, grinning, and switched off the TV, a feeling of jubilance buzzing through him like an electric bolt. The first death had been a coincidence after all; he hadn't murdered one of his favorite footballers, thank Christ.

Moments later, his stepdad, a burly and imperious man with thick greying eyebrows and wrinkles that carved through his face like scars, stumbled into the room.

Half asleep, eyes barely open, he grunted. "What you so happy about?"

"I didn't kill someone," he said.

"What?"

"It's complicated. I gotta get ready for school."

He rushed past his stepdad into the bathroom and quickly showered, then dressed in his school uniform. The burden of the previous night had been lifted; a heavy curtain shifted. Once again, he could collect autographs without worrying he would kill someone. He stuffed his autograph book back into his bag along with the football sticker album.

Hefting it on his shoulder, he caught a look at himself in the mirror.

He'd gone from a murderer to angel overnight, and he liked the transformation. His eyes were brighter, bluer. His smile was wide, gripped by genuine happiness.

On his way out of the house, his stepdad called to him. "Arthur!"

He popped his head in the room. "I can't talk. I'm going to school."

"Look—" Gesturing to the TV. "That Jan Lagos, he's dead."

"What?"

"He's dead. Look."

Arthur tentatively stepped into the room and looked at the TV. "How?"

"I don't know. They only just broke the news. But another one's dead."

Shit-chops, he thought, hearing Billy say it. That cloud of nausea bubbled louder now, popping and exploding. He felt it at the base of his throat. He ran out of the room.

His stepdad called out to him, but Arthur ignored him. He couldn't talk.

Underneath his bedcovers, he screamed into a pillow until he felt veins bulging at the side of his neck. He screamed a second time, but it wasn't helping. It hurt his heart.

Breathing slowly, thinking of Jan Lagos dying in the most terrible way—a knife to the heart, a bullet to the head, decapitated by a stray piece of metal—tears leaked down his face, uncontrollable tears, just flowing and flowing. He wiped them but they wouldn't stop. The tears were silent, and no sniveling or self-pity came along with them, nothing.

He'd unlocked the curse. It was official. This couldn't be coincidence.

Wiping at the tears with his shirtsleeve, he sat up, trying to think of something to mitigate his pain. This couldn't define him. His mother had taught him that a negative was merely an opportunity to find a positive. But how could he twist this in his favor?

He closed his eyes, wondering what good could possibly come from such a horrible, messed-up curse? The thoughts came slow; his head hurt from the crying. And then, like a screen drawing back to reveal a prize, the answer came to him in color.

Arthur whipped back the bedcovers, went into the kitchen, and spied his mother's purse on the side, open, waiting to be looted. Checking for his stepdad, he crept up to it and slipped his hand in, pulled out the moneybag, withdrew ten pounds, and put it back.

Then he left the house with his cursed notebook and a grim idea.

In the charity shop, Arthur angled straight for the Polaroid camera.

He brought it to the counter and the same woman as before greeted him with her warm smile; her eyes were like melted chocolate. "How you doing this morning?"

"Good," he said, pulling out the folded ten-pound note. "Here you go."

She took the money and punched the amount into the till. She eyed him curiously, like she could see right through him and understood his reason for purchasing the Polaroid camera. As she bagged the item, she said, "So the curse didn't work then."

"What?"

"The autograph curse. I'm still here."

"Yeah," he said, avoiding her eyes.

"You got any more autographs yet?"

"Not yet," he lied. "I have to go. Thanks." And he lifted the plastic bag off the counter and headed for the door, his steps feeling slow, as if he were walking in mud.

Her voice stopped him. "Hold on a second," she said.

His back tightened. She knew; she could see it in his eyes. He turned. "Yeah?"

She waved a piece of paper. "Your receipt?"

"It's okay. I don't want it," and he hurried out, the door tinkling behind him.

Then, before she had a chance to put the pieces together, he veered left, going toward school. Predictably, Billy was outside the front gates, pestering and harassing everyone like a security guard with an attitude problem. Arthur walked over to him.

"Hey Billy," he said, and when Billy spun his way, Arthur lifted the Polaroid camera and took his picture. The flash momentarily blinded Billy, and he angrily grasped at air, aiming for Arthur. The front slit on the camera spat out the Polaroid, and Billy lunged for it but Arthur got there first. He tore it out and said, "*Fuck you,* Billy."

Then he turned with the camera and jogged back the way he'd come, but Billy wasn't about to give up that easily; he chased after him, a hulking, asthmatic, sweaty pig-boy, wheezing as he called out Arthur's name. "I'll catch you, you ugly fuck-stick!"

At the end of the road, Arthur turned left and sprinted up the hilly street.

Billy wasn't far behind, chugging along, his face blossoming red from exertion. He puffed but wasn't giving up. He lifted his legs higher, pumped his arms harder.

Near the top of the hill, Arthur cut a swift right and pushed his way through a jagged opening in a wired fence. It surrounded a wooded area, which eventually led down to train tracks. Some of the older kids hung out here at lunch, smoking weed or cigarettes and trying to feel up girls or each other. Either way, nobody was here this early.

Arthur waded deep into the forest, and Billy followed, not far behind, panting loudly and heavily. He shouted out: "I'm gonna beat the shit out of you in a second!"

Arthur ignored him, weaving between bald trees and twisted mazes of toppled oak, being careful not to break his ankle on an outstretched branch or clatter into a web-work of treacherous vine. Gold leaves crunched underfoot, giving away his position.

His breathing choppy now, Arthur realized he'd trapped himself in a corner. The only way out was either back where he'd come from—which would mean somehow getting around Billy—or across the train tracks down below. He wouldn't take the risk.

Instead, he crawled behind an intimidating tree trunk and hid away.

If he was lucky, Billy would bypass him, and then Arthur could slip past and run to the top of the forest, going out the way he'd come. But Billy was only meters above him, no longer panting. He crept along, a thick log in his right hand like a baseball bat.

"I know you're down here," he said, voice booming. "I can smell you."

In less than a minute, Billy would spot Arthur and batter his brains in. Sneering now, Billy inched closer, his log-bat at the ready, a violent predator closing on its prey.

Arthur scrabbled for his autograph book, flipped to the page with Billy's signature on it and pressed the Polaroid against it. He searched his bag for glue and found a Pritt Stick right at the end of its use. After smearing the page as best he could, he pressed and held the Polaroid against it for two seconds, then a further three seconds. It stayed there.

He closed it, and when he looked up, Billy stood above him with the bat.

"I knew I'd find you," he said. "Time to die, you little fuck-rat."

For a second, Arthur was too stunned to move. His breath caught in his chest.

Then Billy swung the piece of log towards his head.

Arthur ducked, and the thick wood clattered against the tree trunk, missing him by a few inches. Billy pulled back for a second swing, but Arthur didn't stick around to feel its brunt. Still gripping the notebook, he exploded away from the tree and heard the crack of bat-on-wood behind him; he'd been a split-second from having his head bludgeoned.

Billy resumed the chase.

Arthur's only option was to go down, toward the train tracks, and sprint to the other side and up the embankment. He hesitated, scanning the area around him—nothing, no other way to get to safety. And Billy was lumbering after him like a wild bull.

Pushing his fear aside, Arthur clambered down the marshy hill and clumsily stumbled through muddy piles of wet, yellow leaves, slipping, until he reached the bottom. Billy shouted from up high: "I'm gonna fucking kill you, Artie! You watch!"

With mud caked around his trainers, Arthur clumped over to the tracks, glancing behind him. Billy was coming, wielding a cracked log with a pointy end like a bayonet.

Just do it, he thought, hearing the roar of an approaching train, feeling the vibration in the floor by the tracks. *Just remember to skip the third rail*, he told himself.

He did it. He leapt across the tracks in one bound. He had no other choice.

The train rattled along at speed, and Arthur felt the rush of air slamming against him. He twisted to see if he'd made it, just in time to see Billy try the same maneuver—

The train thumped into Billy like a 2-ton bullet.

It happened in a fraction of a second.

Arthur saw Billy's red-face fixed in a sneer as he lunged through the air—then slam, he was gone, the train punching through the air at 100 miles an hour or more, not slowing on impact. Blood splattered everywhere, splashing Arthur in the face.

He stood on the spot for a long time, droplets of blood on his cheeks, breathing heavily—in shock. The train rippled past him for at least a minute, a speeding weapon.

And then, gradually, after it disappeared into the distance, the sound returned to Arthur's mind, and the life returned to his body, and he wiped his face on his shirtsleeve. When he looked at the liquid, he realized it was a mixture of bone and brain matter.

Finally, still dazed, he opened up his autograph book to Billy's page.

It worked, he thought. *I killed him.*

And this time I meant it.

Arthur arrived home just after lunch.

He'd been walking around town, in circles, feeling both jubilant and despondent in equal measures. He'd accomplished his task, but it was bittersweet.

When he stepped through the front door, his stepdad grabbed him by his T-shirt and dragged him into the living room. Arthur hadn't rinsed off the blood, but thankfully his stepdad was so consumed with a red rage, he hadn't noticed any of it. He chucked Arthur onto the sofa and loomed over him, his fist held up high like an iron hammer, ready to break every bone in Arthur's body. "You stole from your mother," he said.

For a moment, Arthur was silent. He thought he was being thrown about because of the murder; he thought, somehow, his stepfather knew what he'd done with Billy.

He frowned. "What?"

"Your mother," he said. "You took money from her purse."

Is that it? he thought. "Yeah. Sorry. I needed it for lunch."

"You know you're not meant to steal. I *hate* thieves."

"I just borrowed it," he said, standing up. He straightened out his clothes, still worried his stepdad would see the bloodstains and flip. "I'm going to my room—"

"No, you're not." His stepdad pushed him back on the couch.

"I said I'm sorry! I just borrowed it for lunch."

His stepdad looped the belt out of his jeans and began wrapping it tightly around his right palm. "I wish I didn't have to do this," he said, "but you need to learn."

Instinctively, Arthur held up his hands, and the first blow whipped at his thighs. The pain was instant—the belt hitting his leg with the force of a swinging wrench—and it bloomed in a large circle, then diffused, spreading all the way down his leg like liquid. The second whack hit the first in the center, making the pain ripple further.

By the time his stepdad finished, the man had red cheeks like Billy's when he ran. He was out of breath. Sweat dripped down his forehead. "Go to your room," he said.

Arthur could barely walk, his right leg numb with pain. Fire radiated from his thigh to his spine. He hobbled to his room, using the furniture to help him along the way.

For the next few hours he stayed in bed. He didn't cry; after all, he'd deserved to be punished, just not for the money stealing. This was punishment for killing Billy.

Then, later that evening, with his stepdad calm now, Arthur pushed his notebook across the table for him to check out. "Could you sign it? I want your autograph."

"Yeah?" He grinned; it lit the darkness in his eyes with delight.

"I just think it will be cool," he said.

"Of course." He squiggled down a signature.

"Can I get a picture of you too? To put by it?"

"Of course," he said again, and when Arthur produced the Polaroid camera his stepdad didn't ask where he'd bought it. He merely posed for his death photo, happily.

And Arthur felt cold in his chest, ice forming around his heart in a shell.

After dinner, he excused himself and went to his room. For a long time, he stared at the picture of his stepdad, then slotted it in his drawer and put the notebook elsewhere.

He probably wouldn't use it. On most days, he loved his stepdad. The man cared about him and usually treated him well. Sometimes, like today, he crossed a line.

But he wouldn't use it; he just liked to have it there.

He liked to know he had that power.

Just in case.

)(o)(o)( )(o)(o)( )(o)(o)( )(

About the Author

George Kelly is a married father-of-four who's been toiling away at his keyboard for over a decade trying to make it in the cutthroat world of publishing. His work has been showcased by a number of online and print magazines around the globe. He was recently signed to Piers Blofeld of Sheil Land Associates and is currently in the process of preparing his latest crime novel *One Knife Stand* for traditional publication.

ABOUT J. S. WATTS
Guest Editor

J.S. Watts is a U.K. writer. Born in London, she now lives and writes just outside of Cambridge. In between, she read English at Somerville College, Oxford and spent many years working in the British education sector.

Her poetry, short stories and book reviews appear in a variety of publications in Britain, Canada, Australia, New Zealand and the States including *Acumen, Envoi, Mslexia,* and *Popshot* and have been broadcast on BBC and independent Radio. She has been Poetry Reviews Editor for *Open Wide Magazine* and Poetry Editor for *Ethereal Tales*.

J.S.'s debut poetry collection "Cats and Other Myths," a multi-award nominated poetry pamphlet "Songs of Steelyard Sue," and her latest collection "Years Ago You Coloured Me," are published by Lapwing Publications. Her novels, *A Darker Moon* – dark literary fiction, and *Witchlight* – a paranormal tale with a touch of romance, are published by Vagabondage Press. For further details, see her website: www.jswatts.co.uk